USA TODAY bestselling author **Margaret Moore** has written over forty historical romance novels and novellas. She graduated with distinction from the University of Toronto, has served in the Royal Canadian Naval Reserve, and is a past president of the Toronto chapter of Romance Writers of America. For more information about Margaret, including a complete list of all her books, please visit her website at www.margaretmoore.com

Novels by Margaret Moore:

THE OVERLORD'S BRIDE
COMFORT AND JOY
  (in *The Christmas Visit*)
BRIDE OF LOCHBARR
LORD OF DUNKEATHE
THE VAGABOND KNIGHT
  (in *Yuletide Weddings*)
THE UNWILLING BRIDE
THE DUKE'S DESIRE
HERS TO COMMAND
HERS TO DESIRE
THE DUKE'S DILEMMA
MY LORD'S DESIRE
THE NOTORIOUS KNIGHT
KNAVE'S HONOUR

And in Mills & Boon® Historical *Undone!* eBooks:

THE WELSH LORD'S MISTRESS

Kimber Chin,
savvy businesswoman and writer,
with many thanks for her advice and support.

'I hardly think a simple kiss is cause for such an extreme reaction.'

His unrepentant cavalier attitude cut her to the quick—until she realised it was another proof of his degeneracy. 'It was a kiss that I did not want, did not invite and did not enjoy. It was also an affront to my dignity, as well as a sign of gross disrespect.'

The man grinned. 'Good God, all that? Was it treason, too?'

'How would you like it if I reached over and started pawing at you?'

'Why don't you try it and we'll see?'

She was horrified, appalled, disgusted—and tempted, which was surely wrong and sinful.

'Or do you fear for your virtue?' he asked. 'If so, rest assured. You're the last woman in England I would ever want to seduce.'

'As if you'd have any hope of succeeding!'

'Careful, Miss McCallan,' he replied. 'I like a challenge.'

HIGHLAND ROGUE, LONDON MISS

Margaret Moore

First published in Great Britain 2012
by Mills & Boon, an imprint of Harlequin (UK) Limited.
Large Print edition 2012
Harlequin (UK) Limited, Eton House, 18-24 Paradise Road, Richmond, Surrey TW9 1SR

© Margaret Wilkins 2010

ISBN: 978 0 263 22523 5

Harlequin (UK) policy is to use papers that are natural, renewable and recyclable products and made from wood grown in sustainable forests. The logging and manufacturing process conform to the legal environmental regulations of the country of origin.

Printed and bound in Great Britain
by CPI Antony Rowe, Chippenham, Wiltshire

Chapter One

London
February 1817

Esme McCallan paced restlessly in the solicitor's office in Staple Inn. From beyond the closed door she could hear the hushed voices and footsteps of clients coming to meet with other attorneys. Some of the steps were as brisk as Esme's, others slow and shuffling and defeated.

None of them belonged to her brother.

Esme hated waiting, as Jamie well knew, yet here it was almost 3:30 p.m. on a wet, chilly afternoon and Jamie was not here to meet her, even though he himself had set the time. There was only one thing that could irritate her more and—

It happened.

Quintus MacLachlann strolled into the office

without so much as a tap on the door. Of course she hadn't heard him approaching; the man moved as silently as a cat.

Dressed in a brown woollen jacket, indigo waist-coat, white shirt open at the neck and baggy buff trousers, one could easily assume he was the son of peasants and earned his keep bare-knuckle fighting. Only his voice and lord-of-the-manor self-importance suggested he was something else, if not the truth—that he was the disgraced, rake-hell son of a Scottish nobleman who had squandered every advantage his family's wealth and station had provided.

"Where's Jamie?" he asked with that combination of arrogance and familiarity she found particularly aggravating.

"I don't know," she replied as she perched on the edge of the small, serviceable, oval-backed chair her brother kept for his clients. She smoothed out a wrinkle in the lap of her dark brown pelisse and adjusted her unadorned bonnet by a fraction of an inch so that it was more properly centered on her smoothly parted, straight brown hair.

"That's not like him," MacLachlann unnecessarily observed as he leaned back against the shelves holding Jamie's law books. "Was he meeting someone?"

"I don't know," she repeated, silently chastising herself for her ignorance. "I'm not informed of all the appointments my brother makes."

MacLachlann's full lips curved up in an impudent grin and his bright blue eyes sparkled with amusement. "What, the mother hen doesn't know every move her little chick makes?"

"I am not Jamie's mother and since Jamie is a grown man with a fine mind and education that *he* has not wasted, no, I don't keep watch over his every move."

Her words had no effect on the wastrel, who continued to grin like a demented gargoyle. "No? Well, he's not with a woman, anyway, unless she's a client. He never indulges in that sort of thing during the day."

Esme's lips tightened.

"So there's something else the mother hen doesn't know, eh?" MacLachlann said with a chuckle that made her feel as if she'd stepped into some kind of low establishment where all manner of indecencies occurred—probably the sort of place MacLachlann spent most, if not all, of his evenings.

"My brother's private life is not my concern," she said, sitting up even straighter and fixing MacLachlann with a caustic glare. "If I made all his business mine, I would know why he ever hired a rogue like you."

The sparkle in MacLachlann's blue eyes changed into a different sort of fire. "Is that supposed to hurt, little plum cake?" he asked, thickening his brogue and using an epithet she hated with a passion. "If it is, ye've missed the mark entire. I've been insulted in ways that'd curl the toes of your thick-soled boots."

Tucking her boot-clad feet under her chair, Esme turned her head toward the square-paned window that overlooked the soggy inner garden and didn't deign to answer.

She must speak to Jamie about MacLachlann's insolence. If MacLachlann wouldn't treat her with the proper respect, there had to be other men in London who were equally capable of finding out information. Her brother need not employ MacLachlann for that purpose, even if he had gone to school with Jamie.

With a self-satisfied smirk, MacLachlann strolled over to the desk and, with one long, ungloved finger, tapped the documents she'd placed there. "I wonder what your brother's clients would say if they knew his sister was as good as a partner in the business? That it was a woman who wrote the contracts, wills, entailments and settlements and did most of his research for him?"

Esme jumped to her feet. "I merely help him compose the first draft of such documents and find legal precedents for him. Jamie *always* writes the final documents and checks everything I do. If you dare to say or imply otherwise to anyone, we'll sue for slander. And if you write it anywhere or tell any member of the press who reports it, we'll sue for libel—not that you'll be able to pay any damages."

"Settle down, Miss McCallan, and put your lawbook mind at ease," MacLachlann replied in his most patronizing manner. "I won't tell anybody about all the work you do for your brother." His customary smirk left his face for the briefest of moments. "I owe him too much."

Just what? she wanted to ask. Jamie had never told her exactly where or how he'd encountered MacLachlann in London. Jamie had simply brought the obviously inebriated man home, let him sleep in the spare room and then given him employment as a sort of investigative associate. Naturally she'd had questions, most of which Jamie declined to answer, saying only that MacLachlann had fallen on hard times and was estranged from his family. Only later, through snippets of conversation between the two men, had she learned that MacLachlann had disgraced his family with his wastrel ways.

She'd also discovered, through firsthand observation, that he could be very charming when he wished to be, especially with women, who then responded as if he'd somehow turned their minds to porridge.

Not hers, of course. She was far too wary and sceptical to be swayed by his shallow charm, should he ever have attempted to sway her with it.

She glanced at the gilded clock on the mantelpiece and saw that it was now nearly 4:00 p.m.

"Impatient, are we?" the wastrel inquired.

"You may have nothing better to do than loiter," Esme declared as she started for the door, "but *I* do. Good day."

"What, you're going to leave me here all alone?" MacLachlann demanded with bogus dismay.

"Yes, and gladly," she snapped as she opened the door and nearly collided with Jamie.

"Ah, here you are, then, the pair of you and no blood spilled," her tardy brother said with a smile, his stronger accent telling her that despite his apparent good humor, he was upset.

"I finished the documents you wanted," she said, curious about what had happened, although she would never ask such a question with MacLachlann in the room. Hopefully she could find out later, when she and her brother were alone. "I discovered an interesting precedent in a case from 1602, concerning a sheep whose ownership was disputed due to lack of an earmark."

Jamie hung his tall hat on the wall hook by the door. "I'll deal with Mrs. Allen's suit tomorrow," he said, running his hand through his close-cropped brown curls as he went around the scarred and ancient desk they'd found at a used furniture shop. "And while I thank you for bringing the papers, I have another matter with which I hope you'll both assist me."

A swift glance in the wastrel's direction proved

he was no more keen to have anything to do with her than she was with him.

"Sit down, Esme, and let me explain. You, too, Quinn, if you please," her brother said, nodding at the chair.

Regarding her brother with a combination of curiosity and dread, Esme did as he asked. She again perched on the edge of the chair, while Quinn sat on another equally small chair and tilted it back so that all the weight rested on the back legs.

"You're going to break that chair if you lean back in such a fashion," Esme charged.

"Care to make a wager on it?" MacLachlann replied with that mocking grin she hated.

She didn't give him the satisfaction of answering.

"I've asked you both here," her brother began as if neither one had spoken, "because I need your help with a matter that requires legal expertise and discretion, as well as a certain amount of subterfuge."

"Subterfuge?" Esme repeated warily.

"Surely you're not so naive as to believe the practise of law doesn't occasionally require some creative espionage," MacLachlann said, "at least when it comes to finding out facts that some people would prefer to keep buried."

"I understand there may be facts that need to be ferreted out, but subterfuge sounds illegal," she protested.

MacLachlann rolled his eyes and looked about to say more, but Jamie spoke first. "It's not the method I would prefer. However, I fear that in this instance, subterfuge may be the only way to find out what I must," he said. "Certainly it will likely be the fastest, and the sooner the matter is resolved, the better."

Esme forced her qualms, along with her dislike of MacLachlann, into a corner of her mind and focused on her brother.

"I had a letter from Edinburgh this morning. Catriona McNare needs my help."

Esme's mouth fell open as she stared at her brother. "Lady Catriona McNare asked for *your* help? After what she did to you?"

Jamie winced before replying. Although she felt her indignation more than justified, she was sorry she hadn't been more circumspect.

"She needs the help of someone she can trust,

and a solicitor's confidential opinion," he said. "To whom should she turn but me?"

Anybody except you, Esme thought, remembering the night Catriona McNare had broken her engagement to Jamie.

Poor Jamie's face had been as white as snow and his eyes full of such mute misery, she'd spent all night outside his bedroom door, afraid he might harm himself.

"There are plenty of solicitors in Edinburgh she could hire," she said.

A resolutely determined look came to her brother's usually mild coffee-brown eyes. "Catriona's asked for *my* help, and she's going to get it."

"Help with what?" MacLachlann asked, reminding Esme that he was still there.

A studious expression had replaced his mocking smirk, and it made an astonishing difference. Not an improvement, exactly, for smirking or otherwise, MacLachlann was a good-looking man. It did, however, hint that there might be some measure of sincerity in him after all.

Probably about a teaspoon's worth.

"It seems her father has suffered some financial setbacks," Jamie explained. "Unfortunately the earl won't confide in her or reveal exactly what he's been doing with his money or what documents he's been signing. She's afraid the situation will get worse unless something is done.

"I would go to Edinburgh myself, but if I arrive and start making inquiries, people will wonder why. Nobody will know you, though, Esme. We didn't have a chance to introduce you to anybody before…" He hesitated for the briefest of moments. "Before we left for London."

And a new life, far away from Lady Catriona McNare, the Mistress of Duncombe.

"There's nobody I trust more when it comes to assessing legal documents than you, Esme," Jamie continued. "You'll be able to tell if there's anything wrong with the ones the earl's been signing."

"I suppose you'll want me to get the documents?" MacLachlann asked.

"I don't want you to steal them," Jamie clarified, much to Esme's relief. "I want you to get Esme into the earl's house so she can see the documents."

So much for her relief.

"What exactly do you mean, get me into his

house?" Esme demanded. "House-breaking is against the law, punishable by—"

"I don't mean break into the house," Jamie interrupted. "I simply want Quinn to help you get near the documents so you can read them."

"Hence, subterfuge," MacLachlann supplied.

"But what *sort* of subterfuge?" Esme persisted.

"We need an excuse to get you into the earl's house without raising suspicion. If I wouldn't be welcome there—and I certainly would not— neither would my sister," Jamie said. "Quinn, you've mentioned that your older brother, the Earl of Dubhagen, has been living in the West Indies for the past ten years, although he still keeps a town house in Edinburgh. It's occurred to me that if he returned to Edinburgh, he'd surely be invited to any fetes or parties or dinners Catriona and her father would host. I've heard that all the sons of the Earl of Dubhagen were remarkably similar in appearance, so I thought—"

MacLachlann straightened as if Jamie had slapped him. "You want me to impersonate Augustus?"

"In a word, yes," Jamie said, "and since your brother is married, you'll need a wife."

The full implication of what her brother was proposing hit Esme like a runaway horse.

"No!" she cried as she jumped to her feet, every part of her rebelling at this ludicrous plan and especially at the thought of pretending to be MacLachlann's wife. "That's ridiculous! And illegal! There must be some other way. Some *legal* way to—"

"Perhaps—*if* we knew what exactly was happening and who's behind it, if indeed there's anything illegal going on at all," Jamie replied with remarkable patience. "It could be that Catriona is mistaken and her father's losses are simply the result of poor business decisions. If he's legally competent to make those decisions, there's nothing she can do. But she has to know, one way or the other, and that's the assistance I intend to give her—or rather, that I hope you'll help me to give her."

"But why must we impersonate anybody?" Esme protested. "MacLachlann is still a nobleman, isn't he? Wouldn't he be invited? Couldn't we say I'm a friend of his family who's come to visit? Why must we pretend to be other people?"

"I'm a disgraced, disowned nobleman,"

MacLachlann said without a hint of shame or remorse. "I can't move in the same social circles anymore. Augustus and his wife can."

To her chagrin, he no longer seemed upset or even slightly dismayed by this incredible scheme.

"What if we're caught?" she demanded. "I'm not going to prison for Catriona McNare!"

"I have no intention of going to prison, either," MacLachlann said with infuriating calm, "but since it's my brother I'll be impersonating, I have no fear of that. As Jamie no doubt took into consideration when he concocted this scheme, Augustus has a holy horror of scandal. He'll never charge his own brother with a crime. He'd be only too happy to pass it off as some sort of joke on my part."

Jamie's little smile and the looks the men exchanged told her that Jamie was, indeed, well aware of this possible outcome.

Nevertheless, that didn't satisfy Esme. "Your brother might not want to see you imprisoned, but he might have no such qualms about charging me with impersonating his wife."

"No need to worry, little plum cake," MacLachlann said with what could be genuine joy. "I know—and can prove—a few things about my dear brother's past indiscretions that he won't want revealed to the general public. That should keep you safe from prosecution."

"Surely people will realize I'm not the earl's wife."

"Nobody in Edinburgh's ever met her," MacLachlann said. "They met and married in the West Indies."

He sounded as if he thought there were no more objections to be made, but there were other considerations—important ones, if they would be living together as husband and wife. They would be cohabiting the same house, sharing the same domestic arrangements. People would assume they shared more than that. Who could say what an attractive wastrel like MacLachlann might also assume? That he would be able to...? That she might even be eager?

The thought was...horrifying. Yes, terrible and awful and she would never succumb to any attempted seduction by him, or any man, no matter how handsome or charming he was. "I have no wish to pretend to be your wife, in any capacity or for any reason!" she firmly declared.

MacLachlann coolly raised a brow. "Not even if your brother asks you?"

He had her there, and he knew it. She could see it in his mocking blue eyes.

"Esme," Jamie quietly interjected. "Never mind. I can see my plan isn't going to work."

Her brother came to her and took her hands in his. Only once before had Esme seen such an expression of defeat in Jamie's eyes, and this time, *she* had put it there. "I know I'm asking a tremendous boon, so if you refuse, I won't blame you. Quinn and I will find another way to get the information we seek."

Yes, they probably could—but it might be another way that would send Jamie to Edinburgh and bring him back into Lady Catriona's orbit, to have his heart broken again, or that old wound reopened.

To be sure, Jamie's plan was not without risk, and she didn't want to help Lady Catriona McNare, but how could she deny his request when he had never asked anything of her before? He was the only family she had. Their mother had died of a fever two days after giving her birth and their father of heart trouble when she was twelve and

Jamie an eighteen-year-old solicitor's clerk. Not only that, he allowed her liberties few other men would. What was this risk when measured against all that he had done for her and the way he let her almost practise law? "Very well, Jamie, I'll do it."

MacLachlann picked a piece of lint from his lapel. "Now that that's all settled, I'll write to my brother's solicitor informing him that the Earl of Dubhagen has decided to return to Edinburgh and ask him to hire suitable servants, as well as see that the house is made ready for our arrival.

"Your sister's going to need some new clothes," he added, addressing Jamie as if she wasn't there. "Her current wardrobe is hardly suitable for an earl's wife."

Esme opened her mouth to protest, then realized his observation might have some merit. While her clothes were clean, tidy and serviceable, an earl's wife would have more fashionable garments made of more expensive material.

"Esme will have plenty of new clothes," Jamie assured MacLachlann as he went to his desk and pulled out a book of cheques. "You should, too. I'll also pay for the hire of a coach to take you to

Edinburgh, and you'll have some household expenses, as well."

He wrote out a cheque, the size of which made Esme gasp. Jamie was in charge of their finances and always had been, so she knew little of that part of his business, yet although he had always been generous with her pin money and paid the household expenses without complaining, she'd tried to keep house as frugally as possible. Then to see him hand over so much money to a man like MacLachlann…!

Even more frustrating, when MacLachlann took the cheque, the man didn't so much as bat an eye at the amount.

Instead, he tugged his forelock and said, "Thank you, sir! When are we to depart on this mission?"

"Do you think you can be ready in a week?"

"I can. The question is, can my charming wife?"

Esme ground her teeth and reminded herself that she must put up with MacLachlann's insolence for Jamie's sake. "I'll be ready."

"The coach and driver will be waiting at our house in a week," Jamie said. "Come as early in the day as you can to get a good start on the journey."

"I hear and obey," MacLachlann replied as he strolled to the door, then turned back and gave them a theatrical bow. "And so, my little plum cake and dearest, bogus brother-in-law, I bid you adieu until we depart for Edinburgh. I only wish I could take my lovely bride to the ancestral seat in the Highlands, but alas, I fear time will not permit."

The scoundrel was enjoying this far, far too much!

"Careful, my love," MacLachlann said as he straightened, "lest your face remain permanently in that most unflattering expression."

Then, with another aggravating smirk, he sauntered out of the room.

Esme immediately turned to confront her brother, but before she could say anything, he spoke with heartfelt sincerity. "I do appreciate you're taking a risk for me, Esme, and I'm more grateful than words can express."

Her frustration diminished; nevertheless, she had to voice her concern. "That was a lot of money to simply hand over to such a man, Jamie."

"It will be well spent and if there's anything left over, duly returned to me," her brother replied.

He went to his desk, opened the top drawer and took out a ledger she'd never seen before. "Quinn keeps excellent account of everything he spends when he's doing a job for me, so I know where every ha'penny has gone. Here, see for yourself."

He opened the leather-bound book and turned it toward her. On the ruled lines were itemized expenses written in a hand even neater than her own.

On the surface, the list looked extraordinarily complete, down to a loaf of bread and pint of ale for a dinner. And yet… "How can you be sure that was how the money was spent?" she asked.

"Receipts. He gives me receipts, for everything. I have them here." Jamie opened another drawer and took out a large folder full of pieces of paper of various sizes and in various conditions. Some looked as if they'd been crumbled into a ball, others seemed quite pristine.

"Very well, he may be fiscally responsible," she conceded, "but there are other elements of his character, of his past, that are far from exemplary."

"There's no denying that he's made mistakes in his past, as he'll fully acknowledge. But he's committed no crime and the only person he ever harmed by his actions has been himself."

Esme pushed the folder back to her brother. "Yet his own family has cast him out, have they not?"

"It's their loss more than his. His was a most unhappy childhood, Esme."

"His family are rich and titled. Many people grow up in far more terrible conditions, yet don't lose their money gambling or waste their days in idleness and drinking to excess."

"A boy raised with wealth can still be lonely and miserable," her brother observed. "And he never uses his childhood as an excuse. Indeed, he very rarely speaks of it. I found more out about his family from other friends at school than I ever did from him."

Jamie put the ledger back in the drawer and raised his eyes to regard her steadily. "While he gambled and drank too much, that was in the past. He's been absolutely trustworthy and done everything I've ever asked of him, and well." Her brother sat on the edge of his desk. "He feels remorse, too, although he rarely shows it. Do you know where I found him that night I brought him home?"

She shook her head.

"On Tower Bridge. He never said what he was doing there, but the way he was standing there, looking down at the water..." Jamie shook his head before turning to stare out the window, unseeing. "I don't think he was taking the air, and if I hadn't been searching for him and found him..."

Quintus MacLachlann had been about to kill himself? She found it difficult to accept that a man of such vitality would ever seek to end his existence.

"Thank God I did find him, and I've been more than glad ever since," Jamie said as he pushed himself off the desk.

He looked back at Esme and studied her face. "Is that all you're worried about, Esme? Or do you think he might try to take liberties with you? If so, rest assured that he won't. He's had...well, there have been women in his life, I know, but he's never been cruel or lascivious. If I thought there was any chance of that, I'd never let you go with him, especially in the guise of his wife. Besides, if there's a woman alive who's immune to any man's attempted seduction, it's you."

Yes, she would be immune to any man's seductive efforts, especially those of a man who teased and mocked her.

Jamie put his hands on her shoulders as he looked deeply into her eyes. "You can trust him, Esme. Please believe me when I say that beneath Quinn's devil-may-care exterior is a good, honest man, or I'd never have suggested you go to Edinburgh with him."

Esme nodded her head. She wanted to believe Jamie. She wanted to believe she was going to Edinburgh for a just cause with a trustworthy man.

But she really wished neither Catriona McNare nor Quintus MacLachlann had ever been born.

Chapter Two

A week later and attired in new trousers and Wellington boots, a shirt of brilliantly white linen, black silk cravat, double-breasted vest in a black-and-gray horizontal-striped satin, black woollen jacket, and an equally new bottle-green greatcoat with three capes, the formerly Honorable Quintus Aloysius Hamish MacLachlann strolled up the street toward Jamie McCallan's town house, a valise bumping against his thigh.

Jamie's home was a well-kept little establishment on the edge of Mayfair, close enough to impress the *ton*, but far enough away to be affordable if a man made a good living, as Jamie obviously did.

As Quinn trotted up the steps to the front door and raised the polished brass knocker in the shape of a thistle, the curtain at the front bow window shifted. The movement was barely noticeable, yet it was enough to suggest that somebody was keeping watch.

Esme, no doubt. The woman was like a prison guard. She was also beyond prejudiced, always ready to believe the worst of him, regardless of any evidence to the contrary and despite the necessary work he did for her beloved brother.

Since she thought him beneath contempt, was it any wonder he was always tempted to say outrageous things to her? To tease and mock and goad her until she gave him the edge of her sharp and clever tongue?

Jamie's butler, a tall, slender fellow of indeterminate age, opened the door and took Quinn's hat and valise. "They're waiting for you in the drawing room, sir."

"Thank you," Quinn briskly replied, darting a passing glance at his reflection in the pier glass in the spotlessly clean foyer. In this rig he *did* look like his brother, certainly enough that the ruse should work.

He'd never imagined Jamie had such a devious streak. Well, there had been hints of it at school, he supposed. A few times Jamie had gone with him to sneak a bit of food from the buttery, and once even told him when the cook would be away, but he'd never gotten drunk on the cooking sherry, or cheated on tests, or lied to the headmaster.

The drawing room was as neat and tidy as the foyer. It was simply, but tastefully, furnished, with nary a figurine or knickknack in sight. He had never seen a speck of dust or dirt in either Jamie's home or office. He suspected even dust and dirt were too intimidated by his sister to linger. Books there were in plenty, however, and what furniture there was had been well-crafted. The camelback sofa and chairs were worn, but comfortable, and the mantel—

Esme stood by the mantel, but Esme as he'd never seen or imagined her. Her eyes were downcast, her dark eyelashes fanning over smooth, pink cheeks and her slender, yet shapely, figure encased in a well-fitting traveling gown of soft pale blue wool. The bodice, bordered by a band of scarlet ribbon, accentuated perfect breasts. Glossy, chestnut-brown tresses were beneath a charming bonnet decorated with small scarlet rosettes, and a few even more charming tendrils of soft curls fell upon her cheek and neck.

She looked young, pretty, fresh, modest—the very picture of Youthful Femininity, until she raised her head and glared at him with irate hazel eyes, her bow-shaped lips turning down in an equally irate frown.

"Although I see you at least remembered to shave, you're late," she snapped, running an imperious gaze over him.

He sauntered farther into the room, just as fiercely determined to prevent her from seeing that he was even remotely disturbed by her disapproval. "I went to a barber, so now my cheeks are as smooth as silk. Care to feel?"

"Certainly not!" Esme exclaimed before she abruptly turned away.

But she was blushing, and she'd lowered her eyes again, as if she was tempted to touch him but didn't dare.

Good God, could Esme McCallan secretly want to touch him? This was a most interesting development and one definitely worth exploring. "You look lovely, Esme."

"I'll thank you to keep your unwelcome remarks to yourself!"

"You're the first woman I've ever met who didn't appreciate a compliment."

"If I thought there was any sincerity to your observations, I *might* be flattered."

Despite her contempt, he tried again. "I *am* being sincere. You look very nice. I never realized what a difference a change of clothes could make."

She whirled around to face him.

And then, a miracle. She smiled—a warm and genuine smile. His heart leapt with what might be joy, although it had been a long time since he'd felt anything like true happiness, so he could be wrong.

"Jamie," she said, walking past him.

She'd been smiling at her brother, who had entered the room behind him.

Of course. He must have been momentarily mad to think Esme would ever smile at him like that, and he must not be disappointed. After all, there were plenty of other women who were eager for his attention.

"I'm sorry I'm late, Jamie," he said before Esme could condemn him. "I was delayed by the tailor."

"Never mind. There's still plenty of time to get

out of London and a good distance before dark," Jamie replied. "The money was well spent, I see."

"So was yours. I confess I had my doubts about your sister's ability to pass for a titled young lady, but in those clothes, I think she could."

"How delightful that my garments meet with your approval," Esme said coldly. "Now might I suggest we be on our way? The sooner we reach Edinburgh, the sooner we can conclude our business and return."

Quinn couldn't agree more.

As the hired town coach rattled along the road north, Quinn didn't bother to hide his scowl or attempt to make conversation. Why should he exert himself with a woman who was so obviously determined to detest him?

Water from the puddles left by the heavy rain the previous night splashed up nearly to the windows, and the sky was dull and overcast, with a brisk breeze that did nothing to add to the comfort of the coach.

"If you slouch any more, you'll ruin your greatcoat," Esme noted as the heavy vehicle upholstered with striped worsted jostled over yet another rut in the road. "It must have cost my brother a pretty penny."

"I doubt it cost more than the pelisse you're wearing and probably less," he replied, sliding a little lower on the seat just to spite her. "I'd wager my whole wardrobe cost less than one of your gowns, and I have the receipts to prove it."

She gave him a haughty look. "*I* know how to drive a bargain."

"I'm sure a look from you can freeze the marrow of a modiste's bones and convince her to work at a loss," he agreed. "I, however, believe in paying for a job well done."

"I only want my money's worth."

"*Your brother's* money's worth," he pointed out.

That brought a flush of pink to Esme's cheeks. "If women could have a profession, I'd have been a solicitor, too, and gladly earned my own income."

She'd probably be as good a solicitor as her brother, Quinn mentally conceded. She might be one of the most unpleasant women on the face of the earth, but he couldn't deny her legal expertise.

"I think you'd be a better barrister," he said, and

that was no lie. "I can easily imagine you interrogating a witness on the stand."

She frowned, clearly not pleased with his comment. "Solicitors do all the real legal work, the preparation and research, while barristers unfairly reap the glory—the way noble landlords reap the benefits of their tenants' labor, even if those landlords are wasteful, drunken gamblers."

God give him patience! And the remembrance that he himself had made her criticism possible. Nevertheless... "Unless you want the servants to gossip about our marriage, you're going to have to at least *pretend* to like me when we get to Edinburgh."

"I see no reason why," Esme replied. "There are plenty of unhappy marriages in Britain. Ours can simply be another."

"Not if we're to be invited to balls and parties and things, and we should be, so we can find out if other gentlemen are experiencing financial woes, or if that's unique to the earl."

Esme shook her head. "I rather think the opposite. A squabbling couple is sure to be an object of curiosity and if people think we'll give them something to talk about, we'll be more likely to be invited. Haven't you noticed that people are more curious about a quarrelling, bickering couple than a happy one?"

"If that's the case, the hatred you harbor for me is indeed fortunate and we stand an excellent chance of being the most popular couple in Edinburgh."

"I don't hate you, MacLachlann," Esme said with infuriating composure. "I'd have to care about you to hate you."

It was like a slap to his face, or a blow to his heart, to hear her calm dismissal of him. But he would die before he'd allow himself to show that she—or anyone—could hurt him.

"Whatever you think about me, Miss McCallan," he said just as coolly, "your brother's asked for my help and he's going to get it. It would make that task easier for us both if you would refrain from condemning me every time you speak to me. And while I don't expect you to respect me, can you not at least cooperate? If not, we should return to London."

Esme got a stubborn glint in her eye. "I *am* co-operating, or I wouldn't be here." She took a deep breath and smoothed down her skirts. "However,

I agree that continued animosity will not be beneficial to our task. Therefore, let us begin again."

He kept his relief hidden, too, even as he wondered exactly what she meant by "beginning again."

"If I'm supposed to be your wife, I should learn more about your family. As it is, all I know is that your father was an earl and your older brother is the heir. Have you any other siblings?"

Of all subjects, his family was the last one he ever wished to discuss. Unfortunately, she had made a point that he couldn't refute—she should know something of his family history. "I had three more brothers—Marcus, who was the second oldest, then Claudius and Julius. Marcus died in the war with France, Claudius died of a fever in Canada and Julius fell from his horse and broke his neck when he was sixteen. I had a sister, but she died in infancy before I was born."

If he were looking at any other woman, her expression at that moment might indicate sympathy. However, since it was Esme, her furrowed brow probably meant she was simply memorizing the information.

"And your oldest brother's name is Augustus?"

"My father had an unfortunate love of Latin and Roman history."

"So he called his fifth son Quintus."

"Yes."

"A name you dislike quite intensely, to judge by that expression."

"Not just the name. I had little love for my father—and he for me."

"I'm sorry."

She actually sounded sincere.

"Don't be," he said sharply. If there was one thing he didn't want from Esme McCallan, it was pity. He didn't miss his family. He'd always been too different from them—too spirited, too full of life to exist in their staid world of hunting and shooting, exchanging tales of fish caught, pheasants downed and stags sighted. He'd yearned for something different—life in Town, a vibrant, colorful, exciting existence. Expensive. Sensual. Seductive. "I found ample compensation as I grew older."

"With women, I suppose."

He very much doubted Esme would ever understand why a man would try to console himself in the arms of a woman, even if it provided only a fleeting moment of pleasure and forgetfulness.

He couldn't even imagine Esme naked in a man's arms, kissing him, stroking, making love with sighs and moans and whispered endearments, writhing and passionate, crying out at the moment of climax.

Actually, he could.

Which was a very disconcerting discovery.

"How old is Augustus?" she asked, startling him out of his stunned reverie.

"Forty-five."

"Which makes you…?"

"Thirty."

She nodded thoughtfully, and he noted that she didn't seem to find it impossible that he could pass for a man fifteen years his senior.

What did it matter if she thought he looked older than he was? "His wife is twenty-seven. It's fortunate you can easily pass for that."

She didn't seem the least bit upset by his observation.

On the other hand, maybe he shouldn't be surprised by her lack of reaction. He'd never met a woman less vain of her looks. "She was seventeen when they married," he added. "Augustus always liked his women young."

Esme didn't look nonplussed by that, either. "They have no children?"

"Not yet, but if I know Augustus, it isn't for lack of trying."

A spark of interest lit Esme's hazel eyes, which gave him another shock. He'd expected her to react with prim condescension, disgusted by the mere suggestion of the physical relations between a husband and wife.

"What was in the marriage contract?" she asked eagerly. "There was one, I assume."

He should have known it wasn't the sexual nature of a relationship that excited her, but the legal. Still, it was rather interesting watching her when she was talking about the law and her hazel eyes became vibrantly, intelligently alive. He could easily envision her brain as a sort of well-oiled machine, all whirring gears and levers.

But as for any marriage settlement or contract his brother might have made… "I have no idea. Nor do I care."

She frowned. "You should. If he dies before you and there are no children, the inheritance—"

"I won't get a penny and the title will probably go to my cousin Freddy. I was disinherited, remember?"

Finally something dulled those shining eyes.

"I should mention that my brother prefers his women pliant and ignorant, so his wife is likely as uninformed and stupid a young woman as you're ever likely to meet."

"Oh?" Esme replied as if about to write a treatise on the MacLachlanns. "Is that a family trait?"

Once more feeling the need to be on the offensive, MacLachlann inched forward so that their knees were nearly touching. "I prefer intelligent women who know what they want and aren't afraid to ask for it. In fact, intelligent women who are interested in the law *fascinate* me."

Especially if the woman regarding him had shining hazel eyes in a pretty, heart-shaped face, with full lips and soft cheeks, and her head proudly poised above a slender, yet shapely body, the proximity of which was proving more of a temptation than he ever would have expected.

An expression flashed in Esme's bright eyes, but it was gone before he could tell what it was, and the rest of her expression didn't alter. "I don't believe you."

He sat back and laughed as if she were right.

Esme gave a long-suffering sigh. "If we *are* to work together, you should cease attempting meaningless, flirtatious banter or trying to elicit a reaction from me. Simply convey the information I require if people are to believe you are Augustus and I am your wife."

Despite his increasing frustration and his own resolve to remember that she hated him, suspicion was not what was being aroused.

"For instance," she briskly continued, clearly and blessedly ignorant of her effect upon him, "what did your family call you? Quinn? Quintus?"

"Several epithets I don't care to remember. Since we're going to be husband and wife, you'd better start referring to me as 'my lord' or some form of Dubhagen."

"*Pretending* to be husband and wife," she immediately corrected.

Of course she would want to be precise.

A different sort of expression came to those hazel orbs. Almost…mischievous.

"Dooey," she declared. "After Doo-agen," she unnecessarily clarified.

He knew how the name of his family's title and estate was pronounced.

But Dooey sounded like some sort of dim-witted beast. "You can call me Dubhagen, or my lord. If you call me anything else, I'll ignore you—or refer to you as my little haggis."

As he expected, she didn't like that. "Very well, my lord," she grudgingly conceded. "What is your sister-in-law's name?"

This was going to be interesting. "Hortense."

Esme reared back against the squabs, then her eyes narrowed. "Is it really, or are you just saying that to upset me?"

"It really is," he honestly admitted. "However, I think it would be best if we avoided the use of first names, even in private. That way, should our ruse be discovered prematurely, nobody can say we were using their names.

"I could call you Horsey," he proposed as if seriously considering it, although her features were not at all horse-like. "Or my little plum cake."

He had called her that last Christmas to tease

her, but now, when he considered how delectable she looked, it seemed rather fitting.

Good God, had he just thought of Esme McCallan as delectable?

She glared at him as if she could kill him where he slouched. "If you do, I shall call you my dearest ducky."

Eager to get his feelings back to normal, he not only took up the challenge, but he also upped the ante. "I could call you my sweet encumbrance."

"My darling incarceration."

He frowned and sat up straighter. "My beloved shackles."

She shifted forward, as if being nearer to him spurred her imaginative efforts. "My handsome millstone."

He told himself not to notice how pretty she looked, or think about her rosy lips, or how it would be to have her looking up at him with desire instead of annoyance.

Or how his traitorous body was responding to her excitement, her appearance and her proximity. "My adorable…punishment."

"My wonderful pestilence."

"My dearest—"

"I've used that already!" she cried, eyes aglow and full of triumph.

There seemed only one way to snatch victory from defeat—a way that was simply too tempting to resist.

He took hold of her face with his gloved hands and kissed her right on the mouth.

Never had Quintus MacLachlann felt such an immediate, powerful jolt of desire as the one that hit him the moment his lips touched hers. It was like being struck by liquid passion, hot and all-encompassing, enveloping him and filling the air around them.

He would never have guessed how soft and kissable Esme McCallan's mouth might be. He'd had no idea how much he'd want to keep kissing her, for as long as he could.

Or that he wanted to be the only man who ever kissed her.

But so it was, as he moved his mouth over hers in a hired coach lumbering northward toward Scotland.

Chapter Three

Esme had never been so confused and discon-
certed in her life.

Quintus MacLachlann was kissing her and it
wasn't terrible. His mouth was on hers intimately,
his lips gently gliding over hers, and she didn't
find the sensation repellent.

Indeed, it was completely intoxicating, as if
she'd imbibed the entire contents of Jamie's
brandy bottle in one gulp.

She'd never been kissed before. Never once, in
all her life. No man had ever wanted to, or dared.
Only MacLachlann—the rogue who'd probably
kissed a thousand women in his time, and with
no more genuine affection than he'd bestow on a
horse or dog he found of use.

Shame and disgust at her own weakness drove

Esme backward. Indignation at his bold, disgrace-ful act followed just as swiftly.

"How dare you?" she demanded as she retreated to the farthest corner of the coach. "You...you... cur! Don't you *ever* do that again! If you do, I shall write to my brother immediately and you'll never work for him again!"

Instead of being upset, MacLachlann crossed his arms and regarded her with mild amusement. "I hardly think a simple kiss is cause for such an extreme reaction."

His unrepentant, cavalier attitude cut her to the quick—until she realized it was another proof of his degeneracy. "It was a kiss that I did not want, did not invite and did not enjoy. It was also an affront to my dignity, as well as a sign of gross disrespect."

The man grinned. "Good God, all that? Was it treason, too?"

"How would you like it if I reached over and started pawing at you?"

"Why don't you try it and we'll see?"

She was horrified, appalled, disgusted—and tempted, which was surely wrong and sinful.

"Or do you fear for your virtue?" he asked. "If

so, rest assured you're the last woman in England I would ever want to seduce."

"As if you'd have any hope of succeeding!"

"Careful, Miss McCallan," he replied with a leer she wanted to slap off his face. "I like a challenge."

"You disgusting, vain oaf! Even the thought of you touching me makes my skin crawl! You are impossible! I should order this coach to turn around at once."

The sardonic amusement disappeared from Mac-Lachlann's face. "Are you forgetting that Jamie is counting on us? Is that how you'd repay him for all he's done for you? I can't think of one man in a thousand who'd let his sister take such a place in his life, let alone his business."

He was right. Nevertheless, so was she. "Then I must insist that in the future, you treat me with respect, not like one of your dockside dollies."

"Although I admit I made an error by acting without warning, I don't consort with prostitutes," he said without a hint of remorse or apology. "And if we're to pass as Augustus and his wife, you had better get used to the occasional spontaneous kiss. The men in my family are known for their passion and public displays of affection. If I don't ever touch you when we are in public, people will surely wonder why."

As if she were that naive. He was just trying to find an excuse for whatever lustful impulse seized him. "I don't believe you."

"Why else would I kiss you?" he countered.

Since this was Quintus MacLachlann, who enjoyed teasing and tormenting her, it couldn't be because he found her attractive. There had to be another reason, and she found it. "To silence me in the only way a man of your ilk would, because I was besting you in an argument."

His expression told her she'd guessed correctly, which was… No, she wouldn't find it disappointing. Not when the man who'd kissed her was Quintus MacLachlann.

And then a slow smile spread across his face. "Which just goes to prove my point. My brother is of the same ilk, Miss McCallan, and he would use the same method to silence his wife in a similar situation."

"*If* that is true," she sceptically replied, "we should have a signal of some sort, so I can steel myself in preparation for your assaults. Otherwise, I'm liable to recoil in horror."

His dark brows lowered and his lips turned down in a frown. "You enjoyed that kiss or you would have stopped me the moment I touched you. Don't try to deny it. We both know it's true."

It *was* true, as Esme well knew, yet to acknowledge the veracity of his statement would be to give him the upper hand, and that she would not do. He was, after all, a man and men believed they had every right to rule over women. Moreover, he was a very virile, powerful, confident man whose kiss had completely overwhelmed her reason. She must take care that such a thing never happened again or he would no doubt try to take command of the entire enterprise. And her. "I cannot deny that you have a facility in that regard, MacLachlann, and one I found momentarily interesting. However, I am not like the sort of women with whom you usually consort. I suggest you remember that and give me some sort of indication that you are about to embrace me before you again take such liberties in the name of verisimilitude."

MacLachlann folded his arms and regarded her

with his usual and infuriating insolence. "How about a wink?"

"Hardly subtle, although my brother seems to think you are a paragon of discretion."

"I am," he replied. "Otherwise, you would know all about my private life, which you don't."

"I have no wish to know about your private life."

Despite her honest response, she couldn't deny that she'd sometimes wondered where he lived and with whom he passed his leisure time, especially after he'd spent an evening with Jamie and she had heard them laughing in the library. MacLachlann had an attractive laugh, rich and deep and merry.

"I shall look at you like this," he said, bringing her back to the present.

Was it possible for a look to raise one's body temperature? How else to explain the rush of heat that overtook her as he regarded her with an expression of apparently genuine desire?

She definitely didn't want to encourage *that*. "If that's the best you can do, I suggest something else."

As she expected, that loving expression died instantly, replaced with mocking insouciance. "How else do you propose I convey the full measure of my desire for my wife?"

"By treating her with courtesy and respect," Esme returned. "That is how a gentleman shows his regard for his wife."

"Or his mother, or his sovereign," he replied. "A man should show a little something more passionate toward his wife, don't you think? Or maybe you don't, in which case I shall pity your husband, if you ever get one."

His words stung, because she secretly did want to marry, and have children, too. But she wasn't about to let him discover any chink in her armor. "If you must demonstrate your spousal affection in company, a simple kiss on the cheek will suffice."

"Very well," he conceded with a shrug—and to Esme's vast relief. "A little peck on the cheek it will be."

Then he turned to look out the window and said not another word.

Quinn was glad Esme stayed silent for the rest of that stage of their journey. He didn't want to endure another quarrel with her, or be bombarded by her caustic observations. It was enough that she'd made it clear that pretending to be his wife was something she considered abhorrent. As for that kiss... Although she'd reacted as if he'd ravished her right there on the seat, she'd responded with shocking passion, at least at first.

He would not imagine making love with Esme McCallan right here on the seat, her body against his as he thrust, hot and hard, driving them both to ecstasy.

God help him, what was wrong with him? Was he fatigued? Feverish?

Really that lonely?

Fortunately, they had only a few more miles to go before the coach entered the yard of an inn in Stamford through its high, arched gate. It was a bustling, busy, half-timbered place, with guests, servants, grooms, stable boys and maids going about their work. Vines covered the stone wall surrounding the yard and straggled around the edges. Large stone troughs stood filled and ready, and smoke billowed from the chimneys of the public rooms and kitchen. Although it was not yet evening, the glow of the windows foretold bright lamps, warmth and candles within.

Glad it was no longer raining, Quinn dutifully helped Esme disembark from the coach, as their roles demanded. Meanwhile, the innkeeper, a thin, sallow fellow in plain homespun jacket, neatly tied cravat, white shirt and dark trousers, rushed toward them. A beefier servant in a yoked smock appeared from the stable and started to take their baggage from the boot.

"Good day, good day!" the innkeeper cried, making a swift survey of their clothes and the coach. Quinn didn't doubt the middle-aged man could gauge the value of their garments and equipage almost to the penny. "Staying the night, sir?"

"Yes," Quinn replied with his most charming smile. "My wife and I require two rooms."

The innkeeper frowned and rubbed his nearly bald pate. "Two, eh? I'm sorry to say, sir, we're nearly full up. I have only one room left that'll be good enough for you and your wife."

That was a problem.

"I'm sure one will be sufficient," Esme replied sweetly, slipping her arm through Quinn's.

It took a mighty effort not to stare at her, for he'd never in his life guessed Esme McCallan could sound so docile and demure. As for the sensation of her arm in his and the possibility of sharing a room…

Gad, how long had it been since he'd made love to a woman? Too long, clearly. What else could explain the way his body seemed to leap to life the instant the scornful, prudish miss, who never looked at him except to frown, touched him? She could barely tolerate him, while he'd been more excited by that one kiss, and now this touch, than by a practised courtesan's most seductive efforts.

Determined to act as if he wasn't aroused and their relationship was perfectly ordinary, he patted her gloved hand. "Yes, one will be quite all right. Please show us to the room and have our baggage brought up. And we'll require a supper, of course." He'd already decided on one point of procedure for this part of their journey and saw no need to change it. "We'll dine in our room."

Esme's grip tightened. He ignored that, and her, as they followed the innkeeper across the yard, through the door and into the crowded taproom. Not surprisingly, several of those inside turned to watch the new arrivals and more than one of the men regarded Esme with open admiration.

He could guess what they were thinking—that

she was lovely and desirable. That they'd gladly bed her, if they could only have the chance.

A rush of primal possessiveness filled him and he glared at them all as if they were thieves attempting to steal his most valuable possession.

Not that Esme needed that sort of assistance. She could cut a man down to size with a look, or a few sharp words. Indeed, he'd pay good money to witness that…except she couldn't see them. That fancy bonnet she was wearing was like blinkers on a horse, shielding her from their attention, and him from seeing her face.

"Here you go, madam, sir," the innkeeper said after they'd gone up the stairs and he opened the door to a small, but comfortably appointed room. Although there was a commode and a washstand with plenty of fresh linen, most of the space was taken up by a large curtained bed that looked at least two hundred years old. "When would you like supper?"

"Eight o'clock," Quinn replied as Esme walked over to the small, mullioned window and looked out at the yard. "We'll breakfast at six."

"Right you are, my lord. Boots outside the door for cleaning, if you like."

"Thank you."

With a nod, the innkeeper went out and closed the door, leaving Quintus MacLachlann alone in a room with a large, probably very comfortable bed.

And a beautiful woman who hated him.

Out of the corner of her eye Esme watched MacLachlann stroll toward the curtained bed covered with a brown woollen blanket. He pushed down on it as if checking its softness…or stability.

Good heavens, surely he didn't think…! "You will, of course, be sleeping on the floor tonight," she said as she turned to face him.

MacLachlann flopped on the bed like a landed fish and cushioned his head with his hands while crossing his long legs. He still had his boots on, too—the typical behavior of a selfish, inconsiderate man who thought only of his own comfort and not of the person who would have to clean the covering.

"Have you forgotten we're supposed to be married?" he asked, as if she was stupid.

Her hands balled into fists as she turned back to glare at the massive oak tree at the edge of the yard. How she'd dearly love to wipe that smug, arrogant grin from his face! "Supposed to be, but most definitely are not. You're the last man on earth I'd ever want to—"

A vision popped into her head, of Quintus MacLachlann in that same pose and place, naked and smiling with a come-hither look in his eye.

"Ever want to what?" he prompted, his voice low and husky and rather close, too.

She stiffened. Had he gotten off the bed?

Wherever he was, she didn't want to let him know she was curious about him in any way, so she didn't even move her head to glance in the small framed mirror over the washstand to try to locate him.

"Ever want to marry," she continued. "If you're the best I can hope for, I'll gladly be a spinster. You're far too insolent, rude, crude and barbaric, as exemplified by your behavior in the coach."

"I assume you're referring to the kiss."

Of course she was. How could he possibly think that kiss was appropriate, or that she would enjoy such an unwelcome familiarity?

Except that she had. Far, far too much. Even now she couldn't stop thinking about it and wondering if she'd feel that same surge of longing

and excitement if he did it again. "I'm also referring to your impudent manner of speaking. And
slouching."

"Saints preserve me!" he cried with a mockery
that was impertinence personified. "I had no idea
that even my posture was damning me in your
fine eyes!"

Determined not to be cowed or intimidated by
him, she turned into the room, to find him only
about two feet away, looking like the epitome of
a Handsome Gentleman—except that he was no
gentleman, as she well knew.

Nor was she a trollop or loose woman. She was
Jamie McCallan's sister and a virtuous woman,
and she expected to be treated with respect. "Your
language is most inappropriate, as was that kiss."

"Inappropriate, but enjoyable."

"For you perhaps, but not for me."

His eyes seemed to glitter with feline satisfaction and his smile would have done credit to a
satyr. "Liar."

"You are insufferable!" she declared, turning
her back to him and wrapping her arms around
herself.

"You liked it when I kissed you."

She glared at the window. "Leave me alone."

"I liked it, too."

She mustn't listen. Anything he said couldn't be taken at face value, and any feelings a man like MacLachlann aroused must be suspect. Despite his new apparel and clean-shaven appearance that had suddenly and vividly reminded her that he was the son of an earl, he was still a disgrace and a scoundrel who had probably seduced scores of women. That was what she must remember, not the yearning she felt when his lips slid softly over hers. "Go away!"

"You don't mean that."

"I assure you, I do!"

There was a knock on the door.

Grateful for the interruption, Esme darted past MacLachlann and opened the door, to find the beefy servant waiting with her trunk full of new clothes on his back.

"Please put that at the foot of the bed," she directed.

Another servant, twice the weight and age of the first, followed with MacLachlann's much smaller valise. "Put that beside my wife's baggage," he said, reaching into his pocket for a few coins. He gave them to the men, who tugged their forelocks, then departed.

Ignoring MacLachlann, Esme pulled off her bonnet, set it on the dressing table and started to tug the pins from her hair. She would feel better when her hair was down; she always did.

She realized he was watching her. "Must you stare at me?"

His lips lifted in another of his insolent grins. "Make you anxious, do I?"

"It's rude."

"If you're going to criticize me for staring," he said, "you shouldn't look at a man the way you were looking at me this morning."

"I don't know what you mean."

"You were looking at me as if you were imagining what I looked like naked."

"I was not!" she exclaimed—and she hadn't been. When he first entered the drawing room, she'd been thinking that he looked even more handsome in his new clothes and freshly shaven. It would surely increase his considerable vanity if she admitted that, though, so instead she told a partial truth. "I was worried about this journey and what we have to accomplish."

"You don't find me handsome?"

What a conceited question! He didn't deserve an honest answer. "No."

Instead of looking suitably quashed, his lips curved up in the most devilish, triumphant smile she'd ever seen as he moved toward her. "One of my particular skills is being able to tell when somebody's not being completely honest and forthcoming, and you, Miss McCallan, are not."

She backed away. "I was *not* picturing you completely nude this morning."

She had later, but not that morning.

"Not *completely* nude?"

"Yes! No, that is…" She hit the windowsill and could go no farther. "You stay away from me! Don't you dare kiss me!"

With a look that combined astonished innocence with devilish satisfaction, he spread his arms. "Miss McCallan, I assure you I have absolutely no intention of kissing you again—unless you'd like me to, of course. Then I place no limits on my actions."

"You…you…*you!*" She jabbed her finger at him as if that would ward him away. "Stay back or I'll call for help!"

He didn't move, and his smile turned into a leer. "You could call for help, but we're supposed to be husband and wife, remember? That gives me the right to do whatever I like with you."

At his arrogant, yet ignorant, answer, a thrill of triumph surged through her. "No, it does not. Among other things, the Habeas Corpus Act of 1679 renders it illegal for a husband to imprison his wife in order to force conjugal relations."

That sobered him, and his leer became a scowl. "I suppose if any woman alive can be counted on to know such a thing, it's you. Fortunately for us both, I wasn't going to kiss you."

"Now who's lying?" she charged, even though she had no idea if that was really his intention, or not. "Not that it would be a compliment if you were," she added primly. "You would probably kiss almost any woman over fifteen and under seventy, and for the most minor of reasons."

"While you'll probably never be kissed again!" he retorted as he turned on his heel and went out, slamming the door behind him like the arrogant, spoiled wastrel he was.

Even if he kissed like a tender, compassionate lover.

Chapter Four

"I've brought your supper, madam," a man called out from behind the closed door of the bedroom of the inn sometime later.

MacLachlann hadn't returned and Esme wouldn't have been surprised to learn he intended to remain below for the entire night.

"Come," she replied, setting the law book on the table beside her chair near the window. After MacLachlann's childish exit, she'd decided to brush up on the differences between Scottish and English law so she would be prepared. She certainly wasn't going to waste any time pondering MacLachlann's mental state, or any abilities—sexual or otherwise—he might possess.

Then MacLachlann himself strolled into the room. He was carrying a large tray holding covered dishes, as if he were a waiter.

This was hardly the behavior of a nobleman, and one possible explanation instantly came to mind—except that he didn't appear to be drunk. Indeed, his gait was remarkably steady, as if the tray and its burden weighed next to nothing.

Not sure what to say or do, she picked up her book and got out of the way so he could put the tray on the table.

"You're going to ruin your eyes reading in the dark," he said evenly, and as if they hadn't quarrelled earlier.

If he was going to ignore what had happened, so could she. "It was still light enough to read. And I note an earl would hardly carry a tray."

"He does if he's hungry. I also told them that I wanted to make up for a silly quarrel with my wife."

That would explain the slammed door, if others had heard it, and they probably had.

He gestured for her to sit. "Dinner is served, my lady."

Although she didn't consider their quarrel silly, they needed to work together, so she would behave as if there was a truce between them. She put her book on top of her trunk and took her place at the table before removing the napkin covering a small basket of freshly baked bread. It smelled heavenly.

Meanwhile, MacLachlann slid into his chair with his usual lithe, masculine grace. He always moved like that, as if he were part cat. "I don't suppose that's a novel," he said, nodding at her book while buttering his bread.

"It's about mortgages and promissory notes," she replied, lifting the covering over the plate before her to reveal a dark, rich beef stew, with carrots and potatoes in thick gravy. It smelled nearly as good as the bread.

"Heaven spare me! And you didn't fall asleep?"

"I enjoy research."

"I dare say there are some people who enjoy having a tooth pulled, too," MacLachlann reflected as he lifted a spoonful of stew.

Despite the necessity of getting along with him, both his tone and his words rankled. "Just as I suppose there are some people who enjoy drinking to excess."

"I was never one of them."

"Really?" she pointedly replied as he continued to eat with relish.

"I don't deny I used to get drunk, and often. I deny that I ever enjoyed it."

"Then why did you do it?"

He raised his eyes and regarded her with a disarming frankness. "To forget."

What? she wanted to ask. What did he want to forget? His family? Some past misdeed? A woman?

But if she asked and he answered with that apparent honesty, she might find herself caring about him.

He looked down at his food. "I was a fool, wallowing in self-pity and blaming all my misfortunes on others—the gamesters who won what money I had, my supposed friends who deserted me when I had nothing left. My father, who never liked me. The rest of my family, with whom I had nothing in common. I believe I even blamed my mother for dying when I was a child. It was easier to do that than admit that I'd made terrible mistakes. Then one night I found myself on Tower Bridge, alone, drunk, penniless, thinking I would do the world a favor if I jumped and never surfaced."

He raised his eyes to look at her again. "That's

when your brother found me. He'd heard I was in London from one of my false friends he was representing, and sought me out. He took me to an inn, bought me dinner, told me he wanted my help, and that he would pay me for it. I've never gotten drunk since."

As MacLachlann made this unexpected confession, Esme discovered she could no longer meet his steadfast gaze. She'd always thought he felt no shame and no remorse for his wasted youth. How wrong she'd been! She'd never heard such sincere regret.

Yet all the answer she dared make to his confession was a subdued "Oh."

If she said more, what might she confess? That she'd never seen such excellent accounts? That she thought he was astonishingly handsome? That when she heard him laugh, she wanted to laugh, too? That she'd been overwhelmed with desire when he kissed her in the coach?

"Finished?" he asked, his voice as casual as if they'd been discussing the price of tea.

As hers ought to be, despite the rapid beating of her heart. "Yes," she said, pushing the plate away.

MacLachlann rose and went to the bell pull by

the small hearth to summon a servant, then returned. "I don't expect you to understand why I drank," he said quietly, regarding her with a furrowed brow. "I don't imagine you've ever done anything wrong in your life."

She couldn't meet his gaze, and she couldn't lie. "Once I stole a shilling from Jamie. I felt so guilty, I never spent it. I still have it, in a box in my room at home."

Even now the guilt of that small sin tore at her and made her feel ashamed. Nevertheless, she risked a glance at MacLachlann, to see him smiling with delight. "Dear me, I'm consorting with a criminal!"

While what she'd done was no great crime, she immediately regretted having revealed her secret.

MacLachlann stopped smiling. "Good God, I think you feel worse about that than I do about…" He shrugged his broad shoulders. "Some of the things I've done that are much worse. I do appreciate your confidence, little plum cake," he said, "and rest assured, your secret is safe with me."

He spoke so earnestly, she was sure he would keep her confidence.

Although that was a relief, she couldn't help

wondering why he was suddenly being so kind, so sincere, so serious and chivalrous. And why was she finding it so easy to believe that he was being honest about keeping her secret, and that he really would?

As she looked into his eyes, trying to decide if she could truly trust him, another unwelcome knock heralded the arrival of a servant to take away the tray.

As MacLachlann wordlessly waited, Esme reached for her book and pretended to read. She was trying to act as if nothing extraordinary had happened, and as if she stayed with a man—a handsome, compelling, seductive man—every night.

After the servant had gone, she held her breath, expecting MacLachlann to leave, too.

He didn't. He sat in the chair across from her, and he didn't say a word.

His silence was tense and unnerving, filling her with uncertainty and stress, because…because he was there. Watching her.

Finally, after reading the same paragraph five times, she'd had enough. She closed her book and said, "I'd like to retire."

"Please do," he replied as he stretched his long legs out in front of him.

"I wish to go to sleep," she added pointedly.

"So do I."

"You should go below until I'm in bed. Then you may return and sleep on the floor. You can have the blanket."

"How very generous. However, I've seen quite enough of the taproom and its patrons for today, especially if you're expecting me to sleep on the floor."

"Where else could you—?"

His gaze flicked to the bed.

Good heavens! "Never!" she cried, jumping up. "Not here and not in Edinburgh, either!"

"Calm yourself, Miss McCallan," he said, rising as well. "I have absolutely no desire to make love with you tonight, or ever."

She believed that, too, and felt a most ridiculous pang of disappointment.

And although there was no obvious change to his expression, she had the sudden horrible feeling that he could sense that disappointment.

She immediately straightened her shoulders. "If

you did touch me, I would have you charged with attempted rape."

"I doubt that," he said as he went to the door. "That would mean telling the world we aren't really married."

With his hand on the latch, he paused and looked back at her, his expression enigmatic. "Good night, little plum cake."

After he was gone, Esme sat on the bed and rubbed her temples. Even for Jamie's sake, how was she ever going to endure this untenable situation with the most insolent, infuriating man in Britain?

Who tempted her beyond reason.

It seemed MacLachlann might be regretting his revelations, for he apparently had no more desire to converse than she did as they continued their journey north to Scotland. Unfortunately, she couldn't easily ignore him. During the day, when MacLachlann hunched in the corner of the carriage, either asleep or staring moodily out the window, she could fill her mind with legal precedents and possible scenerios that could explain the earl's financial distress; at night, though, when they stopped at an inn and had to play their roles of husband and wife, it proved more difficult to pretend he wasn't there.

At least MacLachlann never again made a fuss about sleeping on the floor. Every night, he went below while she prepared to retire, then returned when she was already in bed and presumably asleep.

But she only feigned sleep to avoid another confrontation. More than once she'd been rewarded— or cursed—by the sight of MacLachlann's naked back, all hard muscle and sinew, with a few scars marring his marble-smooth skin. His shoulders and bare arms were likewise muscular, as if he'd spent several years at the oars of a boat. Or boxing. Or fencing.

The rest of him was equally fit, muscular and well-formed.

So now during the day she was too often aware of his body beneath his fine new wardrobe, even as she reminded herself that he was still Quintus MacLachlann and they had a job to do that required her utmost attention.

At last, however, Edinburgh Castle appeared in the distance and the city beneath it came into view. She wasn't surprised when the carriage went toward the New Town, where all the gentry and aristocracy lived since the Great Flitting at the end of the previous century, when they'd abandoned the older, inner part of the city for fine new houses.

MacLachlann continued to stare out the window, a deep, disgruntled frown darkening his features. Either he was annoyed with her, or as concerned about their purpose and their ability to achieve their goal as she, or else Edinburgh held no happy memories for him. Given what she'd learned of MacLachlann, she wouldn't be surprised to discover all three reasons brought that expression to his face.

The carriage came to a halt outside a large, imposing three-story stone house with a huge fanlight over the door. She'd assumed that the town house of an earl would be a large and fine one; even so, she was not quite prepared for a house as big as a palace, with an abundance of windows and black double doors that gleamed like liquid pitch. No doubt there was an enclosed garden at the back and a coach house and stables off the mews for horses and carriages, too.

"Home sweet home," MacLachlann muttered with an absence of anything remotely like joy as the doors of the house opened and a butler appeared on the threshold, looking suitably austere and grave.

MacLachlann hissed a curse and before she could ask what was the matter, he said, "It's McSweeney. Been with the family forever."

"Do you think he'll recognize you?" she asked, trying to hide her own dismay at this unforeseen turn of events.

"If he does, we'll just have to brazen it out. If he doesn't, he'll probably go out of his way to avoid me. He never liked Augustus.

"And remember to act vapid and stupid," he added. "I daresay all the servants will be more curious about you than they will be about me."

That wasn't exactly comforting, Esme thought as a liveried footman came out from behind the butler, trotted down the steps and opened the door.

MacLachlann got out of the coach, then held up his hand to help her down.

She tried to ignore the warmth of his touch, and his expression that could be encouragement as she stepped onto the pavement.

"McSweeney, you old dog!" MacLachlann cried as they started up the steps. "I thought you must be dead by now."

"As you can see, my lord, I am not," the butler replied, sounding exactly like an undertaker in a house of bereavement.

"Nor hired by another family?" MacLachlann asked.

"I was, until your solicitor inquired about the possibility of my return to Dubhagen House, my lord."

"He offered you a pretty penny, too, I don't doubt. That's a solicitor for you, always ready to spend a client's money."

Esme's grip tightened at the insult, but MacLachlann ignored her as they continued into the house.

MacLachlann glanced over his shoulder as the butler ordered the coachman to drive around to the mews, then whispered with obvious relief and delight, "McSweeney didn't bat an eye. If we can fool him, we can fool anybody."

She was relieved, too, but she couldn't share his confidence. For one thing, he'd been raised to his role. She had not.

Nor had she grown up in such opulent surroundings. A round mahogany table with an enormous oriental vase full of roses stood in the center of the marble-tiled foyer, their scent lost amid the stronger odors of beeswax and lemons. Pier glasses hung on sea-green walls decorated with ornate white plaster work.

Two middle-aged maids holding brooms and dustpans were in the corridor leading to the back of the house, a hall boy with an empty coal scuttle lurked by a door that probably led below stairs, another footman in scarlet livery waited by the door to what was likely the drawing room and three more maids peered down from the landing above, reached by a wide hanging stair.

"See that our baggage is unpacked at once," MacLachlann ordered with a casual flick of his hand. "I'll show her ladyship to her bedroom myself. I trust it's ready?"

"Absolutely, my lord," the butler replied. "Your solicitor has hired a most excellent housekeeper, so all is quite prepared despite the lack of time."

MacLachlann turned on the butler with a speed that was shocking. "Are you presuming to criticize me, McSweeney?" he demanded.

The poor man took a startled step back. "No, my lord. Of course not, my lord."

"Good." MacLachlann addressed Esme as if that confrontation had never happened. "Come along, my dear."

He gave her that...that *Look.* She stiffened, waiting for a kiss. He pulled her close—and squeezed her bottom.

It took every ounce of self-control Esme possessed not to slap him, especially when she saw the sly look of amusement on his handsome face, and his bright eyes gleaming in a way that sent the blood rushing through her veins.

Then, without a word or even a look of warning, he scooped her up in his arms and started toward the stairs.

Appalled and afraid he was going to drop her, Esme threw her arms around his neck. She was going to demand he put her down *at once,* until she saw the butler's shocked expression.

She had a part to play and play it she must, so instead she whispered loud enough for the butler and other servants to hear, "Put me down, dearest ducky, or what will the servants think?"

He didn't answer as he continued up the stairs.

Not sure what to do, she started to babble like a ninny. "Oh, you're such a romantic fellow! I'm glad you're so strong. And you didn't tell me your house was so magnificent, Ducky, or I would have asked you to bring me here sooner. All that time courting me and you never said. And your servants—so very proper. I do hope they like me!"

Still he was silent as they passed the maids, who dutifully bowed their heads.

Perhaps Augustus was not a loquacious man.

MacLachlann carried her along a corridor full of portraits and paintings of landscapes, the walls behind painted sky blue, until they reached a room nearly at the end of the hall. Finally he spoke as they crossed the threshold. "This is my lady's chamber."

Distracted as she was being carried like an invalid, she couldn't help noticing that it was a beautiful room. The walls were papered with a delicate design of pale green and blue, the draperies green velvet and the cherry furniture polished to a gleaming gloss.

Nevertheless, her surroundings were less important than the fact that he was still holding her in his arms. "You may put me down now."

He did, slowly setting her on her feet. Very slowly. Her body close to his. Very close.

Suddenly his expression darkened and her heart seemed to stop beating as she wondered what she'd done.

"Who the devil are you?" he demanded, and she realized he wasn't addressing her, but someone behind her.

She turned swiftly to see a woman in a plain gray woollen gown and white mop cap with a pillow in her hand standing on the other side of the bed curtained with pale blue silk.

She must be a maid, Esme thought, and a very pretty one, too, although not so young as Esme first supposed. She immediately hoped she didn't have to worry about her alleged husband seducing the servants.

"I am Mrs. Llewellan-Jones, the housekeeper, my lord. I wasn't informed you had arrived," the woman replied with a Welsh accent as she dipped a curtsey and met MacLachlann's genial smile with a frown.

Esme was suddenly quite sure that even if MacLachlann tried to seduce the housekeeper,

Mrs. Llewellan-Jones was quite ready and able to resist him.

As she, apparently—and to her chagrin—was not.

"Ah. The solicitor hired you as well?" MacLachlann asked.

"Yes, my lord. I was recently working for Lord Raggles."

"How is old Rags?" MacLachlann asked with one of his more charming smiles, while Esme sidled toward a huge armoire near the door.

"His lordship was quite well the last time I saw him, my lord," Mrs. Llewellan-Jones answered evenly.

"Glad to hear it. Now if you'll excuse us, Mrs. Jones," he said, "my wife and I would like to rest before dinner."

Esme darted him a sharp glance, then flushed when she saw The Look on his face.

"It's Llewellan-Jones, my lord, and what would you like done with your baggage?"

"It can all be taken to the dressing room and un-packed—but no one should enter this room until we ring for a maid."

Until…? What was he thinking?

"As you wish, my lord. My lady," the house-keeper replied, her expression serene as she left the room and closed the door behind her.

Chapter Five

On guard and ready for anything, Esme waited with bated breath.

Fortunately MacLachlann didn't come any closer. He shoved his hands into his trouser pockets and rocked on his heels as he surveyed the room. "I see Augustus hasn't paid for any redecorating."

Determined to act as if she were perfectly calm, Esme began to remove her gloves. "Was it really necessary to be quite so primitive? I'm not one of the Sabine women to be carried over the threshold."

"It seemed appropriate," MacLachlann absently replied as he strolled toward the cheval glass that was cracked in one corner. "Gad, this place is in worse condition than I imagined. Augustus should have sold it if he was going to let it fall into ruin."

"Perhaps he expects to return and repair it someday."

"Perhaps, but I doubt it," MacLachlann said as he continued toward the barren dressing table, running a finger along the top as if checking for nonexistent dust. Despite the slight state of disrepair, the room had obviously been recently cleaned.

"Your solicitor seems to have hired a considerable staff."

"Augustus always had a considerable staff."

"For which, I assume, my brother is paying?" Esme asked as she began to pull the pins from her hair and set them one by one on the dressing table, making a tidy little pile.

"I certainly couldn't afford it," MacLachlann shamelessly admitted. "Jamie was well aware there were going to be considerable costs, no matter how much I try to economize."

"And are you?" she asked.

"As much as possible. Everything will be accounted for."

As she pursed her lips with disdain, for the money would still be gone, he strolled to the window and pulled back the draperies, peering into what must be the back garden.

"I don't think I'd be quite so willing to pay so much to help a woman who jilted me," he said under his breath, as if thinking aloud.

She wouldn't be so willing to help a man who'd broken her heart, either, Esme silently agreed, but she wasn't going to make any more confessions to MacLachlann. "My brother is a very kind and generous man."

"Obviously," MacLachlann replied, "or he would have left me on Tower Bridge."

He turned back into the room, and she was sorry to see that the usual sardonic, mocking expression had returned to his features. "Makes me damn glad I've never been in love."

He hadn't?

"What about you, Miss McCallan? Has any young gentleman ever stirred your heart?"

As if she would ever tell him if one had! "No."

"Thought not," he said with another infuriating grin.

Then, without a word of warning or explanation, he suddenly launched himself at the bed and rolled around on it as if he were possessed.

"What on earth are you doing?"

"Making it look as if we've been engaged in intimate marital relations."

"Whatever for?"

"I warned you that the men in my family are passionate."

Passionate was not what she would call it. "How unfortunate for the women in your family, to be always put upon."

"Put upon? There speaks a virgin."

Esme wouldn't let him make her feel ashamed or ignorant. "Of course I am, and so I shall stay until I'm married."

He rolled off the bed and onto his feet in one fluid motion. "Until that day, should it ever come to pass—or, I should say, the day after that blessed event—I wouldn't presume to comment on how other women feel about their husbands' passionate attentions."

As she flushed and tried to think of an appropriate response, he started toward a door in the wall to Esme's right. "Now if you'll excuse me, my little plum cake, I'm going to change."

"Isn't that *my* dressing room?"

"We have adjoining rooms. As I said, the men in

my family are passionate," he replied, giving her
another mocking smile before he left the room.

That evening, delicate bone china sparkled upon
the long table covered by fine linen, silver, crys-
tal and lit by candles in silver holders in the earl's
enormous dining room papered in burgundy and
with mahogany wainscoting. Footmen stood ready
to wait upon the lord and lady, with the butler to
oversee them.

Esme, however, was blind to the glories of the
expensive setting and scarcely tasted the excellent
meal. She was discovering it wasn't nearly as easy
to pretend to be ignorant and silly as she'd supposed. Not only did she have to guard her tongue
constantly, but wearing costly clothes like this
beautiful, low-cut gown of emerald green silk was
also a nerve-wracking torment. She worried she
was going to spill wine or soup, a piece of sauced
fish or roast beef, on it and ruin it.

It didn't help that MacLachlann was revelling
in the role as lord of the manor, while she was so
constrained by hers as his ignorant, vapid wife.

Or that he looked even more handsome in evening dress. The cut of his black evening jacket

accentuated his broad shoulders, while his tight-fitting knee breeches and stockings emphasized his leanly muscular legs.

"Yes, the finest gelding I think I've ever seen," he said, referring to the saddle horse he'd bought in London with Jamie's money and had sent to Edinburgh, as if there weren't any good horses in Scotland.

She mentally shuddered as she considered how much such an animal and its transportation must have cost.

"Should bring a tidy profit if I ever decide to sell it," he noted.

Was he telling her that would be the horse's fate when their task was complete? "You'd sell it?"

"Of course. If I could get the right price, I'd sell it tomorrow."

So, he didn't intend to keep it—thank goodness.

"I should be able to get a damn good price for it here. There's no finer beast in Edinburgh—probably all of Scotland. I trust your mare will be just as fine."

Esme nearly dropped her sterling silver fork. "You bought *two* horses?"

Then she remembered she was supposed to be

dim, so she added a giggle and widened her eyes. "You don't mean you bought a horse for me? I don't ride."

That was quite true. When she'd been growing up in the Highlands, they hadn't been able to afford a horse. Jamie had learned to ride later; she never had.

MacLachlann laughed, and this time she did not find the sound of it nearly so appealing. "Well, now that we're home, you'll have to learn."

If ever there was a time to be vapid… She clasped her hands together like a penitent supplicant. "But, Ducky, horses are so big and prancy, I'm sure I'll fall. You wouldn't want your dearest love to hurt herself, would you? And you wouldn't make me do something I really don't want to do, would you?"

He looked mildly annoyed. "There's nothing to be afraid of. It's just a horse."

Undeterred, Esme put her napkin to her eye and sniffled as if she were weeping. "Is Ducky going to be cruel to his dearest, sweetest love?"

MacLachlann scowled as he reached for his cut-crystal goblet of excellent red wine. "If you really don't want to ride, very well, don't."

"And you'll sell the mare?"

His frown deepened for a moment, then it was as if he'd suddenly seen an angelic vision. "I should be able to make an even better profit on it," he declared with obvious satisfaction, "so yes, I'll sell the mare."

A predatory gleam came to MacLachlann's blue eyes. "Dry your tears, my sweet, and come give your husband a kiss."

With the servants in the room, what could she do except obey? So she did, keeping her eyes demurely lowered and sliding an apparently bashful glance at the nearest footman before she gave MacLachlann a peck on the cheek.

Before she could move away, he slid his arm around her and pulled her close, The Look fully evident as he gently caressed her cheek. His touch was warm and gentle, light as a feather, yet enough to disturb every nerve in her body and make her remember him lying on the bed.

"How can I deny you anything?" he asked softly, sounding as if he truly meant it.

Her heartbeat quickened and her legs seemed weak as jelly. How she wished he meant it....

No, she didn't! She couldn't! This was still Quintus MacLachlann, and he was only pretending. There was no real sentiment behind that action or that look. The man was simply a superb actor—and she must remember that.

"Not in front of the servants, Ducky," she murmured, pulling away.

He didn't protest as she hurried back to her chair. Thank goodness the meal was nearly over—although what would happen after that?

She found out soon enough. MacLachlann downed the last of his wine, pushed back his chair and got to his feet.

"Good night, my dear," he said briskly. "I'll see you at breakfast."

She hadn't expected that. "You're retiring already?"

He shook his head. "I'm going to my club. I don't know when I'll be back. Sleep well, my little plum cake."

"I shall try," she replied, trying to hide her annoyance that he hadn't informed her of this plan. "Don't be out *too* late, Ducky. It's been a long and tiring day."

The leering expression on his face wouldn't have been out of place on a Roman in mid debauch. "For you perhaps," he said as he swaggered from the room.

Early the next day, Esme paced in the countess's morning room. She was too agitated to pay much heed to the wallpaper depicting peacocks and nightingales, or the ornate plasterwork. It barely registered in her mind that the delicate chairs were gilded, nor had she been as enthralled by the intricacy of the inlaid ebony of the writing desk as she might have been otherwise, because she was exhausted. She'd lain awake for hours waiting for MacLachlann to return. She'd finally fallen asleep near dawn, only to dream of Quintus MacLachlann as a satyr, with horns and furry legs and a V-shaped beard. He had chased her and caught her, laughing as he laid her down on the ground and…

Worse, instead of being horrified, she'd been excited by his wild embrace. Passionately so.

She pressed her fingertips to her closed eyes, trying to forget that vivid dream.

It had to be the wine. She didn't usually drink

more than a single glass in the evening and last night she'd had three.

Now it was well past breakfast and MacLachlann still had not returned.

Had he really gone to a gentlemen's club, she asked herself for the hundredth time, or somewhere else? Had he returned to familiar Edinburgh haunts, and if so, how long would it be before somebody realized he wasn't the earl, but the man's brother?

"Good God, what a night!"

She whirled around to see MacLachlann leaning against the door frame. He was unshaven and unkempt, his cravat undone and lying loosely around his neck, the top of his shirt unbuttoned and exposing his neck and too much of his clavicle. He also looked utterly exhausted—yet even then, he was still more attractive than the majority of men she'd met.

As for his weary, dishevelled state, he had only himself to blame. If he hadn't gone out, he could have spent the night sleeping between clean, pressed sheets in a soft bed in a finely appointed chamber near her own. *Very* near her own.

Esme watched as he walked to the nearest chair

and slid into it as if his legs were liquid. He closed his eyes. "I've never been so bored in my life!" he said with a long-suffering sigh. "All they talked about was dogs and horses—and not even racing horses. Just hunters. I thought I'd go mad."

It certainly sounded as if he really had gone to a gentlemen's club, which came as a greater relief than she cared to acknowledge. And yet… "If it was so boring, why did you stay so long?"

He cracked open his eyelids. "Because I thought I might hear something useful, of course. And I did. If the earl is having financial difficulties, it's not the general state of things among the nobility and gentry here. If it was, I doubt they'd be spending so much on their hounds and horses." His eyes closed again. "At least I found a buyer for the mare willing to pay a good price and I'll be able to sell the gelding to him for a handsome profit, too, before we go back to London."

Esme sat on the edge of a slender gilt chair near the writing desk and absently lifted the lid of the inkpot. It was as dry as the Sahara. "Nobody questioned your identity, I hope."

"I hardly recognized any of them myself, so no, nobody questioned my identity, little plum cake."

She crossed her arms. "Please don't call me that."

He came to stand before her, his arms crossed, his weight on one leg. "Are you going to keep calling me Ducky?"

She would not allow him to be intimate…intimidate her. "I'll stop calling you Ducky if you'll stop calling me little plum cake."

He nodded. "Very well. We have a bargain. Now I'm going to bed." He started toward the door, then paused and glanced back, smirking. "What, no kiss good-night?"

She stiffened. "As we are alone and it is almost the afternoon, certainly not."

"Too bad. You kiss quite well—for a novice," he said as he opened the door.

Only a few days ago, she would have been tempted to throw the empty inkpot at his head for such a condescending remark.

Now?

Now, she hardly knew what to make of Quintus MacLachlann.

Two hours later, Esme sat at the writing desk. Where before the delicate piece of furniture had been as empty as the inkpot, now it was equipped with several sheets of blank foolscap, quills and a penknife for sharpening points. The inkpot had been filled with the finest India ink, and the sand shaker prepared. She'd given some of her pin money to the butler to purchase the necessary writing supplies.

She did not include that detail in the letter she was writing to her brother, only that they had arrived, their ruse seemed to be working and MacLachlann had already gleaned some useful information at his brother's club.

She'd just noted MacLachlann's observation about the gentry's apparent prosperity when McSweeney arrived bearing a card on a silver server. "Are you at home, my lady?"

She took the card and frowned when she saw who was waiting before she raised her head. "Yes, I am."

As the butler departed, Esme closed the writing desk, rose and smoothed down her pretty gown of pale green sprigged muslin. So attired, she felt on more equal footing with Lady Catriona McNare, the Mistress of Duncombe, breaker of her brother's heart and destroyer of his happiness.

Chapter Six

As Catriona glided into the room, Esme tried not to stare. To be sure, she had known Catriona would be older—they all were. And Catriona was as stylishly dressed as ever, in a lovely dove-gray pelisse with black-frog closing and a matching gray bonnet with black velvet ribbons. So it wasn't her clothes or her deportment that surprised Esme; it was the alterations to her features. Esme had seen her only once, on that fateful evening when Catriona had jilted Jamie, but she would never forget the youthful beauty who had broken her brother's heart.

Catriona's face had been soft and round, her cheeks plump and pink. Now she was pale and gaunt. Her green eyes had a haunted look, not un-like Jamie's when he thought Esme wasn't watching as he stared out the drawing room window on a rainy Sunday afternoon.

"Hello, Miss McCallan," the Mistress of Duncombe said after a swift glance assured her they were alone. "I can't thank you enough for coming to Edinburgh to help me, or your brother for sending you."

However she had changed and however grateful she was, this was still the woman who had rejected her brother because he was too poor and unimportant for the daughter of an earl to marry. "He is a very generous, *forgiving* man."

"But you don't forgive me," Catriona said with quiet wistfulness. "I don't blame you. I treated your brother very badly, and I—"

"Well, well, who have we here?" MacLachlann jovially asked as he strode into the room.

Although it had only been two hours since Esme had last seen him, he appeared remarkably well-rested. He was also shaved, his hair brushed, and he wore a fresh white shirt, cravat, black trousers and dark green jacket and waistcoat. Indeed, he looked every inch the rich, confident gentleman.

"This is Lady Catriona McNare, the Earl of Duncombe's daughter."

"I'm delighted to meet you, my lady," MacLachlann replied as he bent down to lift Catriona's gloved hand to his lips.

"You must be Quintus MacLachlann," Catriona said. "Jamie told me all about you in his letter."

"Dear me, I hope he didn't tell you *everything*," MacLachlann cried with mock horror, "or you'll never speak to me again."

Looking more like the beauty she'd been in the first flush of youth, Catriona gave him a warm smile. "I shall always be happy to speak to any friend of Jamie's."

Not wanting to waste any time with idle chit-chat and the sharing of meaningless compliments, Esme got right to the point. "Have you been able to find any pertinent documents?"

Catriona shook her head, making the little blond curls on her forehead dance. "Unfortunately, no. My father keeps his library door locked most of the time."

MacLachlann darted an inscrutable glance at Esme, then gestured to a chair. "Please, sit down."

Was he implying she'd been remiss? Or rude? She didn't care. She wouldn't care what he or

Catriona McNare, ruin of her brother's peace and happiness, thought about her.

"Most of the time? But he doesn't keep the door locked *all* the time?" MacLachlann asked Catriona once they were seated.

"No. Sometimes he leaves it open, although only for a little while if he's temporarily called away." Catriona delicately cleared her throat. "It's my understanding that a locked door should present no hindrance to you, Mr. MacLachlann, so when I heard when you'd be arriving, I arranged to have a dinner party in your honor tonight. My father was quite a good friend of your father's, I understand."

"Yes, he was."

Esme tried not to reveal her dismay at only hearing of this now. "You never mentioned that he knows you."

"He knows *of* me, but we've never met," MacLachlann explained. "I was rarely in Edinburgh when I was a boy. My father considered me too rambunctious, so he made me stay at school."

Esme had enjoyed school, but she had enjoyed her holidays at home more. It would have been upsetting to be forced to remain there all year 'round.

She told herself to concentrate on the business at hand, not MacLachlann's childhood. "Will he have met your brother?"

"Yes, I suppose."

At his cavalier response, the blood warmed in her veins, and not with desire. "And yet you didn't think that was something I ought to know?"

"We're going to be introduced to many people who've met Augustus," MacLachlann said lightly. "He'll be no different from the others."

"Except that we're going to try to see his private papers. If the earl has any reason to suspect you're not Augustus—"

"It's my job to make sure nobody suspects we aren't who we claim to be, and I'm very good at my job. If we're discovered in the library, we'll simply say the door was unlocked and we slipped away for…" He waggled his eyebrows suggestively. "A few moments alone."

That explanation might be plausible, but sneaking into the earl's library was still dangerous. "Our absence might be noticed."

"Not right away," Catriona said hopefully. "I've invited twenty couples."

That sounded more like a ball than a dinner party to Esme.

"Father likes large parties," Catriona explained, "and given your purpose, I thought it best to have as many guests as possible."

"Right you are," MacLachlann said with a reassuring smile. "The more the merrier, I always say."

"Fortunately most of your set and your brother's acquaintances are in the country this time of year," Lady Catriona continued. "I've invited friends of my father, as well as our solicitor, Gordon McHeath."

Although Esme wanted to believe no solicitor would ever cheat or defraud a client, she knew human nature too well to believe it impossible. "If your father is being defrauded or otherwise tricked in contractual matters, it's possible Mr. McHeath is involved," she said.

"I wouldn't like to think so," Catriona replied with every appearance of dismay. "His family's reputation has been without blemish for three generations and Gordon McHeath seems a fine young man. I haven't heard a word against him."

Which didn't make him an honest man. "Some of the people Jamie has represented have been cheated by men who were supposedly paragons of virtue," she duly noted.

"It's a bit early to be casting aspersions on anybody," MacLachlann said. "As a matter of fact, my family uses the same firm."

Esme stared at him. Why hadn't she been told this, too? It would help their investigation to have a connection to the earl's legal representation.

What else had MacLachlann and Jamie kept from her?

"I'm *sure* Mr. McHeath is trustworthy," Catriona said with a shy smile, as if too modest to voice an opinion. "And perhaps you're right and I've been worried about nothing. I do hope so! Is there anything else you'd like to know?"

"What time should we arrive?"

"Seven o'clock." Catriona looked from one to the other and toyed with the tassel on the bottom of her black velvet reticule. "I cannot possibly express how grateful I am to you both," she said, her dulcet voice as soft and pleasant as Esme remembered, her green eyes moist, as if she were about to weep. "I fear our financial situation is even more precarious than I thought."

"It can't be so very bad if you're hosting a dinner party for forty people," Esme pointed out. And Catriona's clothes were clearly new, as well as expensive.

Despite her logical observation, MacLachlann slid her another censorious glance. Like most men, he was obviously willing to accept anything that came out of a beautiful young woman's mouth at face value.

"Father pretends everything is fine and we have no need to worry about money," Catriona said as a blush tinted her cheeks. "Even after he tells me of another loss, if I try to economize, he insists on spending as we always have. But I fear we're deeply in debt, and our property mortgaged beyond the capacity of the estate to repay."

"Don't worry, my lady," MacLachlann assured her. "We're here to help you, and it may be that you're worried for nothing. Men can sometimes say things without considering the effect on others and imply a situation is worse than it is.

Without all the information, it's easy for a woman to worry."

"If a *man's* father was losing money and he wouldn't tell him the exact details of the situation, I daresay his son would worry, too," Esme coldly observed.

MacLachlann ignored her. "For tonight, I think it will be enough that we meet this McHeath fellow and get into your father's library to examine any documents we can find. If we find evidence of suspicious dealings, we'll figure out our next step."

He gave Catriona another encouraging smile. "But as I said, it may well be that by keeping you ignorant of his business dealings, your father has worried you unnecessarily. Let's hope so, shall we, my lady?"

Looking almost as youthful as the Catriona Esme remembered, the young lady stood up and held out her hand to MacLachlann. "Thank you so much—both of you," she added with a glance at Esme, as if she—and by extension, Jamie— weren't as important.

"Jamie's the one who deserves your thanks," she said as she, too, got to her feet. "We wouldn't be here if it weren't for him—and his money. He's paying all our expenses."

Catriona had the grace to blush. "Of course I'll see that he's repaid out of my own funds."

"I'll make sure he sends you a bill."

Catriona nodded and, still blushing, gave them another tremulous smile. "Until tonight, then," she murmured before she glided from the room.

The moment the door closed behind her, MacLachlann turned on his heel and glared at Esme. "What the devil was that all about?"

Esme was fairly certain she knew what his question referred to, but she was in no mood for his criticism. She had seen too many men fall under the spell of a pretty young woman to be surprised that it happened. The only surprise today was that a man like MacLachlann would be susceptible. She had assumed he would be too worldly and have too much experience with women to succumb to any woman's charms. Obviously, she was wrong.

"As it was a long conversation, please clarify to which point you refer," she replied as she went to the writing desk, sat down and opened the lid.

"Why did you have to mention money and bills?"

Refusing to be ashamed of anything she said to Catriona McNare, Esme swivelled on the chair to regard MacLachlann. "It was simply a reminder that this is costing Jamie money and he should be repaid. Or do you think he should pay all the costs himself? She did jilt him, you know, and it didn't look as if she's lacking for pin money."

"Did you have to raise that subject today? At our first meeting?"

"Why delay? Better she should understand her obligations at once than claim ignorance later. Indeed, if I had my way, Jamie would have written a contract for her to sign outlining exactly what we were to do and how he would be reimbursed."

"God!" MacLachlann exclaimed, throwing out his arms. "Women and the law—what a combination! It's a damn good thing women can't be lawyers, or we men would have our heads handed to us on a legal platter!"

"If you deserved it, I should hope so," Esme calmly replied. The more he lost control of his emotions, the easier she found it to restrain hers. "If women could be lawyers, the world would be a different place—especially for women. And it would also be better if men didn't keep unnecessary secrets. Why didn't you tell me that your father was a good friend of Catriona's and that your family used the same firm of solicitors?"

"I didn't think of it," MacLachlann growled.

"If this is how you conduct your business, I should warn Jamie that he might not be getting all the necessary facts."

"He gets all the necessary facts. And so do you, when you need them. I'm in charge of this investigation, Miss McCallan, not you. You are here to provide legal expertise regarding documents, and nothing more."

Esme could hardly contain her anger. "Oh, so you are captain of this ship?"

"Yes! And you know it, Esme, so don't try to tell me I'm overstepping."

"You've been overstepping since we started. And if you're the captain, I shall ensure I have a lifeboat and my own compass, because you're sure to run us aground!"

"I've had enough of your insolence," he snapped.

"*My* insolence?" she replied. "You've been nothing *but* insolent since the day we met—as well as disrespectful and rude and uncouth, with your countless, unwelcome innuendos."

"I confess myself surprised that, given your limited experience, you can even understand my innuendoes."

"I most certainly do—and they're disgusting, just like you."

With a muttered curse, he marched to the door.

"Where are you going?" Esme demanded.

"Back to bed." He turned around and jabbed his finger at the writing desk. "If you're writing a letter to Jamie, tell him that he should be paying me *double* for putting up with his martinet of a sister."

His insult stung, but she wouldn't let him see that. "Are you attempting to change the terms of your employment arbitrarily and without prior agreement? If so, Jamie could sue you for breach of contract."

MacLachlann wrenched open the door. "Women and the law!" he muttered as he strode from the room.

Esme flounced onto the chair and stared at the letter she had yet to finish.

What else didn't she know, about MacLachlann

and the earl, Jamie and Catriona…and her own wayward heart that, even when she was enraged, still found Quintus MacLachlann so attractive?

Gad, this place hadn't changed at all, Quinn thought as he walked into the gambling hell that Augustus had frequented. Although at one time the establishment had been well-maintained, the wallpaper was now shabby, the rugs on the oaken floor worn and the smoke-laden air smelled as if a window hadn't been opened since Quinn had left Edinburgh ten years ago. The noise was the same, though—the half-drunken cheers when somebody won, the mutters of discontent when somebody lost, the hushed conversations in other parts of the room, the low rumble of men's semi-embarrassed laughter that suggested a bawdy joke had just been told. And, as always, one or two men slumped in the corner, either passed out from drink or too dismayed by losses to do anything but stare.

Esme probably believed this sort of place was his preferred habitat. Although he'd gambled in his youth, he hated hells like this, with the noise and the stench and the thinly veiled air of desperation. He'd gambled at more private, exclusive places…the better able to delude himself that he wasn't doing anything disgraceful, not even when he was down to his last farthing. Before he'd lost the respect of his family and all his friends except the one who had saved his life.

It wasn't as if Esme was without fault. Would it have hurt her to be polite to Lady Catriona? Did she have to regard the worried young woman like a judge at the Old Bailey about to pronounce a sentence of death?

Legal expertise or not, he never should have agreed to let Esme accompany him to Edinburgh. He should have insisted he come alone. He could have found a way to make copies of documents and taken them back to Jamie, or at least the pertinent parts. He did know how to read. How hard could it be?

"Good God, is that you, Dubhagen?" a man shouted from across the room.

Fervently hoping he'd recognize the speaker, Quinn peered through the smoke, trying to identify the stocky figure hurrying toward him through the tables of card players, most of whom barely glanced up from their games. The man looked vaguely familiar and he wracked his brain for a name.

"Ramsley?" Quinn suggested as the fellow who appeared roughly the same age as Augustus came to a halt in front of him, narrowly avoiding a collision with a waiter carrying a tray of drinks.

"Yes, b'God, it's me," Ramsley cried, his eyes watering and his nose red, more than half in his cups although it was barely noon. "I never thought to see you again! We all thought you'd stay in Jamaica for good. What brings you home?"

Quinn suppressed a sigh of relief that this fellow thought he was Augustus. On the other hand, perhaps he needn't have been so anxious. He'd tricked McSweeney, after all, although there'd been a brief instant when he thought McSweeney was starting to smile. The butler never would have smiled if Augustus had returned.

"I've come back to Edinburgh to see about some investments," Quinn explained as Ramsley threw his arm about Quinn's shoulder, as if they'd been the best of friends before Augustus had sailed. Quinn, however, knew for a fact that Augustus had hated the man. He'd only tolerated Ramsley because of his family connections, and the money Ramsley had inherited.

Probably not a lot of that left, Quinn thought, if Ramsley was in a gambling hell and drunk before noon.

"Investments, eh?" Ramsley repeated as, with his free hand, he grabbed a passing waiter's arm.

"Two brandies for my friend and me," he ordered as he started steering Quinn toward a corner of the room. "Nothing wrong, I hope? I'd heard you married a rich girl over there."

"Oh, I did," Quinn answered as they reached a velvet sofa that had clearly seen better days. "That's why I've come. I've got to make sure I invest the dowry well, don't you know."

"Substantial, was it?" Ramsley asked.

"Considerable," Quinn agreed.

Ramsley got a greedy gleam in his eye. "I don't suppose she has a sister?"

"No," Quinn answered, thinking Ramsley was the last man on earth he'd ever want to marry any relative of his. "Aren't there any suitable young women in Edinburgh anxious to ally themselves with an old, established family? What about that daughter of the Earl of Duncombe? She's not married, I heard."

Ramsley scowled. "I'd take the girl and her dowry in a heartbeat. It's the father I can't stomach."

As if the lady was simply waiting for him to ask. Nevertheless, Quinn looked suitably concerned. "What's wrong with him? I always thought he was a genial sort."

"He is, unless you pay attention to his daughter," Ramsley replied, leaning back against the sofa. "Then he treats you like a leper."

"I did hear something about a young man who wanted to marry her. Nothing came of that, eh?"

"I should say not. The fellow was only a solicitor. Talk about gall!"

It sounded as if in some things, Ramsley would side with Catriona's father.

Again Quinn wondered how Jamie could find it in his heart to want to help a woman whose father held him in contempt.

What would it be like to love a woman so devotedly?

He'd never been in love. He'd experienced lust, of course, a few times. And he certainly wasn't celibate. But to love a woman as Jamie must have loved Lady Catriona… That was something he'd probably never know, just as no woman would likely ever feel that sort of love for him.

So although Esme would probably call it foolish sentiment, knowing that Jamie was capable of such devotion made Quinn that much more determined to help him.

If that meant putting up with Esme, so be it. He would ignore her as best he could, or at least not let her upset him, as she was particularly capable of doing. And he certainly wouldn't kiss her again, not even if he wanted to.

Even if her kisses were surprisingly…excellent.

"The earl's turned into a regular hermit, too," Ramsley said, reminding Quinn he was there. "Hardly goes to balls or parties and keeps his daughter close to home, too."

Quinn decided to put out a little bait. "I wonder…?"

"What?" Ramsley demanded as the waiter brought their brandies.

Quinn lowered his voice to a confidential whisper as the waiter moved away and Ramsley downed his drink in a gulp. "I've been hearing rumors that the earl's financial situation might not be as good as it used to be."

Ramsley laughed with scornful derision. "Whoever told you that is a fool. My father's gone to the earl for advice about investing his money for years and never had a moment's regret."

"Not even this year?"

"Never."

Ramsley sounded absolutely sure of that.

But then, he was more than a little drunk and had never been particularly bright. It wouldn't surprise Quinn to learn that Ramsley was as ignorant of his own family's financial situation as Catriona was about her father's.

Chapter Seven

Several hours later, after Quinn had managed to get away from Ramsley and the gambling hell without drinking more than two brandies or betting a penny, he waited for Esme at the foot of the staircase.

McSweeney stood by the door and the French valet McHeath had also hired was ready to hand Quinn his hat and assist him with his greatcoat.

As much as he enjoyed having servants and fine clothes, there was much about this assignment that made it unpleasant, not the least of which was having to endure the company of men like Ramsley, in places like that gambling hell. He was absolutely determined to get this job done as quickly as possible, and to pay as little attention to Esme as he could while he did.

He hadn't expected his resolve to be tested the

moment he looked up to see Esme descending the stairs. She wore a soft, shimmering concoction of pale pink silk with a low, rounded neck that revealed her cleavage. The ribbon beneath her breasts seemed designed to accentuate their plump fullness. The puffed cap sleeves and long evening gloves covered most of her arms, save for a tantalizing glimpse of flesh in between. Her hair, piled on her head in an intricate style of braids and curls, with a ribbon the same pale pink as her gown woven through it, made her look like a goddess. Venus. No, Athena, the goddess of wisdom, come to Scotland in mortal form, beautiful and serene, calm and confident, able to deal with any problem, whether human or supernatural.

He immediately wanted to kiss her again, and to do more than that. He wanted to caress and excite her, to show her all the intimate joys a man and woman could share, to lay her down on his bed and make love with her until they were both sated and completely satisfied.

"Is something the matter with my gown, Ducky?" Esme asked, her brows knitting with concern as she reached the bottom step.

He reminded himself that this was still Esme

McCallan, the same woman who usually treated him with scorn and derision and disrespect.

"I was just thinking that pink suits you," he replied. "It makes you look...younger."

A brief flare of annoyance flashed in her eyes. Thank God. He had to do something to quell his desire, and making her angry would surely work. It had to. "Nobody would guess you're twenty-seven, my dear. You don't look a day over twenty-six."

Esme McCallan had, as he well knew, recently turned twenty-two.

Instead of replying with a sharp retort, she giggled.

He'd never before found giggling appealing, yet he found hers unexpectedly pleasant, like water bubbling over rocks.

Then she spoke. "And you don't look a day over forty, my love. Losing five stone on the voyage home has made such a difference!"

Five stone? Seventy pounds? He would have been as fat as a hog ready for market.

"I feared you'd never be able to eat a full meal again," she continued in that slightly daft manner she'd adopted while a maid helped her into her cloak and he allowed the valet to assist him into his greatcoat.

"It was only seasickness," he lied for the benefit of the servants while McSweeney went to open the door.

Was that a smile twitching at the corners of McSweeney's lips?

"We're going to be late," Quinn snapped, leading Esme outside.

Mercifully she didn't say another word as they got into the waiting barouche that belonged to his brother. Once inside, he settled into the corner, arms crossed, while she adjusted her skirts with the most smug expression he'd ever seen on her face.

"I had no idea you could play the fool so well," he frigidly remarked.

"Neither did I," she replied. "It's quite easy, really. I simply pretend I'm about five years old. How do *you* manage it?"

He scowled and slouched lower in the seat as the carriage lurched into motion.

"Sit up straight or your clothes will be wrinkled."

He neither moved nor answered.

"Now who's acting like a five-year-old?"

"Why shouldn't I act like a child when you're acting as if you're my mother? 'Sit up straight, mind your manners, what's wrong with you?'"

He hadn't meant for that last to slip out.

"Enough, my little plum cake," he growled. "I owe Jamie my life, but I won't be made the butt of a joke by you, or anyone."

She glared at him as if he'd asked for the Stone of Scone. "You dare say that to me, when you make a joke out of everything I say?"

"I do not!" he protested.

"As good as," she returned. "You ignore me, keep important information from me, insult me and have the effrontery, the insolence, to kiss me—and yet you then insist I treat you with the same respect I accord other men?"

Quinn crossed his arms and glowered. She'd probably be quite happy to shoot him and spit on his corpse, if only it wasn't against the law. "If you'd rather that I treated you like a vestal virgin, so be it. That will be no hardship for me, I assure you."

The carriage stopped outside a brightly lit mansion of dark gray stone and bow windows, even more immense than Quinn's family's town house.

"We've arrived," he unnecessarily growled. "Remember why we're here."

"You remember that, too—and that I'm Jamie McCallan's sister."

As if he could ever forget.

Once out of the barouche, Esme took MacLachlann's hand with a vicelike grip and marched stoically beside him into the house, looking neither to the left or the right. How dare he speak to her that way? What unmitigated gall to demand that she treat him with respect, when he mocked and teased her, chided and…and kissed her!

She moved away from him as soon as she could when servants hurried to help them remove hat, coat and cloak. Then it was on to the finely appointed drawing room full of expensive furnishings of royal blue and silver damask and hothouse roses in a variety of tall, oriental vases. Several well-dressed men and women were already milling about, resplendent in evening attire. The men were almost uniform in their dark jackets, brilliantly white shirts, intricately tied cravats and white knee breeches and stockings, with polished and buckled shoes. The ladies, however, were like a collection of flowers, the hues ranging from dark purple or black to the brightest, lightest pinks and yellows, with a smattering of green that could represent foliage. The hairstyles were likewise fashionable, with curls and ringlets and ribbons and flowers interwoven in the glossy locks. Some of the older women sported turbans, with flowers and jewels attached. Indeed, there were so many jewels of so many kinds and sizes, Esme was quite dazzled, although she thought her simple string of pearls, given to her by Jamie when she turned twenty-one, was finer than any necklace here because it had been given with love.

"Ah, here you are!" Catriona cried, hurrying toward them through the crowd.

She wore a gown of soft green velvet that brought out the color of her eyes. Her hair was dressed with pearls that matched the string at her throat, and her long gloves were spotlessly white, like the toes of the slippers peeking out from beneath her gown. She moved with lithesome grace and her smile was all that a woman's welcoming smile ought to be.

No wonder the young men flocked to her, and Jamie had fallen deeply in love.

What man would find *her* attractive, Esme wondered, if he knew the truth about her love of the law, the joy she found in researching legal precedents, the triumph she experienced when she'd written an excellent draft of a will or settlement, her lack of concern for her wardrobe or hair, or saw the ink that so often stained her fingers?

Apparently, MacLachlann did—except that she couldn't believe his kisses meant any sincere affection on his part. Lust, perhaps—and although even that was surprising, it was hardly the long-lasting feeling she hoped to inspire in a man's heart.

"You must come and meet my father," Catriona said, taking Quinn's other arm and steering them toward an elderly gentleman with white hair, as wrinkled as a raisin and as thin as a barge pole, seated near the marble hearth carved to look as if it was held aloft by half-naked nymphs.

As they walked across the room, Esme could feel the scrutiny of the people watching. In spite of her anxiety, she did her best to look as if she belonged there, among this glittering, wealthy crowd. She risked a swift glance at the man beside her, to see that he didn't look the least bit uncertain or out of place. Indeed, given how fine he looked, she could well believe that the women were watching out of admiration for a handsome man, not because they suspected anything was amiss. And Catriona would draw the attention of any male older than fifteen.

"Papa," Catriona said when they reached the elderly gentleman, "this is the Earl of Dubhagen and his wife, who have recently returned from Jamaica."

"Who?" the older man demanded, frowning as he looked at them and cupped his right ear. A few stray white hairs protruded from each ear, and a few more grew equally as wild in his eyebrows, looking not unlike antennae.

"Lord Dubhagen and his wife," Catriona repeated a little louder. "Come back from Jamaica."

"Dubhagen, eh?" the earl cried with sudden understanding and a smile. "Back from Jamaica at last! Everybody thought you'd never return. And this is your wife. Pretty little thing, I must say."

He leaned toward Esme. "He looks strong enough," he whispered loudly, "but young men today don't know anything about pleasing women."

Esme couldn't quite mask her shock, and it was no hardship to feign an embarrassed giggle. "He suits me, my lord."

"You're a lucky man, Dubhagen, but then your family always was, except for that young scamp. What was his name? The fifth one that ran off with the Gypsies."

"Quintus, my lord," MacLachlann matter-of-factly supplied. "But it wasn't with Gypsies. He took my father's best horse and rode to London."

"Whatever happened to him? Came to a bad end, no doubt."

"I have no idea, my lord. I haven't had any communication with him for the past decade."

Esme had known MacLachlann was estranged from his family, but that was a long time to be alone.

"Not since before your father died, eh? There was a man for you—your father. Not like these young fellows today who are all spit and boot black. *That* man could fight!"

"Yes, he was very strong," Quinn replied, and in a coldly distant tone she recognized. She'd heard it often enough from the adult children of parents and guardians who'd been neglectful, harsh, or even brutal.

A tawny-haired, broad-shouldered fellow approached and bowed. The earl nodded in return, so clearly he knew the man, while Catriona gave him a little smile more indicative of friendship than desire, or so it seemed to Esme.

When he spoke, however, he addressed neither the earl nor Catriona, but MacLachlann.

"Please forgive the rudeness, my lord," he said. "I should have come by your house as soon as you arrived from London, but I've been working on a very difficult contract up in Inverness. I'm your solicitor here in Edinburgh, my lord. Gordon McHeath."

Another lawyer at last! Now she could have some intelligent conversation that wasn't fraught with…anything.

"I've been so looking forward to…!" she began with heartfelt sincerity before she remembered she was supposed to be shallow and ignorant, and that although she hated to believe a solicitor could be complicit in illegal activities, it was certainly possible. "To meeting my husband's solicitor," she added with another silly giggle.

McHeath smiled. "Really? Well now, that's not something a solicitor usually hears."

She was well aware of that. Attorneys were often held in contempt as grasping, greedy charlatans—until they were needed, of course.

"Not that I understand at all what you do," she continued with another giggle. "I wanted to thank you for hiring all the servants and seeing that the house was ready for us. It must have taken a lot of effort on your part in addition to your other tasks."

"It was no trouble, I assure you."

His accent was broader than either hers or MacLachlann's, and he had excellent teeth, too. No doubt a solicitor with his good looks, muscular build and manners didn't lack for clients, especially women.

"Your work must be so very interesting!" she said, turning the conversation to matters of business. "Ducky, here—oh, I mean Lord Dubhagen— doesn't do anything at all, you know."

"I wouldn't say that, my lady," the solicitor gravely replied. "He has many decisions to make over the course of a year, and that requires some effort."

Esme waved her hand dismissively and took McHeath's arm, leading him away from the others. "But entailments and wills and contracts—it's all so complicated. Do you compose all the documents yourself, or do you have help?"

Despite the excellent meal of several courses and various wines, the longer Quinn sat in the earl's opulent dining room, the more he remembered exactly why he preferred meals in pubs and taverns, or alone in his rooms in Cheapside. He'd never been comfortable with the constraint of formality and had chafed at the meaningless rules and social hierarchies even in childhood.

Nevertheless, those meals now seemed like child's play as he pretended to be Augustus and feign an interest in the conversation.

It didn't help that he'd been seated to the right of their hostess, who was beside her elderly father, while Esme was at the far end of the table beside that damn handsome solicitor.

Quinn had never thought much about a solicitor's appearance until McHeath—comely as

Adonis with wavy brown hair—had walked up to them and smiled. Put the man in a kilt and give him a claymore and Quinn didn't doubt half the ladies in the room would swoon. The man had the deep, velvety voice of an actor, too.

He'd thought Esme more impervious than most women when it came to a man's looks—she'd certainly never reacted to his outward appearance, which he knew most women found appealing—until he saw her smile at Gordon McHeath as if he were a knight in shining armor coming to her rescue.

He'd told himself she was excited and pleased to meet the man because he was a solicitor, then been afraid she would forget that she had a role to play and it was not Lady Lawyer. He hoped that she wouldn't inadvertently reveal a level of knowledge that would rouse McHeath's suspicions, or anything else. Fortunately, she seemed to have adopted a strategy of saying nothing, batting her long lashes and smiling like a simpleton.

It could be worse, he told himself. If Catriona wasn't as spirited as Esme, at least she was pretty to look at. Indeed, it was easy to see why Jamie had fallen in love with her, especially when he considered what she must have been like five years ago—young and fresh as the first rosebud of spring, innocent and blooming and sweet.

Esme, on the other hand, had been full of thorns and as imperious as an empress from the first time he'd met her. She always dressed in drab, ill-fitting garments that masked her figure. Her usual severe hairstyle—the smooth locks drawn back so tight he'd often wondered if it hurt—didn't do much for her features, either, although it did emphasize her remarkably bright, intelligent eyes.

Fortunately, Esme's manners were impeccable and she seemed far more at ease in these surroundings than he ever would have expected as she sat listening with rapt attention to whatever McHeath was saying, although perhaps it was the man's nearly constant attention that made her so relaxed, as she never was with him.

What was the solicitor thinking about Esme? He obviously found her attractive, but any man alive would find Esme attractive tonight, with her hair dressed in the latest style, her eyes modestly downcast, her cheeks aglow with excitement or the heat of the room and dressed in that gown that exposed far too much cleavage.

He wanted to be able to look into her shining, shrewd eyes, to hear what she was really thinking about the company, and to have her decently covered from men's lustful gazes, even his—perhaps especially his, if he couldn't subdue the desire that surged into life whenever he looked at her.

The earl cleared his throat as his guests finished their dessert of crème brûlée and fruit.

"Tell me, Dubhagen," the old nobleman said, "what do you think of these abolitionists? Surely you won't be able to manage your sugar plantation without slaves."

Quinn was very aware of his brother's attitude toward slavery. Augustus had often used Quinn's opinion on slavery as proof of his younger brother's ignorance of the ways of business. Unfortunately, his brother's opinion would be well known to the earl and perhaps others here, so tonight he would have to espouse it.

"Quite right," he replied, hating to say the words even if they were necessary. "Men who condemn the use of slaves are softheaded fools who have no idea what's required to bring sugar to their tables."

Esme frowned and so did McHeath, who said, "Surely, my lord, in these enlightened times, there are alternatives to slavery, especially when the sugar trade is so lucrative. Why not pay for the labor required?"

"We do pay," Quinn replied, repeating his brother's well-remembered words. "We give them food and clothes and tend to their wounds and illnesses, give them places to live, as well as make them Christians. They are much better off under our care than left to live as heathens in Africa."

"But they are human beings, my lord," McHeath protested, "not dumb animals to be abducted and shipped off like so much cattle."

"Then what do you, as a solicitor, think of the earl's right to remove his tenants from his Highland estates so the land can become pasture for sheep?" Quinn asked. "Should the tenants be allowed to disobey the law?"

"Something may be right under the law, yet morally unjust," the solicitor replied, "and the law must change to reflect that. I'm confident that one day, slavery will be regarded as the abomination it is. Tenants will have more and better redress under the law. Women will cease to be regarded as chattels and will be persons under the law, with full legal rights and privileges."

Her hazel eyes full of approval, Esme stared at McHeath as if she wanted to kiss him. Or more.

"Never," Quinn growled before he remembered what he was supposed to be talking about. "How can savages have rights? Or peasants? Or women? They wouldn't know what to do with them even if they had them, and this country would descend into ruin and anarchy. Look what's happened in France."

"Surely you don't think women should be able to vote," another gentleman demanded of McHeath, laughing as if that was the best joke he'd every heard. "Why, only handsome politicians would ever stand a chance of election!"

Instead of wealthy ones, or those with the backing of a rich patron or family, Quinn wanted to retort. Instead, he said, "Perhaps Mr. McHeath would run for office then."

"Perhaps I would," the solicitor returned, "although I give women credit for being able to consider important issues as well as any man. And men can be equally influenced by popularity."

"Or wealth and family," Esme suggested.

"Well, I see no harm in it," another man smugly asserted, tucking his thumbs into his waistcoat. "My wife would vote as I told her."

Esme batted her long eyelashes at him. "If the

ballot was a secret one," she asked with apparent wide-eyed innocence, "how would you know?"

Before that man, or any other, could summon a response, Catriona swiftly got to her feet, signalling that it was time for the women to retire to the drawing room.

Esme was slow to rise, as if she didn't want to leave.

Thank God she couldn't stay. Who could guess what she might say in defence of women's rights? Although he agreed with her and she was doing her best to sound daft, he didn't know how long it might be before she lost her temper and with it, her facade.

After the ladies had left the room, McHeath shoved back his chair and bowed to their elderly host. "If you'll excuse me, Lord Duncombe, I have some documents at home that require my immediate attention. Please express my regrets for my hasty departure to your daughter."

"My word!" Quinn said after the man had marched from the room. "Rather a hothead, isn't he?"

"With some radical ideas," the earl agreed. "Still, he's the best solicitor in Edinburgh, so it's worth putting up with his eccentricities. I can't make head nor tails of a contract without his explanations."

"Is that so?" Quinn replied. "As good as that, eh?"

Or as devious?

Chapter Eight

Having no choice, Esme followed her hostess to the drawing room, even though she hated the upper class custom that required women to leave the dining room before the men, as if the women couldn't and shouldn't be expected to take part in discussions about politics and social issues. Although MacLachlann was proving he could act every inch the wealthy, titled gentleman, she wished she was back in London and home with her law books.

Several young women clustered around Esme after she sat on a blue silk-covered cabriole sofa.

"Such a lovely gown! Is it from Paris?" one of them asked.

Esme recalled that the questioner was the youngest daughter of a magistrate. In London, she and her family would probably not have been considered of high enough rank to be at such a gathering. In Scotland, though, members of the legal profession were held in better esteem—as they deserved to be.

"No, London," Esme answered, wondering how much longer it would be before the men returned. She found fashion a boring subject and it was one reason she was rarely comfortable with members of her own sex, for it seemed the one subject to which feminine conversations always diverted.

Not that she blamed her fellow women entirely for their limited topics of conversation. What could one expect given the education most women received? Even those of the upper class were taught only a smattering of French, a bit of drawing or instruction in watercolors, how to play the piano or, if they were capable, sing. Most of their time was spent preparing for social occasions, so what else should they think about but clothes and hairstyles, fans, reticules and gloves?

"Who was the modiste?" another young woman asked eagerly. Lady Eliza Deluce had on a beautiful gown of soft, flowing scarlet silk with several rows of blue and green ribbon around the hem.

Over her arms she'd draped a cashmere shawl, and her hair glowed like a golden coronet.

Unfortunately, neither gown nor hair could hide the moles upon her chin and forehead.

Esme quickly made up a modiste's name and did her best to look interested as the conversation drifted onto the more general subject of dress-makers and fabrics and trims and styles even as she retreated into silence. While the other young ladies chattered on, her gaze wandered to a few older women deep in discussion on a pair of sofas at the far end of the room. They reminded Esme of a cabal of thieves, and every so often one would glance her way, convincing her that she, and her supposed husband, were likely the topic of dis-cussion.

Did MacLachlann really believe what he'd said about slavery, or was he saying such things to maintain their ruse? And what about the earl's handsome solicitor? Could a man who spoke with such feeling about the evils of slavery be a thief or embezzler, swindling the earl out of his money?

Of course he could. She'd been privy to enough of her brother's business to know that a deter-mined hypocrite could easily mask self-interest.

A plump, middle-aged woman wearing a biliously purple turban with a droopy ostrich feather dangling over her left ear and encased in a gown of similar mind-boggling hue trimmed with bright green, began insinuating herself between Esme and the arm of the sofa. "May I join you, my dear?"

She was Lady Stantonby, Esme recalled, a very wealthy widow. Unfortunately, she couldn't think of a reason why the woman shouldn't. "Of course."

"Are you quite well? You look a little piqued," her companion said in a sympathetic tone that was more appropriate to a deathbed than a drawing room.

She would feel better if she had more room, Esme thought; nevertheless, she smiled insipidly and replied with the truth. "I'm not used to such large dinner parties."

Lady Stantonby gave her a knowing smile and got a sly look in her eye that set Esme instantly on guard. "I suppose being married to Dubhagen is exhausting, too."

"I'm not sure what you mean," Esme replied innocently, although she could guess what the woman was hinting at.

Lady Elvira Cameron, who was sixty-five if she was a day and trying to look twenty in a gown of thin pale pink silk and with powder and rouge on her cheeks, settled on an oval-backed chair opposite and leaned forward as if she'd been desperate to speak to Esme all evening. "No doubt he's changed since he married. You're so lovely, he's surely felt no need to stray. I certainly hope so. He was *quite* the merry gadabout in his youth."

"I'm sure Lady Dubhagen doesn't need to hear every skeleton in her husband's family's closet," Lady Stantonby mildly protested.

"Well, she should be glad she married the eldest and not the youngest—Quinine or Quentin or whatever his name was," Lady Elvira said. "Sent down from school, spending his days in gambling hells and drunken revelry." She lightly tapped Esme's arm with her delicate fan made of carved ivory. "Quite the rascal he was, I assure you. No wonder his father disowned him—but I'm sure you know all about that."

"Indeed, I don't. I don't know very much at all about the earl's youngest son," Esme truthfully replied, suddenly glad the men weren't there and hoping they would be in the dining room a little longer yet.

Lady Elvira's eyes widened. "No? Poor man must be too ashamed to speak of him."

"Or sorry," another older woman said as she sat on the other side of Esme.

Unlike Lady Elvira, Lady Marchmont was tastefully attired in a gown of jonquil silk and satin, with topazes at her throat and a peacock feather in her jet-black hair. Only the few small wrinkles at the corners of her mild gray eyes suggested that she was older than twenty-five. "My husband's cousin knew Quintus MacLachlann at school. He thinks the poor fellow has been much maligned."

"If *my* son had gotten sent down from school for public drunkenness, I should have disowned him, too," Lady Stantonby said with a scornful sniff.

"My husband told me Quintus got drunk because he'd just learned that his mother had died and he wasn't to be allowed home for the funeral. He thinks Quintus did that so they would *have* to send him back to Edinburgh."

Esme clasped her hands in her lap and her heart filled with sympathy for both MacLachlann and his mother, who had died with her son away at school. "He loved his mother then?"

"Oh, yes, very much."

"They were much alike," Lady Elvira waspishly observed. "She was very pretty and quite useless, except to bear children, of course. At least there was never any doubt her children were also the earl's—every son looked just like him. Otherwise, well…she was forever going to balls and parties."

"Any opportunity to be out of the house," Lady Stantonby agreed. "The earl was a hot-tempered fellow and could be most unpleasant, even though it was *her* dowry that allowed him to keep his estate."

If their marriage had been an unhappy one, Esme wouldn't blame MacLachlann's mother a bit for wanting to get away from her husband any and every chance she could. Indeed, Esme would have advised the woman to seek a divorce, although she supposed fear of never seeing her children again would prevent that. Women always faced that threat in divorce proceedings, for men had the upper hand in law there, too.

"Ah, here come the gentlemen," Lady Stantonby murmured as Catriona's father entered the room, followed by the rest of the gentleman, including MacLachlann. As before, he seemed perfectly comfortable and at ease in his formfitting, expensive evening dress and looked every inch the noble lord.

"Your husband is certainly the handsomest fellow here," Lady Elvira said, drawing Esme's attention once again, "so I suppose that even if he has his father's temper, there are certain compensations."

"I suppose," Esme agreed with a giggle even as she tried not to imagine exactly what those compensations might be or how it would feel to be receiving them.

Catriona immediately went to her father, leading him to the choicest seat by the hearth. The other gentlemen, with one notable exception, scattered around the room.

MacLachlann strolled directly toward Esme and she rose to meet him. With what looked like an eager gleam in his eye, he immediately drew her away from the others toward a shadowed alcove. She had no choice but to go with him, she reasoned, with so many people in the room. The young ladies watched every step and began whispering eagerly, while more than one regarded her with blatant envy.

But what was he doing, and why, and why did he have that particular expression? And where was the solicitor? So far, all she'd discovered was that he enjoyed his work and found the differences between Scots and English law fascinating.

"What happened to Mr. McHeath?" she asked in a whisper.

"He had business that couldn't wait," MacLachlann quietly replied.

"That's most unfortunate. I shall have to arrange a meeting with him some other time."

MacLachlann's expression turned to irritation. "Why?"

She thought this should have been obvious. "As the earl's solicitor, he has a lot of influence over the earl's decisions—or could have, if he chooses to exercise it," she explained. "I hope he's not involved in any bad dealings with the earl, but I'm not so naive as to believe he couldn't be simply because he's a solicitor. If he *is* a swindler, I intend to give him the opportunity to attempt to ensnare us, as well, and how better than through your rather dim wife?"

"What reason would you give to meet with him?" MacLachlann asked, his brow furrowing.

"I shall tell him I have concerns about your disposal of my dowry."

"You would have no say in such a matter," he pointed out.

"I'm well aware of the limits of a wife's rights under the law," Esme replied. "However, given how I've been acting, I doubt Mr. McHeath will be surprised if I profess complete ignorance as to what's become of it."

"And if he tries to seduce you?"

As if she was some gullible innocent fresh from a convent!

"As you should know by now, I'm not easily swayed by looks or a charming manner. I simply mean to provide him the chance to expose any criminal enterprises in which he may be involved."

"He might be keen to expose *something*," MacLachlann sourly agreed.

"Don't be disgusting."

"That's a warning," he murmured, running a finger along her cheek.

She flinched, not because his touch was unpleasant, but because it was unexpected—and too pleasant. She lowered her eyes, blushing. She could smell his cologne, a wonderfully woodsy scent that mingled with the starch of his shirt and the wool of his coat, and felt his body close. "What are you doing?" she demanded with quiet annoyance.

"Being about the business of acting like your husband, and giving those old cats something to talk about," he murmured, leaning closer, his body mere inches from hers. "What's the matter, Esme? Are you afraid I'm going to kiss you again? Or are you hoping that I will?"

His last words were too close to the truth. Much too close. "Stand back," she warned.

"Have no fear, little plum cake. Even I wouldn't kiss you with those gossips looking on."

She breathed again and raised her eyes to find him looking at her with the most unusual expression on his face. Why, he looked almost…wistful. "McHeath will probably jump at the chance to meet with you, even if he's tempted to withdraw his services after our little discussion in the dining room."

She had to ask, had to know. "Were those your opinions?"

"Gad, no—my brother's, and they would be well known, so I had no choice but to say what I did. And I didn't expect McHeath to get so angry. I thought all solicitors could keep a cool head."

Usually so could she, except when she was around MacLachlann.

"It may well be that there's nothing illegal going on with the earl's affairs," MacLachlann continued, still close enough to kiss. "Did you notice how much wine he drank at dinner? Perhaps if he's having financial difficulties, it's because wine is clouding his judgment."

She hadn't noticed, although she should have. She shouldn't have been so distracted by the urge to discuss the difference between Scottish and English law with McHeath, or been so acutely aware of how fine MacLachlann looked in evening dress, or how often he leaned close to Catriona to hear what she was saying.

He nodded toward the far end of the drawing room, where Lady Marchmont was preparing to play the pianoforte and some footmen were moving chairs to clear a space for dancing. "Once the dancing starts, we should go to the earl's library. You leave the room first, and I'll follow a little later. Catriona says the library is toward the back of the house. The door is to the left of the painting of Edinburgh Castle."

Mercifully he drew back without touching her. "Until then, I suggest you talk to those biddies who are no doubt deciding that Jamaica was not good for my health, you're too thin and our marriage is a disaster. I shall engage the earl in a discussion about his estate in the Highlands. After a little while, excuse yourself and head for the library. I'll follow shortly and meet you there."

"Very well," she replied, having no alternate plan and finding it difficult to think with him so close.

He cupped her cheek with his palm. "Don't worry. Just ask them questions about their families and you won't have to say a word about yourself."

His touch and reassuring words were more welcome than she cared to acknowledge. "Until later, then."

He nodded and sauntered off toward the earl and Catriona, who was sitting beside her father and surrounded by a bevy of young men who were all from rich, upper-class families. More than one had a title and stood to inherit an estate.

Yet not a one of them commanded attention the way MacLachlann did simply by walking across the room.

At the first opportunity and after making sure nobody was watching her, Esme slipped out of the drawing room and into the main corridor. Her heart pounding, she made her way down the hall toward the back of the house, looking for a picture of Edinburgh Castle.

However did thieves stand the strain, the fear of discovery at any moment, the dread of being caught, especially knowing the usual consequences under the law?

At last she spotted the painting of the castle and hurried closer to the earl's library door. She tried the handle and discovered it was indeed locked.

At almost the same time, she heard voices coming toward her from the drawing room. What excuse would she give if someone saw her?

If she said she was lost, that might work.

Or she could say she was admiring the painting

of the castle. She tilted her head and walked forward to study it as the voices mercifully receded. The perspective was off and those clouds looked more like wool than—

"You'd never make a spy."

With a gasp she whirled around, to find MacLachlann right behind her. "Where did you come from?" she demanded in a whisper.

"The servants' stairs," he calmly replied.

"It's a miracle nobody saw you skulking about and raised an alarm."

"Nothing miraculous about it. Good timing and experience," he said as he looked down at her.

"Then I suggest you use some of that experience to get into the library," she replied, anxious to get their task completed. This dreadful excitement was a far cry from her usual thrills—finding obscure legal precedents or the perfect wording for a contract—and it was as disagreeable as she'd expected.

MacLachlann drew something from his breast pocket that he inserted into the keyhole in the door.

She shouldn't be surprised that not only did he

know how to pick locks, but he also possessed the tools to do it.

He wiggled the pick until she heard a soft click, then eased open the door and nodded for her to precede him inside. Hoping she wouldn't hit a piece of furniture or knock something over, she sidled into the dark room.

MacLachlann followed her, apparently with no such worries. He walked swiftly across the room to the window and opened the thick drapes. As she closed the door behind her, a shaft of moonlight fell directly onto a secretary cabinet by the door.

As her eyes adjusted to the available light, Esme noted a beechwood pedestal desk with a cushioned Charles II chair behind it in front of the windows and a dark chaise by the fireplace opposite. The walls were lined with shelves of books and portraits, including one of Catriona over the black marble hearth. It must have been painted around the time Jamie had met and fallen in love with her, for it uncannily depicted the beautiful young woman Esme remembered. In the portrait she was standing in a garden and holding a bouquet of white roses as lovely and fresh as she.

As if they had all the time in the world and had only to ascertain the earl's reading habits, MacLachlann wandered around the room studying the shelves, while she went directly to the desk. She tried to pull open a drawer only to find it didn't budge. "Can you open this, too?" she asked in a whisper.

MacLachlann didn't cease his circumnavigation of the room. "He won't keep anything important in there. Letters and receipts, perhaps, but not legal documents."

"How can you be so sure?"

"Because it's too obvious. While the earl may have lost some of his mental capacity, he was always a wily, suspicious sort of fellow, or so I remember my father saying during one of the few times I recall him speaking of something other than my own faults and failures."

This didn't seem quite the time to tell him what she'd heard about his family. Besides, what exactly would she say? *I'm sorry your father was a brute? I'm glad to know you loved your mother?*

"It's more likely there's some sort of hidden cupboard or perhaps even a fireproof cabinet hidden in the wall or shelves or behind a sliding panel.

Look for anything that seems odd or out of place or something unusual in the woodwork."

"I don't think I can see well enough," she admitted.

He held up his hand and waggled his fingers. "Use your fingertips."

Trying not to envision those same fingertips grazing her face and naked body, Esme did as he suggested, starting with the decorative edge of the desk. "How can you see so well when I can't?" she wondered aloud.

"Perhaps because I don't spend all my time pouring over law books in bad light."

Maybe he had a point. In future she would make an effort to ensure she had better lighting when she did her research.

Unfortunately, her exploration of the desk and the outside of the drawers didn't yield anything that could be considered unusual, nor could she open any of them. Thinking she should feel around the bottom edge of the overlap of the desktop, she sat on the chair—and heard the familiar sound of crinkling paper.

From beneath her.

Standing, she felt around the edges of the chair's

bottom cushion and first found a loose thread, then a hole in the seam large enough to slip her hand into.

"MacLachlann, come here!" she whispered excitedly. "I've found something!"

As he hurried to join her, she pulled several documents of both foolscap and vellum from inside the seat cushion and laid them on the desk. Some were merely folded, while others were folded and sealed with wax and ribbon, with an identifying notification on the outside. The writing was just barely legible in the dim light. One was the last will and testament of the present Earl of Duncombe and another was the last will and testament of his father. There was the marriage settlement between the earl and his late wife, too. She unfolded the papers and discovered several promissory notes and mortgages that the earl had given, some for very large sums.

"Gad, I knew the man was rich, but I had no idea," MacLachlann muttered as he stood close beside her and looked over the notes and mortgage agreements.

"Everything looks completely in order," Esme said. Indeed, from her swift perusal of the papers, she would say that not only were these documents fully legal and legitimate, but they were also as good as anything she—or Jamie—could have drawn up.

"It all looks aboveboard to me, too," MacLachlann agreed.

"None of these involve funds received by the earl," she noted. Indeed, in every case, it was the earl who had provided the money for the promissory notes or mortgages. "Could his financial problems stem from people defaulting on the repayments?"

"Perhaps," MacLachlann said, "assuming these loans were made to actual people."

Esme didn't have to ask him what he meant. Having the earl lend money to nonexistent individuals would be one way to rob him, and it would be a way that would necessarily involve his solicitor.

"We'll have to find out if these are real people," he continued. "If not…"

"Catriona will need to make a formal accusation against Mr. McHeath," she answered for him, and firmly. Although she hated to think a solicitor would abuse his client's trust that way, if he had, he must be stopped. "If they are real people, we'll have to try to learn their financial status, too."

"We'll need a pen, ink and paper to make note of the names," MacLachlann remarked, surveying the barren desktop.

"There's no need for that," she told him as she began to refold the documents. "I'll remember the names."

MacLachlann hesitated for only an instant before inclining his head in acquiescence. "Jamie says you have a remarkable memory."

"Because I've trained it," she replied, trying not to feel so very pleased by his compliment. It was secondhand, after all, based on something her brother had said about her.

MacLachlann reached for the present earl's will, obviously intending to open it. Appalled, Esme grabbed his forearm to stop him.

"We can't open that. It's sealed," she protested, nodding at the red wax blob with the earl's insignia pressed into it.

MacLachlann raised a brow and, taking a penknife from the desk, slid it beneath the seal.

Esme had felt a twinge of guilt slipping into the locked library. Accepting that as necessary, she had even felt a sense of victory when she'd found the hidden documents. But to open and read a sealed legal document...

She had tried to stop him, she reasoned as her curiosity got the better of her. "Bring it to the window so I can see it in more light."

He handed her the will and stayed beside her as she read it as quickly as she dared, lest she overlook something important. The will was detailed, exact, clear—as well-written and precise as anything she or Jamie could have created.

"We can't stay away from the drawing room much longer," MacLachlann said as she neared the end.

"This is an excellent will. I don't think I've ever seen a better one, and although it names Gordon McHeath as executor, he is not to receive a percentage of the estate. It names a clear sum for the task and it's less than Jamie would ask for in a similar situation."

"You think this means McHeath is innocent of any wrongdoing?"

She wanted to answer in the affirmative, but had to be truthful. "I think if he's involved in anything illegal, it's nothing to do with the will, which has to be resealed somehow."

"Oh, ye of little faith," MacLachlann said as he took the document. He sat in the chair, folded the will and laid it down on the table with the seal on the top of the desk, then blew hard on it.

"It won't be well-sealed, but good enough," he said as he put his palm over the paper and pressed down.

"Won't that damage the seal?"

"If it's a bit cracked, who's to say that wasn't because the earl's been sitting on it?"

That was true enough, she supposed.

"Do you recall the order the papers were in?" he asked as he rose.

"Yes," she said, blessing her retentive memory.

She put them in the right order, then returned them to their hiding place. "Ingenious, really," she murmured. "It was by mere chance I sat on the chair and heard that noise."

"Perhaps you should take up gambling."

She was about to reply that she had no desire to wind up penniless, but the memory of his past losses stopped her tongue. Meanwhile

MacLachlann closed the drapes, plunging them back into darkness.

She put her hand on the desk for a guide and started toward the door, then hesitated, unsure, until she felt his hand on her elbow. "Good God, Esme, you *have* been reading too much. You'll go blind if you don't take better care."

Here, in the dark and close beside her, he sounded sincerely worried about her.

Very aware of his body, hearing the soft sound of his breathing, inhaling the masculine scent of his cologne, as well as starch and wool, she could easily believe they were all alone in the house and there was nothing and no one to prevent him from taking her in his arms and…

"You won't be much help to Jamie if you're blind," he noted, his matter-of-fact tone like a splash of cold water, waking her up and bringing her back to reality as he guided her forward.

He eased the door open and peered into the corridor. "The way is clear. You go first and I'll follow."

She slipped out of the room and waited as he, too, made his exit. She relaxed and let her breath out slowly as he locked the door.

Until she heard people talking and footsteps coming toward them from the drawing room and more voices coming from the other end of the corridor, trapping them in between.

She looked at MacLachlann desperately. "What are we—?"

He pushed her back against the wall, then covered her mouth with his.

Chapter Nine

Esme's stunned shock lasted a mere moment before she put her hands up to push him away.

He slid his mouth closer to her ear. "We're supposed to be married," he whispered as he angled his knee between her legs, creating a pressure of a sort she'd never experienced before, a pressure as exciting as his touch and as arousing as his kiss. His mouth found hers again and he insinuated his tongue between her lips.

Her protests and any thought of merely pretending to be aroused drifted away as her body responded to the sensation of his lips on hers and the feel of his muscular body against her own. Desire took hold of her. Passion consumed her as she leaned into him fully, relaxing against him so it seemed only his strong arms were holding her upright.

His hand grazed her hip, then her torso, moving to cup her breast. It was shockingly intimate and unbelievably exhilarating and—

"Well!" Lady Elvira ejaculated, the sudden explosion of sound and scorn yanking Esme out of her haze of desire.

MacLachlann let go, and Esme found that her legs were indeed capable of holding her upright. When he stepped back, there was a slight flush in his cheeks and hostile gleam in his eyes.

She wished she knew how much of his reaction was real, and how much was feigned, except... if he really was upset that they'd been forced to stop, what did that mean?

Did she really want an answer to that question?

"Ah, Dubhagen and your pretty wife, I see," the old earl said, while Esme struggled to get her tumultuous emotions back under control.

"*That's* a surprise," Lady Elvira tartly observed.

"It's a surprise that I want to kiss my pretty wife?" MacLachlann coolly replied, arching a brow as a pair of footmen sidled past on their way to the dining room from the back stairs. It must have been their voices they'd heard coming the other way.

"You were doing much more than kissing," Lady Elvira waspishly noted.

"Not nearly as much as I wanted to," MacLachlann countered without a morsel of embarrassment, while Esme blushed right down to the tips of her toes. Not only was the situation humiliating, but her own reactions were also making a mockery of her determination to be in charge of this enterprise, and MacLachlann.

"Perhaps we'd best leave," MacLachlann continued, taking Esme's arm. "Good night, Lord Duncombe. Thank you, and your charming daughter, too, for a most delightful evening. Come along, my dear, before Lady Elvira falls into a fit."

Her arms crossed, frowning as only Esme could frown, Quinn's supposed wife squeezed into a corner of the carriage as if determined to get as far away from him as she could.

If she intended to pretend he wasn't there, he would ignore her, too. It wasn't his fault Lady Elvira and the earl and a pair of servants all happened along the corridor at the same time. Would she rather they'd been caught in the library?

"I couldn't think of anything else to do on the

spur of the moment that wouldn't arouse suspicion, or believe me, I would have," he said, telling himself that was the truth.

Besides, for all her protests, Esme had responded passionately to his kisses. She might claim she was only pretending, but either she was the world's greatest actress, or she was as excited by their embraces as much as he.

Even though he shouldn't be. She was Jamie's sister, after all.

"I find it interesting that you appear to think only of certain intimate activities in times of difficulty," she dourly replied, making it sound as if kissing him was the equivalent of being forced to swallow terrible-tasting medicine. "You are either a slave to your baser nature or have a distinct lack of imagination. And I suggest you take care how you behave toward Catriona. It would hamper our efforts if her father thought you were trying to seduce her—although not as much as it would upset Jamie if you were."

He couldn't believe what he was hearing. "What have I done that makes you think I have any such intention?"

"The way you looked at her during dinner."

"By that measure, you must be passionately smitten by Mr. McHeath."

Her frown deepened. "And you *smiled* at her."

"You stared at him as if he was King Arthur come to life."

"I have no passionate feelings for Mr. McHeath!"

"As I have no passionate feelings or seductive intentions regarding Lady Catriona. And do you honestly think me capable of such ingratitude that I would try to seduce the woman your brother loved?"

"Yes!"

Quintus MacLachlann had been insulted many times and in many ways, but none had pierced his heart as much as Esme's answer, spoken with such conviction. "Well, I wouldn't!"

And it was not as if she was an angel, or had any love in her heart for the woman who'd rejected her brother. "I confess myself astonished that you feel Lady Catriona deserves your unnecessary protection. Your prejudice against the woman has been obvious from the moment Jamie mentioned her name."

"Whatever she's done," Esme snapped, "she's

a woman, and we women must stick together against seductive scoundrels."

He was a seductive scoundrel, was he? And he was never going to be anything else in her eyes, either, no doubt.

Very well, then. He would teach her a lesson about seduction she wouldn't soon forget.

"You wound me, Esme," he said with every appearance of genuine sorrow as he moved to sit beside her. "I would never seduce Lady Catriona, and not only because of Jamie's devotion to her. Why would I, when she lacks so much I seek in a lover? She has no fire, no spark, no passion— not like you. She would be too tame, too easily wooed and won. Not like you."

Esme didn't believe him. She wouldn't. She couldn't, as she slid back to the corner, getting as far away from him as she could.

He moved slowly closer. "I should have thought of another diversion or some other way to avoid detection, but I couldn't. Not when you were so close to me, and so beautiful."

Beautiful? That word told her he couldn't be sincere. She was no beauty. She never had been and she never would be. And she would be a silly fool to think otherwise, when she had the evidence before her in the mirror every day.

"How could I not want to kiss you? How could I not want you—and I do want you," he said softly, the words low and tender.

She wanted to believe him, oh, so much—until she recognized cool calculation in his eyes of the sort she'd seen in a fraudster's eyes as he tried to justify his activities or blame someone else for his crimes after he'd been caught.

Anger replaced yearning and anguish killed desire.

He was, after all, like every other man who had ever belittled and patronized her, who believed himself by nature smarter and wiser than any woman could be. And like many another handsome man, he was sure she would forget everything except desire and the wish to be in his arms if he sounded keen to have her.

What he was really after, she was certain, was control. Over her, and over this task.

Well, she would show him that he wasn't the only one who could play that sort of game. Had she not heard enough from female servants who'd been seduced by employers to know how such a thing was done?

She slid her arms around his neck. "Oh, Quinn," she sighed as she relaxed against him, "I never knew, never dreamed that you could feel that way about me."

She pressed her lips against his, moving them with slow deliberation, as if eager for him to deepen the kiss—something he didn't hesitate to do. He slipped his hand inside her cloak and ran his fingertips over her collarbone, grazing the tops of her breasts.

She mustn't succumb to the desire he aroused. She must not. She must remain in control, here and while they were in Edinburgh.

His tongue slid past her parted lips, dancing with hers, as he pulled her onto his lap. She felt his arousal beneath her, and could scarcely believe how much it excited her to know that he wanted to make love with her.

Make love, not be in love. The difference was important. Had to be. Must be.

He cupped her breast, kneading gently, brushing the taut tip with the pad of his thumb. Her heartbeat sped up even more, her breathing grew more erratic.

Control. She must have it. Must keep it. Mustn't give in to her need. Her lust. Her longing to be in his arms.

In his bed.

The carriage stopped.

His heart racing, Quinn threw open the carriage door and leapt to the ground. Convinced Esme felt more than lust—that she must like him and must not hold his past against him anymore—he didn't care if he shocked the servants as he reached up and grabbed Esme around the waist to help her to the ground. Once she was out of the carriage, he took hold of her hand and pulled her up the steps and through the open door of the house, where the equally surprised hallboy waited. Paying no attention to the lad, he continued to lead her up the stairs and down the dimly lit hall, as longing and desire and excitement combined within him to an almost fever pitch. How many times had he imagined this—or tried not to?

Maybe all these months, she'd only been pretending to hate him, because she thought she should. Or maybe she had hated him until she'd spent more time with him and realized he was no longer the wastrel he'd been in his youth.

Whatever Esme was thinking, she said not a word, not even as they crossed the threshold into her bedroom.

Three candles burned on the dressing table. More were on the table beside the bed and a fire burned in the hearth, leaving the corners of the room in shadow.

Holding his breath, wondering if she would order him to leave, Quinn turned to face her.

She was so lovely, so beautiful and serene, so good and true and…

Could he be less? "Esme, I should go," he said, although it took a mighty effort.

She walked toward him. "After all those things you said to me? Stay," she pleaded softly. "Don't leave me alone tonight, Quinn. I've been alone too much."

As had he. Alone and lonely.

Like a man crossing the desert who sees water shimmering in the distance, he moved toward her, holding his breath as she undid the drawstring of her cloak and let it fall to the ground, until she stood before him lovely and radiant in her beautiful gown that wasn't nearly as beautiful as she.

Unable to wait another moment, he tugged her to him, taking her mouth with fervent, unrestrained desire. Oh, God, how he'd longed for this, even before they'd come to Edinburgh! He'd wanted to do this from the moment she'd first looked at him with those intelligent, vibrant eyes.

She slipped her arms around his waist and leaned into him, while he embraced her as if he never wanted to let her go. With passionate deliberation he moved his lips over hers, then parted them to deepen their kiss.

He broke their embrace to shrug off his coat and jacket, letting them fall to the floor, before he pulled her close again. She tugged his shirt from his breeches and slid her hand under and upward, gliding her palm over his naked chest before she drew back. "Would you do something for me, Quinn?" she asked softly, her hazel eyes shining as she looked at him.

It was the first time she had ever called him by his first name.

"Anything," he replied, meaning it. Right now,

here and alone with her, he would do anything it was in his power to do for her.

Her expression changed to one of speculation, as if she'd finished reading a scientific treatise and was considering the conclusion. "So that is how one uses desire to manipulate another," she coolly remarked. "How interesting."

He gasped with shock. This had been an *experiment?* A trick? Because she assumed— wrongly!—that he was simply trying to seduce her in order to gain her cooperation?

And she then thought nothing of using his desire to hurt him?

Rage, frustration and humiliation swept through him like a tidal wave. How could she? How dare she? Who did she think she was? "It's not wise to toy with me, Esme."

She tilted her head as she studied him. "It's distressing to be used, is it not? Yet you seem to think it's perfectly acceptable to toy with women."

"I don't toy with women, or use them as you imply. I fulfill my natural urges, as they do with me. Any seduction is quite mutual, and it's understood that there are no obligations, for either of us. And *I* would never feign desire merely to prove a point!"

With that, he grabbed up his coat and jacket, threw open the door and went out, slamming the door behind him with a resounding bang.

Hours after MacLachlann had left, Esme lay in bed, wide awake and restless. She'd only been trying to put MacLachlann in his place by the sort of means he employed, until things had gone too far—much too far. Despite her reasons for doing what she had, his anger had been justified.

But it wasn't his anger she thought of now. It was the pain she'd seen in his eyes, beneath the rage. She had hurt him deeply, and that hurt told her that he hadn't just been trying to dominate her. Maybe he really did think she was beautiful and perhaps he truly wanted to be with her, and she had made a mockery of those feelings. To be sure, he had teased and mocked her often enough, but not enough to cause her such anguish as she had seen in him, however briefly.

What would MacLachlann do now? Would he stay, or would he go back to London?

If he stayed, what should she say or do the

next time she saw him? And if he went back to London, what should she do? If they both went back to London, she would have failed Jamie, to whom she owed so much.

Yet how could she remain in Edinburgh if MacLachlann left?

She rolled onto her side. She never should have kissed him or tried to use desire as a weapon. Why had she even considered it? She'd never been even remotely interested in doing anything like that with any other man…but then, MacLachlann wasn't like any other man. He was both sophisticated and wild, intelligent and vulgar, unabashedly masculine, yet he could be compassionate, too.

These were some of the same qualities that made him so useful to Jamie, and another reason she should keep her distance. Not only was she doing things with him no morally upright woman should, but she could also be jeopardizing her brother's relationship with a man who was of great use to him.

The bedroom door began to open. Esme held her breath.

It wasn't MacLachlann.

Her face smudged with soot, holding the coal scuttle and a brush, the chambermaid dipped a curtsey when she realized Esme was awake and watching her. "I—I'm sorry, m'lady! I didna mean to wake ye," the girl stammered. "I'll come back later."

Esme sat up after a brief glance at the small gap in the drapes confirmed that the sun was rising.

"No, it's all right. Make up the fire, please," she said as she got out of bed and washed as she waited for her abigail to arrive to help her dress and do her hair.

As her maid attended to her, it was on the tip of Esme's tongue to ask if MacLachlann was home or if he'd gone out, or if he'd said anything about packing his bags and heading back to Town. However, her reluctance to appear ignorant of her own husband's plans prevented her.

After she had breakfasted alone except for the footmen and butler, she went to the countess's morning room, picking up the Edinburgh news-papers and several invitations from various peo-ple that waited on a table in the hall along the way. Judging by the quality of the envelopes, the invitations were to more dinners and parties and balls. The Earl of Duncombe and his wife were already very popular, it seemed, although whether it was because people were curious about them, or because Quinn was handsome and charming, she couldn't say.

As for the newspapers, she supposed the real Lady Dubhagen didn't read them, but she had to do something until MacLachlann returned.

If he returned.

The countess's morning room was oppressively feminine and full of reminders of the sort of life Esme had never lived and never wanted to. There was a sewing box in a corner with a piece of unfinished embroidery poking out. Several examples of painted china stood on delicate wooden shelves, and some of the watercolors were obviously amateur efforts. A spinet was in one corner and a harp in another, and a wooden box containing what appeared to be items for trimming hats was on a small table by the window. Another large pedestal table, suitable for the serving of tea, rested in the middle of the room, surrounded by well-cushioned sofas and chairs, except for the side nearest the tiled fireplace.

Such an existence—of little hobbies and crafts,

social engagements and meaningless gossip—
would be too dull for her. She would much rather
help Jamie with his legal practice.

Yet as she sat in one of the Louis XVI chairs
upholstered in velvet and looked through the invitations, she realized there were some things that
might, perhaps, provide some compensation for
a wealthy woman's circumscribed existence—
fine food and clothes, servants and other creature
comforts. And if she were the wife of a loving
and devoted husband, there might be even more:
the feel of a man's lips on hers, the sensation of
being in his arms.

Such speculation was useless, she told herself as
she set the invitations aside to be answered later.
Her life here was an aberration and soon enough
she would be back in London living the life she
knew.

And preferred.

Rain began to splatter against the window-
panes, and outside the sky was dull. Where could
MacLachlann be in this inclement weather? One
of the gentlemen's clubs, warm and cozy? Or with
a woman?

Rising, Esme went to look in the mirror hung

over the mantel, studying her reflection as if it belonged to another woman, one who was used to having her hair dressed daily and expensive gowns to wear, like this pretty one of Nile green muslin with three rows of darker green and brown ribbon along the hem. The sort of woman who didn't have ink-stained fingers or spend hours poring over law books.

She wasn't as beautiful as Catriona, but she wasn't as homely as some of the other young ladies she'd met. Her brown hair done up in that simple manner suited her heart-shaped face, and her cheeks weren't overly pale.

She put her fingertips to her lips. They were full and soft, and ruddy. MacLachlann's were full, too, and when they touched hers—

Somebody rapped on the door.

MacLachlann?

She hoped, but in case it wasn't, she hurried back to the chair and shoved the unread newspapers under the cushion.

"Come in," she said, sitting down on the blue velvet cabriole sofa and doing her best to keep her voice steady.

McSweeney entered the room with silver salver in his hand. "A gentleman has called, my lady."

By rights, he should have announced a gentleman's arrival to her supposed husband first, which told her that MacLachlann must not be in the house.

Keeping disappointment and worry from her face, she took the card and read the name upon it. "I shall be pleased to see Mr. McHeath."

After the butler departed, she smoothed down her skirt and prepared to meet the solicitor.

Mr. McHeath entered the room and bowed with the perfect mixture of pleasure and deference. He was attired exactly the way a prosperous young attorney should dress, too, in clothes that were of good material, but not ostentatious. His jacket was a dark blue wool with silver buttons, his vest a subdued stripe of blue and gray, his trousers likewise gray and his boots were brightly polished. He was as tall as MacLachlann and good-looking, although there was something rather… tame…about him, too.

"I hope I'm not intruding too early in the day, my lady."

His brogue was heavier than either hers or

MacLachlann's, no doubt because he'd stayed in Scotland while they had gone to England. His deep voice also lacked the velvet smoothness of MacLachlann's.

"Not at all," she replied. "It's a pleasure to see you again. I was sorry you left the dinner party so early."

"So was I. I'm afraid there are times I find it difficult to restrain my temper, and last night was one of them. Under such circumstances, I thought it best to go."

She moved to make way for him on the sofa. "Please sit down, Mr. McHeath."

He did as she asked, keeping a proper distance between them.

Remembering she was supposed to be dim, Esme adjusted her skirts before heaving a wistful little sigh. "Politics makes for a lot of quarrels. I think such subjects should be banned from social conversation, don't you?"

"I don't wish to cause any further offence, but no, I don't," he replied. "Discussion should always be encouraged. I regret only that I wasn't able to remain calm, not the choice of subject."

"You don't want to talk about slavery again, do

you?" she asked as if the notion horrified her, although in truth, she would dearly love to tell him that she agreed with his opinion about slavery, as well as the rights of women, and all the reasons why.

"I came to ascertain if your husband wishes to find another solicitor to handle his affairs," he admitted. "Naturally I shall understand if he does."

"I haven't seen him this morning," she confessed, "but I hope he continues to do business with you."

After all, they still had to find out if Mr. McHeath was involved in any wrongdoing, although that seemed more and more doubtful.

"Lady Catriona speaks very highly of you," she added.

The young man blushed and, even though she couldn't be absolutely sure he was innocent of any crime, she nevertheless felt duty-bound to try to spare him the same fate as her brother. "She's a sweet girl, isn't she? Such a pity she won't marry anyone without a title—or so I've heard."

The solicitor's blush deepened. "I'm sure whoever she marries will be a fortunate man."

"You would be writing the marriage settlement for her, wouldn't you?"

"Perhaps."

Esme again smoothed down her skirts and gave him an encouraging smile. "I thought you wrote all the earl's contracts and things."

"I do."

"I'm sure that keeps you very busy."

"Busy enough, my lady." Mr. McHeath got to his feet. "I've taken up enough of your time this morning, my lady, so I'll bid—"

"Why, Mr. McHeath, what an unexpected pleasure," MacLachlann declared as he sauntered into the room, making Esme start as if she'd been found pilfering the silver.

Obviously he hadn't left for London. But where had he spent the night? Wherever it was, he had returned in time to change, for he now wore clothes more appropriate to a day spent on errands or an outing—blue jacket, buff trousers, gray waistcoat and riding boots.

Whatever he'd been doing, they both still had roles to play, at least for the time being.

"Look, Ducky!" she cried, hurrying toward him

and taking his arm. She could feel the muscle of his forearm clench, as if her touch was anathema.

She would not let that trouble her. "Here is Mr. McHeath, all concerned you'll dismiss him over a simple difference of opinion. You won't, will you? After all, we disagree on so many things and yet you still love me, don't you, Ducky?"

Annoyance flashed in MacLachlann's eyes before he gave her a condescending smile.

Then he looked at Mr. McHeath.

Although the two men regarded each other with outwardly mild expressions, she could feel the animosity between them. It was like being in a small room with two rams about to butt heads.

If Mr. McHeath disliked MacLachlann so much, why would he regret the loss of his business? Perhaps he couldn't afford to lose any of his clients, and if he was in financial difficulties...

"I see no reason to seek another solicitor," MacLachlann calmly replied.

That didn't sound as if MacLachlann was planning to leave Edinburgh, either, she thought with relief.

"I'm pleased to hear it, my lord," Mr. McHeath replied, although his expression didn't suggest any pleasure as he gave a bow as stiff as a bow could be.

"Pardon me, my lord," McSweeney intoned from the threshold. "Lady Catriona has—"

Her bonnet askew, her hair dishevelled, her pelisse not completely buttoned and without gloves, Catriona pushed past the startled butler and ran into the room.

Chapter Ten

Catriona came to an abrupt halt when she saw that Esme wasn't alone. "Oh! Excuse me! I—I didn't mean to interrupt."

"It's quite all right," Esme assured Catriona as she led her to the sofa, while MacLachlann ordered McSweeney to have tea brought at once.

Mr. McHeath started toward her, then hesitated and stayed where he was.

"No, please, I'm sorry. I should go," Catriona protested. "I shouldn't bother you with my troubles, but I didn't know what else to do, who else I could confide in. So many of the older ladies gossip so and Lady Marchmont said she'd be visiting her daughter this morning, so I…I came here. It's Papa."

"Is he ill?" Esme asked, mindful that Mr. McHeath mustn't realize she knew anything about the earl's financial situation and hoping Catriona would have the presence of mind to be aware of that, too.

"Not physically. Not really, although he's much distressed. I fear he's suffered a serious financial loss, but he won't confide in me."

As her large green eyes filled with tears, Esme darted a glance at the young solicitor, who appeared genuinely distraught. She'd seen enough bogus emotions from her brother's clients to convince her that unless she was very much mistaken, or Mr. McHeath a superior actor, his distress was genuine.

However, it was possible that he *was* a superior actor and if so, they should suggest he leave.

She gave MacLachlann a pointed look but he merely leaned his elbow on the mantel and watched dispassionately, as if everyone else was a character in a play.

Either he didn't care if Mr. McHeath heard what Catriona had to say, or he didn't think the lawyer was involved in any skulduggery. She didn't want to suspect Mr. McHeath, either, but wasn't caution the wiser course?

Unfortunately, since neither Catriona or

MacLachlann seemed to think the solicitor should go, and she wasn't sure how she could make the suggestion without rousing Mr. McHeath's suspicion that all was not as it appeared, he would have to stay for the time being.

Mrs. Llewellan-Jones arrived at the door carrying a large tray bearing a silver teapot, pitcher of cream, sugar and four Wedgwood cups and saucers. Without a word, and as if the sniffling Catriona were invisible, she set the tray upon the round pedestal table in the middle of the room and glided away.

Esme poured Catriona a cup of tea. She didn't know if the young woman took sugar, but dropped a lump in anyway. "Drink this. It's nice and hot," she said, handing her the cup.

"Thank you," Catriona whispered. She had a few sips of tea, then drew in a deep, quivering breath before continuing. "Papa was very agitated at breakfast this morning. He hardly touched his food, and that's most unusual for him. There were some papers on the table, and he kept glancing at them."

"Were they legal documents?" Mr. McHeath asked.

Catriona shook her head. "No, they looked like letters, although when I drew near, he folded them up quickly, so I couldn't see anything of the contents."

She sniffled again and Esme wordlessly took the cup and saucer when they began to shake in her trembling hands.

"Thank you," the distraught young woman said again before continuing. "Papa finally told me, with great agitation, that we wouldn't be going to London for the Season this year." She looked at them with an air of desperation. "You should have seen his face when he said it! I didn't ask him why not—I was too afraid of upsetting him more—and then he said we…we couldn't afford it!"

Mr. McHeath couldn't have looked more shocked if Catriona had announced her father had robbed the Bank of England. "You couldn't afford it?" he repeated incredulously. "He used those very words?"

This response didn't seem feigned, either, although it could be that Mr. McHeath wasn't so much shocked by the loss as that the earl had revealed even that much of his financial situation to his daughter.

Catriona mournfully nodded her head.

"Did he say *he* couldn't afford, or *you* couldn't afford it?" MacLachlann inquired.

"He said *we* couldn't afford it," Catriona clarified.

"You assume he meant financially."

"What else *could* he mean?" Esme asked.

MacLachlann clasped his hands behind his back and rocked forward on his toes. "There are many ways to pay for something, and money is only one of them. Perhaps he meant he didn't think you could spare the time, for instance."

"What else have they got to do?" Esme demanded, too late remembering she was supposed to be dim. She quickly widened her eyes and spoke as if completely baffled. "It's the *Season*, Ducky. There's *nothing* more important than the Season!"

"It may be important for a young woman desperately seeking a husband, but the earl's heiress is hardly in that position," MacLachlann calmly replied. "Perhaps the earl was referring to the cost of living in London. It *has* gotten outrageously expensive."

"But he's rich!" Esme protested in that same bewildered manner. "Surely he can afford it—unless something terrible has happened."

Instead of replying to Esme, Mr. McHeath addressed Catriona. "I doubt that whatever's happened, it's as bad as the earl thinks," he said with what sounded like sincerity. "I fear your father tends to take the most pessimistic view of a situation. I'll go to him at once and see if I can find out exactly what has occurred. He may be more forthcoming to his solicitor than he would be to his daughter."

"Oh, thank you! I'd be so grateful if you would!" Catriona cried, clasping her hands together as if he were the answer to her prayers.

"I can take you both in my carriage," MacLachlann offered. "Perhaps I, too, can provide some assistance to the earl if he's deeply distressed."

"I'll come with you," Esme quickly added, and not just because this could be a good opportunity to find out what was amiss with the earl's finances. Whatever Catriona had done to Jamie, she was clearly at the mercy of her father, a situation that always roused her sympathy.

"I'll gladly accept the offer of the carriage.

However, I believe the earl would prefer to keep his financial business private," Mr. McHeath replied, his tone amicable but his expression determined—a most interesting change and one that made Esme wonder if she'd been too quick to absolve him of being involved in any financial wrongdoing.

"Indeed, I think he would," Catriona agreed as she rose. "I fear he won't want to speak of business at all if you return with me, Lord Dubhagen, or you, my lady, and my own carriage is waiting outside."

Which meant they had no choice but to remain behind.

"Good day, my lord, my lady," Mr. McHeath said. He turned to Catriona with a gentle smile. "Shall we, my lady?"

With her eyes downcast and a mumbled "goodbye," Catriona let him lead her from the room.

As soon as they were gone, Esme sank onto the sofa, not at all pleased with what she had just witnessed. "If Catriona trusts Mr. McHeath as she apparently does, why did she bother to write to Jamie and ask for his help? And if she doesn't trust him, why didn't she let us go home with her? This would have been an excellent opportunity to learn something of the earl's business dealings, and to observe his relationship with Mr. McHeath. We might have been able to determine once and for all if his solicitor is acting improperly."

MacLachlann strolled toward one of the water-colors of a landscape of the Highlands with some ruins in the foreground, then turned to address her. "As you say, it would have aided our investigation, but it was better that she didn't accept our offers. It would have been too unusual if she preferred our assistance when her solicitor was immediately available. We are, after all, supposed to be new acquaintances. It looks odd enough that she came here as she did."

Esme had to admit that might be so, and she did—silently. "Is that why you didn't ask him to leave the room when she arrived?"

"I thought it would make him wonder about our association with Lady Catriona if I ordered him to leave." He tilted his head as he studied her. "Do *you* think he's trustworthy?"

"I was beginning to think so, but I'm not certain."

"Good," he muttered as he started for the door.

He was leaving again, just like that? "Wait!"

He turned back and regarded her expectantly.

"Where are you going?"

"To try to learn more about Mr. McHeath." He raised an interrogative brow. "What do you intend to do today? Read some more law books? I hope you'll light the lamps."

At least he wasn't going back to London.

"I'm going to write another letter to Jamie about this latest development, then I believe I'll pay a call on Lady Elvira."

MacLachlann frowned. "All you'll get out of her is the worst sort of gossip."

"As you discovered at your club and wherever else you've been, gossip can be an excellent source of information. I certainly have no intention of sitting here all day."

"That would be the safest course and the one least likely to raise anyone's suspicions. I also think it wouldn't be wise to write to your brother every day, not unless you want the servants to think you're engaged in an illicit affair."

Unfortunately, he had a point. "Very well. But then you should write to him."

"I will when I return."

"We're invited to a ball at Lady Marchmont's to-night," she informed him. "She apologizes for the lack of notice, but since we only just arrived…" She fell silent for a moment, then spoke with more determination. "We ought to go."

"Absolutely. Augustus would. Indeed, I look forward to it, my little plum cake," he replied before he strolled out the door.

Leaving her alone.

Again.

"Tell her the Earl of Dubhagen wishes to speak to her," Quinn haughtily informed the muscular middle-aged man as they stood in the foyer of an establishment not far from the outskirts of Mayfair.

The man squinted at Quinn, then nodded and started up the stairs. Before he reached the landing, he paused and pointed at the open door to a lower room. "You can wait in there."

Quinn decided he might as well sit down as he waited for Mollie, who had been an older woman of twenty-five the last time he'd seen her, before he'd fled Edinburgh.

The drawing room of the town house was, fortunately, empty. It was also decorated in a way that made it clear it wasn't a family home, with plush red velvet curtains, heavy furniture likewise upholstered in red velvet and a picture over the mantelpiece of a group of plump, naked women.

It was, in fact, a brothel, and the sort of place Esme probably thought he spent many nights. He didn't, and he hadn't been near a whore in years, unless he had questions to ask about her customers, as he was about to do now. He'd spent the previous night at a tavern, dozing in a corner until the owner had told him to leave. Then he'd walked until he'd spotted a cabbie and returned to his brother's house.

"My lord?"

At the sound of the familiar voice, he wondered if it had been wise to come here, even if Mollie would likely be an excellent source of information. It was too late to do otherwise now, though, so he would act his part unless and until she guessed he wasn't Augustus.

"Miss MacDonald?" he inquired as he turned to face her.

She'd changed, of course. It had been years, and

her profession was not a gentle one, although she was still a pretty woman. Whatever else had happened since he'd been gone, she'd earned enough to dress in silks and satins, although in a whore's version of the fashions of the day.

She sashayed toward him, her hips swinging seductively. "I'm Mollie MacDonald. What can I do for you, my lord?" she asked with a smile and clearly not recognizing him. "Or do I already know?"

For a moment, he was tempted to enjoy her many talents, and once, he wouldn't have hesitated. But that was before. Before he'd been found by Jamie on Tower Bridge. Before he'd been given a chance for redemption and become determined to do all he could to deserve it. "I require information."

Mollie frowned, and the change of expression made her look even older than she was. "I don't do nothing for free."

"I expected as much, so I have come prepared to pay," Quinn replied.

She raised an expectant brow as he reached into his jacket and produced his wallet, then a ten-pound note. She snatched it out of his hand and nodded. "All right, ask away."

"I have heard a most disturbing rumor regarding my solicitor, Gordon McHeath, and his visits to your establishment."

It was a lie, but if there was any brothel likely to attract a man of Mr. McHeath's level of income and need for discretion, it would be Mollie's.

"Aye, he's been here," Mollie replied as she tucked the bill into the tight bodice of her green satin gown between her ample breasts.

Quinn had thought he'd be happy to hear an affirmative answer, but he was too aware of Esme's approaching disappointment to be pleased. She wanted to believe all lawyers were models of virtue, like her brother; sadly, she was going to find out otherwise.

"But only the once and not for what most men want," Mollie continued.

She laughed derisively when she saw the surprise he didn't hide. "What, you don't think a whore can have anything to do with the law except break it? I'm dyin', so I wanted to write my last will and testament."

Dying? Quinn stared at her with dismay, suddenly realizing how pale she was beneath the rouge.

"It ain't catchin'," she said with a spark of defiance. "But I won't last the year, the doctor says, so I thought I'd make a will. I own this place, for one thing," she finished with more than a touch of pride.

"I'm…my condolences," he muttered, wanting to say more, remembering the good times they'd shared. When he'd first arrived in Edinburgh after fleeing school for the last time, she'd offered him not just her body, but comfort and solace and laughter, things he had sorely needed then.

Things he still needed, but had learned to live without.

"You can take it from me, Mr. McHeath's a good, kind gentleman who'd no more come to this place, or any like it, for what other men do than he'd rob a coach. Believe me, I'd know it if he did, or if he was up to no good in any way, and I'd have got myself another lawyer." She laughed again, only this time, it ended in a rasping cough. "If there's one thing a whore knows, it's men, and he's a man you can trust."

Quinn reached into his wallet and pulled out another ten-pound note. "Do you have any bankers among your customers? I've heard other things, too, about certain investments that should be avoided."

"What, you think they want to talk business when they're here?" Mollie asked, grinning as she sidled closer. In an instant, that bill followed the other. "Too bad for you they don't, so I couldn't tell you, even supposin' I would. I can keep a confidence, or else I'd have already told you I knew your little brother. Quite well, in fact." Her expression hardened, and now he could see just how unwell she was. "I think it's a damn shame, the way you and your family treated him."

He was supposed to be Augustus. "Not too much of a shame you didn't take my money."

"Because I'm a practical woman and money is money. Now, if there's no more questions, my lord?"

He shook his head and started for the door.

"I hear you've got yourself a pretty little wife," Mollie said behind him.

He slowly wheeled around to face her.

"I'd keep my eye on her if I were you, my lord. Women like that are ripe for the picking and there's some mighty sly fellows in Edinburgh who'd love to pluck her. I don't tell you that for your sake, or to save your precious honor. I'm telling you because your brother was a friend o' mine, and whatever else you think of him and no matter how you treated him, he cared about his family." She took a step toward him and a different look came to her haggard features. "He's not… he's still alive, I hope?"

"Yes, he's still alive."

"Got a wife? Children, maybe?"

"No, he lives alone."

"There's a pity," she said softly.

No, the pity was that a woman like Mollie MacDonald, who'd been as pretty as Catriona McNare and was as clever as Esme, should have had no way to earn money except with her body.

He reached into the wallet and drew out another ten-pound note, since the expense of this visit would be coming from his own funds.

"What's that for?"

Because he was sorry he'd left Edinburgh without a word of goodbye to her, even if their relationship had already ended. Because he was sorry she was sick, and that he would always think of her with respect and sympathy. Because he wished he'd been able to save her from the life she'd had to lead, and that she could have had the opportunities he'd wasted. Instead, he said, "For your information, of course. I'm most impressed."

She tilted her head and studied him in a way that made him fear she was beginning to realize he wasn't Augustus. "You may look like your brother, but you're not half the man he is. You see, I know a few things about you, too, my lord, things that made what he did look like nothing. He never told you what I found out, did he, even though I told him? No, because that's how good and kind he is—better than you'll ever be, that's for certain."

Quinn wanted to kiss her cheek, to take her hand and thank her for all that she'd done for him and wish her as well as could be. He wanted to give her more money, so she could quit this life and end her days in comfort and peace.

But she was as proud as any man, in her way, so he didn't. Nor could he run the risk of revealing who he really was, even to Mollie. All he could do was leave.

And silently vow that somehow, either through

Gordon McHeath or somebody else, he would make sure she spent her last days in peaceful ease. He owed her that, at least.

Chapter Eleven

"Why, Lady Dubhagen, this is such a *surprise!*" Lady Elvira crowed as Esme entered her morning room.

The small chamber on the first floor at the back of the narrow town house was decorated in the most extravagant Egyptian-inspired extreme, from the wallpaper, to the painted screen, to the furnishings, as if Lady Elvira had purchased anything and everything she saw that seemed remotely linked to the land of the Pharaohs.

Esme made her way through the overcrowded room to the orange silk-covered couch and sat on the end of it, beside a gilt table that didn't look strong enough to hold a teacup.

"I was afraid you wouldn't speak to me after my husband was so rude to you last night," she said, gripping her reticule the way she'd seen so many worried women do as they waited to speak to Jamie. "I'm so sorry he was! I fear he is a very... well, he can be...overwhelming and difficult."

"It wasn't *your* fault, I'm sure, Lady Dubhagen," Lady Elvira said as she sat beside Esme and patted her gloved hand with her clawlike fingers. "I'm sure it must be *extremely* trying to be married to *such* a man. The whole family was like that, you know. Well, not the youngest so much. He was the best of the lot—but that isn't saying much. Gambling was his vice, though, not..." Lady Elvira delicately cleared her throat. "Not other things. Still, he was a wild sort of fellow and Edinburgh is the better for his absence."

It came as an undeniable relief to know that even in his scandalous youth MacLachlann hadn't been a lascivious libertine.

But then what did it mean that he seemed to behave so when he was with her? Did he simply consider her an easy target for seduction, or was there something more genuine beneath his desire?

This was hardly the time to consider his motives.

"It *is* difficult being married to a man of such... appetite," she said as if she was relieved to unburden herself to a sympathetic listener. "I didn't know him very well before we married and… well…he's so much older than I and so…so *demanding* in certain ways."

Lady Elvira's eyes fairly glowed with avid interest. "Is he indeed? That must be very distressing for you."

"At least he is a handsome man," Esme said with a sigh, "although I fear that he can be impulsive and impetuous in other ways, as well. For instance, I have no idea what exactly became of my dowry after we married. I don't dare ask my husband, though, in case he gets angry. I know he trusts Mr. McHeath with his legal business— mortgages and contracts and such—and I do hope and pray he isn't wrong to do so." She gave Lady Elvira a beseeching look. "Have *you* ever heard anything to suggest Mr. McHeath isn't trustworthy?"

"Not at all," Lady Elvira assured her with another pat on her hand. "He's from a whole *family* of lawyers and his father was a judge. I'm *sure* you can have faith in him."

"Oh, thank you! You've set my mind at ease."

Which she had, at least a little. If there was

any hint of wrongdoing or bad dealings on Mr. McHeath's part, Lady Elvira was the sort of woman who'd probably know it and even exaggerate the tales. "I thought I was wrong to doubt him, but you can't be too sure about people, can you?"

"No, you can't. It's always wise to be a tad suspicious, especially of handsome men," Lady Elvira said with a meaningful look that suggested to Esme that she wasn't only referring to Mr. McHeath.

Tempting though it was to ask Lady Elvira questions about the MacLachlanns, Esme wasn't there to learn about them. She should find out about the people named in the documents she'd found hidden in the Earl of Duncombe's chair.

"Tell me, do you know if a physician named Kenneth Sutherland lives nearby?" she asked. "I believe he and his family moved to Edinburgh after purchasing a large house and some property not far from the castle."

"Oh, indeed I do! Dr. Sutherland is a surgeon at the Royal Infirmary and his father was a noted minister of the Church of Scotland. A fine family."

"How delightful!" Esme cried, not even trying to suggest a connection lest Lady Elvira ask questions. Let Lady Elvira assume she knew Dr. Sutherland through family or friends, not by reading his mortgage agreement with the Earl of Duncombe. "And do you also know the Miltons? Of the Upper Glen?"

"My daughter is great friends with young Lady Milton. You seem to have a large acquaintance here, Lady Dubhagen."

She giggled as if embarrassed. "Oh, I've never met the Miltons. I heard their name the other night and wondered if they might be related to the poet of that name."

Fortunately Lady Elvira accepted her explanation about the Miltons, as well as the other names Esme could recall. Lady Elvira was apparently more eager and interested in proving her own vast social connections than finding out Esme's. In each case, Lady Elvira knew the family and was more than willing to talk about their financial circumstances, at least as much as she knew.

It was a relief to learn the people really existed. She didn't want to discover that Mr. McHeath— or any solicitor—was cheating his clients.

That avenue of query complete, she couldn't resist the urge to ask the voluble, well-acquainted Lady Elvira another question. "I've also heard about another family of solicitors who used to live in Edinburgh, named McCallan. I gather it's a mistake to mention them in the Earl of Duncombe's hearing."

"Oh, indeed, that would not be wise," Lady Elvira eagerly agreed.

So, Jamie had been right to fear that what had happened with Catriona would taint his reputation in Edinburgh, even though he hadn't done anything wrong.

"The son was a fine fellow, by all accounts," Lady Elvira continued, "but he made the mistake of asking for Lady Catriona's hand in marriage. The earl would never agree, of course. He was only a solicitor, you see, and the earl would never consider anyone in the legal profession— or any profession at all—suitable for his daughter. She must marry a titled gentleman, or no one. And then there was the matter of Mr. McCallan's sister."

Esme fought hard not to betray her surprise, but how could *she* have harmed Jamie's chances with Catriona? She'd only spent one night in Edinburgh and never met anyone else before she and Jamie had left for London. "What did his sister have to do with it?"

Lady Elvira shook her head as if about to announce a very serious failing. "Apparently she's *quite* a bluestocking."

"And?" Esme prompted, sure there must be more.

"Isn't that enough?" Lady Elvira replied as if shocked that Esme wasn't already completely horrified.

Esme struggled to hide her annoyance and dismay at the woman's attitude. "Have you met her?" she asked, knowing full well that she had never been introduced to Lady Elvira until she'd come to Edinburgh with MacLachlann.

"She was still away at school, but we heard about her often. Poor Mr. McCallan was quite proud of her. If only he'd known that the earl cannot abide overeducated, opinionated young women!"

Although Esme was proud of her education and not shy about having opinions, she couldn't prevent the heated flush that spread over her face at the idea that she had been, even inadvertently, the cause of any trouble for Jamie. "But what about love? Did the young man love Lady Catriona and did she love him?"

Lady Elvira regarded Esme as if she'd taken complete leave of her senses. "Lady Catriona stands to inherit too much money to marry solely for love! She must marry someone who knows how to manage wealth and property—and that means a title. And while a solicitor might understand the legalities, he'd never really be accepted by society."

Her level of society, she meant.

"And of course, when fortunes and expectations are so mismatched, there's always the possibility that one of the parties is a fortune hunter."

Esme had to fight not to express her anger. And she was glad Jamie hadn't married Catriona. Whatever anyone else thought, he would never marry for mercenary motives, and he had his pride, too.

"Although perhaps I don't have to tell *you* that," Lady Elvira added with a significant look.

Esme bristled even more at the insult to her husband, then realized not only was she not really married, she herself had implied that her husband had wed her for her dowry.

Lady Elvira moved eagerly forward. "But enough of Edinburgh society. Tell me, Lady Dubhagen, what was it like in Jamaica?"

"Hot," she replied as she quickly got to her feet. She'd had quite enough of Lady Elvira. "Very hot. If you'll excuse me, I fear I've taken up enough of your time."

"Not at all!" Lady Elvira protested. "I do so want to hear about the West Indies." Her smile grew rather sly. "And it must be a relief to you to be away from your most *attentive* husband."

Esme hurriedly came up with an excuse. "I'm feeling a little unwell."

Lady Elvira's eyes immediately flicked to Esme's torso. When Esme realized what she might have implied, she did feel sick.

Fortunately, the woman had some sense of decorum, for she didn't ask any more questions. "You must promise me you'll call again and tell me all about the West Indies," she said as she followed Esme to the door.

"Yes, I will," Esme replied, although she would rather spend a week looking for the most obscure legal precedents in existence than call upon Lady Elvira again.

* * *

As Quinn paced in the drawing room that evening, he wasn't sure if Esme would be attending Lady Marchmont's ball with him or not. Even though she'd told him about the invitation, after what had happened last night and her tense manner this morning, he wouldn't be surprised if she elected to stay in her room. He almost hoped she would, because he wasn't at all sure what he should say, or do, if she appeared.

Nor, after seeing Mollie and learning of her situation, did he particularly feel like another evening spent at a party among the rich.

He heard a noise at the door and turned to find Esme standing on the threshold, watching him. She wore a blue silk gown with a rounded neckline that revealed far too much of her cleavage. The fabric flowed from the bodice to the floor, where the tips of white satin slippers with small blue rosettes peeked out from beneath the hem. Her hair was dressed high atop her proudly poised head, and white roses were interspersed with the ornately dressed brown locks. A pearl necklace, as lovely and perfect as she, lay against her slender throat.

Yes, she was perfect. Perfect not just in spite of her lively mind and sharp tongue, but because of them. Perfect, because of her dedication and devotion. Perfect—but not for him. *Never* for him.

She was Jamie's sister, after all, and he owed Jamie more than his life. Because of Jamie, he'd found some measure of redemption. Because of Jamie, he'd been able to put the skills and knowledge he'd gleaned in the most unsavoury places to good use helping others.

No matter how tempting Esme was, how passionate or how she enflamed his desire, he shouldn't jeopardize the most important friendship of his life by giving in to lust.

Not that it was all his fault. Whoever would have guessed such a fiery passion lay beneath Esme's usually cool, intellectual demeanor? Whoever would have suspected her kisses would be so intoxicating?

Didn't *you?* his heart whispered.

Wasn't that why he'd teased and goaded her, to get beyond that cold wall of indifference? Hadn't he wanted to make the pink flush come to her cheeks, to get any sort of response from her, even if it was scorn?

He could deny it all he liked, but deep in his heart, he knew he'd wanted Esme McCallan, with her ink-stained fingers and furrowed brow, her shapeless dresses and untidy hair, her clever, inquisitive mind and devotion to her brother, from the first moment he'd met her.

So now he couldn't meet her gaze, and she just as quickly looked away before she glided silently into the room.

He'd always been aware, on some level, that she was graceful. Having felt that lithe, slim body along his own, now he was even more aware of the way she moved.

"Is the carriage ready?" she asked.

To anyone else, that question might sound quite calm and dispassionate. Perhaps once it would have to him, as well. But not today. Not now. He could hear her constraint, see it in her body.

"Not yet," he replied, remaining beside the sofa.

She nodded in acknowledgement and wandered toward the window.

The neckline at the back of the gown dipped low, too, exposing an expanse of skin from her nape almost to the center of her back. How soft and smooth it looked! He wanted to run his finger up and down her spine and make her shiver with anticipation. He wanted to let his lips take that same path as she lay beneath him, naked and—

"My lord, the barouche is at the door," McSweeney announced.

Cursing his imagination, that gown and McSweeney for intruding, Quinn wordlessly held out his arm to escort Esme from the room.

From the downturn of her lips, she wasn't happy or pleased to be with him. She probably wished McHeath was escorting her.

After their servants had helped him into his coat and her into her cloak and they were in the carriage, neither of them said another word until they were nearly at their destination, and she finally broke the silence. "Did you learn anything more about the earl's financial situation or Mr. McHeath?"

"Mr. McHeath is apparently exactly what he seems, a fine, honest, upright young solicitor," he replied.

He shouldn't be annoyed at the pleased look that came to Esme's face. After all, McHeath was one of the sacred order of solicitors. Nevertheless, and in spite of his faith in Mollie's assessment of men, it was still too early and there was too much at stake, to trust him completely. "Which isn't to say he is. My informant may be mistaken."

Annoyance flared in her eyes, but he didn't care. Anything was better than that cool detachment. It always had been.

"I'm well aware a handsome exterior can hide a duplicitous nature," she said, gazing out at the street as if she'd rather look at damp gray buildings than him.

Enough, he thought with sudden determination. Enough of this speculation about her thoughts and feelings. He was tired of hoping that one day, she would realize that he'd changed and was no longer the wastrel he'd been in his youth.

Here, now, he would find out if she could see beyond his past misdeeds. "Are you also aware that a man can change? That remorse and regret can affect him and make him see the error of his ways?"

She turned the full force of her inquiring eyes—like a bright beam of the summer's sun—onto him. "Are you trying to tell me you've seen the error of your ways?"

"I'm attempting to tell you that in spite of my

past and any necessary liberties I may have taken with you recently, I'm not a completely dishonorable reprobate. And if you hear I was visiting certain disreputable establishments, that's only been because of the job Jamie sent us here to do, not for my personal enjoyment."

He didn't know if she believed him or not as she continued to regard him as if she was trying to look inside his heart.

Let her, if that meant she would venture past the outer surface to the remnants of the good, honorable man that still existed within him.

If she would make the effort and open her mind, and her heart.

Chapter Twelve

Esme had never been so glad to get anywhere in her life, for their arrival at Lord and Lady Marchmont's spared her the need to answer right away. Her feelings were so jumbled and confused, she had no idea what to say to MacLachlann. One moment, she was sure he was simply teasing and tormenting her, the next she believed he truly liked her and felt something more than lust. Then she would fear she was only seeing what she wished to see, and should know better than to fall victim to his charm and good looks.

Why could she not remember who he was and his wasted opportunities when he looked at her with what seemed like genuine remorse and sincerity? Why did she forget that they were here together because they had a job to do, and nothing more?

Why could she not subdue the longing to be in his arms, to feel his lips upon hers, to give herself up to the passion he inspired?

One thing was clear as they entered the spacious foyer crowded with other guests, maids and footmen and she felt Quinn's steadfast gaze upon her: she had to get away from him, if only for a moment, to calm her racing heart and restore her normal mental processes.

A solemn, plain-faced maid past the first blush of youth helped her from her cloak. "Oh, dear, I fear I've got a tear in the seam of my gown," she lied, tilting her head ever so slightly as if surveying the damage while trying not to ruin her hair.

"The upstairs sitting room is being used as the ladies' dressing room," the maid offered.

"Excellent!" Esme cried. Not waiting for Quinn's response, she hurried up the wide curving marble staircase to the right of the foyer.

The upstairs sitting room was at the top of the stairs, a lovely chamber painted in pale blue, with simple plaster work and light oak furnishings upholstered in light blue satin damask.

At present, the only occupants were three maids waiting expectantly. One had a needle and thread at the ready, another hairpins and combs, and the third smelling salts.

She might require that maid's services before the night was out if she couldn't control her nerves, Esme thought as she went to the cheval glass and pushed a flower more firmly into place.

As she regarded her reflection, she told herself to remember that this gown, this hairstyle and these thin shoes were as good as a costume. Quinn hadn't found her attractive before this journey to Edinburgh and he'd probably cease to find her attractive when they returned to London. He would likely wonder what had come over him, as if his passionate desire had been a sort of temporary madness.

Perhaps it was, and perhaps once she returned to London, her feelings for him would be what they'd been before, too.

Yet deep in her heart, she knew that wasn't true. Something had changed between them, permanently and irrevocably, here in Edinburgh. No, from that first kiss.

"Ah, Lady Dubhagen! I was hoping to meet you here!" a young woman cried, hurrying toward Esme from the doorway, her red silk gown swish-

ing about her ankles and her diamond necklace
and ear bobs sparkling in the candlelight. "Forgive
the rudeness, but I simply cannot *wait* for a formal
introduction. I'm Finula Blackmure, Sir Walter
Blackmure's daughter."

"How do you do?" Esme warily replied, taken
aback by the pretty auburn-haired girl's enthusi-
astic greeting.

"Quite well, thank you."

Another young woman, also likely not more
than twenty and fashionably attired in lavender
satin, came to stand beside Miss Blackmure, who
glanced at her with a smile and said, "This is Lady
Penelope Ponsenby. She's been most anxious to
meet you, too."

"You have?" Esme replied, not sure what the
thrill would be.

"Oh, yeth!" the dark-haired Lady Penelope replied, smiling as she lisped. "We want to hear
what it'th like to live on a thugar plantation. It
mutht be quite thrilling, with so many thervants
and things."

Miss Blackmure giggled as she drew Esme
away from the mirror. "I've heard some of the
slaves are quite…well, nothing like English gentlemen. Primitive and so very…muscular."

As if they were animals in a zoo to be stared at, Esme thought with disgust, not human beings.

"No, they aren't like English gentlemen," she replied. "Unless you took an English gentleman, his wife and children, locked them in a ship for several months, starved and beat them and, should they even survive to reach the shore, worked them like livestock. Indeed, I wonder how you would fare in such circumstances, should you be so unfortunate."

She was about to detail some of the atrocities female slaves were subjected to, but restrained herself. These goosecaps would probably faint.

As it was, Miss Blackmure blushed as red as her gown and Lady Penelope had blanched.

"I believe Lady Penelope requires your help," Esme said to the maid with the smelling salts as she swept to the door, feeling much more like herself and ready to beard a lion in his den.

Or encounter Quintus MacLachlann in a ballroom.

But as Esme surveyed the gathering in Lady Marchmont's glittering ballroom illuminated by two large chandeliers and several wall sconces, the light reflected by mirrors that went the length of the wall from floor to vast ceiling, she couldn't see MacLachlann anywhere.

She couldn't enter unless she was announced, and she couldn't be announced without her husband.

As she surveyed the room again, she also began to regret her intemperate response to the two young women upstairs. She should have controlled her anger. No matter how infuriated, she shouldn't have reacted as she had. They might begin to suspect something was not right.

The sound of low male laughter came from a nearby room and a narrow wisp of smoke drifted from beneath the closed doorway as a masculine voice said something about rum punch.

The gentlemen must have gathered there, including MacLachlann. Or so she hoped.

She rapped on the door, and it was opened by a short, plump man whose barrel chest made her think of a pigeon.

He looked surprised to see her, or perhaps he was taken aback that any woman dared to interrupt the male camaraderie, so she took refuge in her role. Batting her eyelashes, she smiled and said, "Is Lord Dubhagen here?"

"I am summoned!" Quinn announced as he strolled into view, his thumbs tucked into the small pockets of his dark green satin waistcoat. "Gown all fixed, my little plum cake?"

"Yes," she said as the rest of the men stared at her with unabashed interest.

Never had she been more acutely aware of the sort of bold scrutiny that other women endured daily, as if they were no more than a statue to be gazed upon, or an object to be possessed, instead of a person of flesh and blood and feelings. Unfortunately, tonight she had to bear it and act her part. "Shall we go to the ballroom?"

"Until later, gentlemen," MacLachlann said breezily as he took her arm and steered her toward the ballroom.

Yet once he was out of the room, his expression grew grim, as if he wanted to be anywhere else, with anyone else.

This was probably not the best time to mention her conversation with the young ladies. She could do so afterward. Or perhaps not at all.

"The Earl of Dubhagen, Countess Dubhagen," the tall, bewigged butler announced as they entered the ballroom, which had become even more crowded.

Esme noticed Lady Penelope and Miss Blackmure leaning toward the gentlemen beside them and whispering behind their fans while keeping their eyes on Esme and her supposed husband. She could easily guess the sort of thing they would say about the Earl of Dubhagen's hot-tempered wife who had spoken so harshly.

Whatever the others were talking about, she and MacLachlann had to act as if nothing was wrong as they greeted their host and hostess. Lord Marchmont was a healthy-looking, middle-aged fellow in excellently tailored evening dress. Lady Marchmont, clad in a rich, burgundy velvet gown trimmed with gold-tipped lace, with a beautiful ruby necklace and matching dangling earbobs, gave them a welcoming smile.

"Charmed, my dear, truly charmed," Lord Marchmont said before giving Quinn an ap-proving glance. "You've done well for yourself, Dubhagen, I must say. I've heard the tropical heat is bad for women, but it seems your wife has bloomed like a hothouse rose."

"She's beautiful in any climate, my lord,"

MacLachlann gallantly replied, while Esme did her best to smile like a simpleton.

The older nobleman's expression was blessedly paternal as he regarded her. "Trust the handsome fellows to get the prettiest wives."

"As you yourself have done," she simpered, although that was no lie. In his youth, Lord Marchmont had probably been the object of many a woman's fancy and Lady Marchmont had clearly been a beauty. She was still beautiful and, unlike some former belles, didn't seem desperate to cling to her lost youth, an attitude that made her seem not just lovely, but wise.

The butler came and whispered something in Lord Marchmont's ear. He nodded, then spoke to his wife. "It's time to begin, my dear."

As they moved onto the floor for the opening quadrille, Esme drew back closer to the wall. Jamie had tried to teach her how to dance as she prepared for this journey, but she was far from confident of her ability and didn't want to look incompetent.

Fortunately, Quinn didn't seem any more eager to dance than she, until he suddenly took her arm.

"I don't want to dance!" she whispered desperately.

"Calm yourself, my dear. That wasn't my intention. Come with me."

He sounded determined, not seductive, and since she didn't want to draw any attention, she allowed him to lead her toward the terrace and out into the cool night air.

Where they were away from everybody and nobody could see them. Where they could do almost anything...

"Why is everyone looking at you as if you've stolen the silver?" he quietly demanded as he let go of her. "Or is it me? Have I a stain on my shirt? Is my cravat crooked?"

She might as well tell him. He would probably hear about it sooner or later anyway. "I lost my temper in the dressing room and was a little blunt in my reply to some of the young ladies."

"Blunt? What did you say?"

She didn't want to answer, although the words themselves hardly mattered. And they shouldn't linger here anyway, alone in the dark. "This is hardly the time or place for an interrogation."

"I have to know what you said, so I can be prepared if anybody talks to me about it."

He was, regrettably, right.

First, though, she would explain the circumstances, so he would understand why she'd been driven to answer as she had. "Miss Blackmure and Lady Penelope Ponsenby wanted to know about slaves. It was clear they were predominantly interested in the *male* slaves and their physical attributes, not about their suffering. I couldn't contain my disgust and annoyance and spoke accordingly."

His brows furrowed even more. "Did you sound like that?"

"If you mean disgusted and angry, I was."

"I meant did you use language like that? *Predominantly. Interrogation.*"

"I don't remember precisely what I said," she admitted.

"Well, it can't be helped now," he said with resignation. "Let's hope your passionate response is considered an aberration or some sort of personal hobbyhorse."

"But what if their suspicions are roused that I'm

not what or who I claim to be?" she asked. "What should we do?"

He shrugged. "Brazen it out." He ran his gaze over her. "You're already being fairly brazen in that gown."

She flushed with embarrassment, afraid she'd made another mistake. "The modiste said it was the latest fashion," she explained. "I suggested something to cover the back, but she said it would ruin the look. I should have worn a shawl."

"I didn't mean to distress you," Quinn said with what sounded like sincerity. "It's a nice dress—a very nice dress. I just wish there was more of it." He gave her a little grin. "A man doesn't like to see quite so much of his wife on display."

His body was mere inches away, his broad chest and shoulders shielding her from the light and music and noise spilling out of the terrace doors. Something seemed to change, like the temperature or level of moisture in the air. Something around and between them that she couldn't name. "I'm not your wife."

"I wouldn't admit that at a ball, even to me," he whispered, his voice low and husky.

He was so close, she could hear him breathe

and smell the light scent of cologne and tobacco emanating from him. She had but to rise on her toes to bring her mouth to his.

She shouldn't, of course. It would be wrong. A weakness. Giving in to what could only be lust... even if he wasn't still the wastrel she'd believed him to be before they came to Edinburgh.

Now she knew more about the man beneath the charm and mockery and handsome features. He was a man who had suffered and paid a price, and was still attempting to redeem himself. Was it so very wrong to kiss him? To allow herself a moment or two of desire?

After this, after they returned to London, her life would go back to what it had been. Was it so wrong to grasp a little excitement while she could?

Suddenly Esme McCallan didn't want to be right, or correct, or honorable, anymore. She wanted to be wild and wanton, free and passionate. She wanted to desire and be desired. To kiss and caress and experience the thrill of being in the arms of a handsome man, if only for a little while.

So she gave in to her yearning, raised herself on her toes, and kissed him.

Desire exploded. Longing and heat thrilled through her as he gathered her in his arms and returned her kiss with the same fervent ardor.

Their hands caressed, touched, explored as he deepened the kiss and angled her against the stone wall, pressing closer. Their tongues intertwined, danced, licked. He insinuated his knee between her legs, while his hand crept slowly up her rib cage and hers swept over the expanse of his broad back.

He pulled back, panting. "Oh, God, Esme, we have to stop or I'm going to make love with you right here."

Yes, they should stop. That would be the proper, the correct, the honorable thing to do.

Except that she'd never been so fully alive and aware of another person. The feel of his body. The light scent of his skin. The incredible heat of his desire.

Quinn drew back even more, his forehead furrowing with unexpected wariness. "You aren't trying to trick me again, are you?" he whispered intently.

For the first time since she'd known him, she heard true vulnerability in Quintus MacLachlann's voice. She saw the depth of his loneliness and the extent of his anguish in his eyes. She realized the power she held over him if she chose to exert it, and the pain she could give him.

But she knew what it was to be lonely and vulnerable. She had her books and her legal work and especially Jamie, but that was not enough. Not anymore.

"No, Quinn, I'm not trying to hurt you," she whispered. "I simply wanted to kiss you."

A smile curved his lips.

Then another couple walked out onto the terrace and a frown darkened his features. "We had best get back inside," he whispered roughly, "or who can say what rumors will be started about us?"

Esme didn't protest, because he was, unfortunately, right. They were guests at a ball, outside in the dark. They weren't really husband and wife.

She shouldn't be kissing him here, or anywhere. She shouldn't want to be wanton. She was an honorable woman, with a brother who respected her. She had far too much to lose if she gave in to her desire.

So she said nothing as he held out his arm to escort her back inside.

* * *

Hours later, as they waited for the carriage to take them home, Esme was a little more relaxed, because it appeared that her outburst in the drawing room hadn't been a complete disaster. Some of the women had given her the cut direct, but others who shared her views had sought her out. Although she still had to act the fool, she was gratified by their support nonetheless.

Quinn, however, barely spoke to her for the rest of the evening, and even seemed to be avoiding her.

Nor did he speak or make any move to touch her when they were in the carriage. He sat hunched in the corner, head bowed and arms crossed, like a turtle retreating into its shell.

Or as if he was regretting what had happened between them.

It had been her desire, her weakness, that had led to their passionate embrace and caused him to reveal his loneliness and vulnerability. A proud man like Quinn might regret those revelations, and so the feelings that lead to it.

A proud man could even come to resent her for it.

Perhaps even hate her.

* * *

A few days later and shortly before dawn, Quinn sat slumped on a seat of a hackney that was bobbing about like a longboat at sea. In the east, the sky was lightening with the dawn. Bakers, green grocers and fishmongers were beginning to appear with their carts or horse-drawn wagons, while he had spent another wasted night at another gentlemen's club.

Well, not completely wasted. He was now quite certain that if there was anything amiss with the earl's money, it was the man's own doing, and there was nothing criminal behind it.

It also seemed that McHeath was as fine a fellow as any man could hope to meet. Nobody had a word to say against him and his clients were all more than satisfied with his work.

So he had come to one other conclusion tonight, a conclusion that he'd been both anticipating and dreading since that night on the terrace with Esme. The time had come for them to return to London and end this charade, this dream of a life that he could never lead, in a house that had never felt like home until Esme was in it.

It would be better for them both—her to return

to a happy life with her brother and every hope of marriage to a man like McHeath, and he to the lonely, but useful, existence he deserved.

He rapped on the top of the cab and the driver dutifully brought it to a halt.

"We're no' a' th'address you gave me," the cabbie protested when Quinn opened the door and stepped down onto the pavement.

"I want to walk a little to clear my head," Quinn replied as he generously paid the fellow.

"Ah," the cabbie sighed, giving him a knowing smile. "Want to sober up a little before the missus sees you, eh?"

Quinn grinned in response, although he was stone-cold sober.

Too sober. It might have been better if he'd gotten drunk. Then he might be able to forget Esme and how he felt about her. How much he wanted her, and not just in his bed. He could forget all the things he'd done and not done in his life that meant he could never deserve a woman like her.

Thank God they hadn't given in to their mutual desire that night on the terrace. Nothing good could come of it, except a brief slaking of their physical need, even if Esme's passionate desire had been just as strong as his.

He coughed in the thick air that smelled of smoke. The chambermaids had been up early setting fires in the grates, he thought—until he turned the corner and came to a stunned halt.

A thick cloud of smoke was rising from the back of his brother's house.

Chapter Thirteen

"Fire! Fire!" Quinn shouted at the top of his lungs as he broke into a run.

As he got closer to the house, he spotted a gaggle of anxious young women and street sellers in the small park across from his brother's house. The women, who were probably maids, huddled together like refugees, and he recognized one or two. The street sellers were more excited, talking and pointing.

Where was Esme? Why wasn't she with the maids? He didn't see Mrs. Llewellan-Jones, either, he realized as the door of his brother's house opened. McSweeney appeared, his face and clothes smoke-blackened.

"The fire's out and no one is injured, so be about your business," the butler announced as Quinn skittered to a halt.

No one was injured. Thank God, oh, thank God!

McSweeney saw him and, looking as relieved as Quinn felt, trotted down the steps. "My lord! You're back!" He frowned. "You look terrible. Are you ill?"

Taking a deep breath, aware that the onlookers were regarding him with undisguised curiosity and probably silently passing judgment on his arrival at this hour and in such a state, Quinn tugged his waistcoat back into place and tried to tie his cravat with fingers that trembled not because of anything he'd done, but because of what might have happened.

And he had not been there.

"Well enough. What happened here? Where's Lady Dubhagen?" Quinn asked as he led the way back up the steps and into the house.

"I believe her ladyship is in the kitchen having a cup of tea, my lord. It was only a small fire in the garden, I'm glad to say. It looks as if a lantern fell near some of the crates and packing straw that had been left there from the last wine delivery. It was soon put out."

"Thank God it wasn't worse," Quinn said, "although you look as if you've been roasted."

"Soot, my lord, and nothing more. The house will need some repairs—a new window and some paint."

"As long as nobody was hurt," Quinn said as he waved his hand dismissively.

He hurried past the main staircase toward the servants' stairs to the lower level. He had more questions about what had happened, but they could wait until he had seen for himself that Esme was all right.

Entering the kitchen, Quinn felt another surge of relief at the sight of Esme sitting at the large table in the middle of the whitewashed room, her hair in a long, dishevelled braid, her pale blue silk dressing gown blackened from smoke and with a spot of soot on her lovely nose. She was obviously safe and blessedly alive.

If anything had happened to her...

He was so happy and relieved, he couldn't help what he did next. He reached her in two long strides and pulled her to her feet, then kissed her fervently, hungrily, with all the passion he'd been telling himself he should never feel for her. Her hair smelled of smoke and her lips tasted of Earl Grey, but he didn't care. She was well and alive and precious and for one glorious moment, she relaxed against him and let him kiss her—although it was only a moment before she broke away.

"Ducky!" she cried, blushing and breathless. "Where were you? You smell like a taproom."

"I was at a club. Are you quite all right? I saw the smoke and feared—"

"I'm quite all right. Nobody was hurt and the damage appears to be minor," she replied, glancing around the room and reminding him they weren't alone.

In addition to the cook hovering near the ovens, the housekeeper stood beside the pantry and the scullery maid watched wide-eyed by the back door.

"I'm glad it wasn't worse," Quinn said as matter-of-factly as he could, even as he noticed the cracked glass in the kitchen window.

"I shall summon a glazier and painter as soon as possible," Mrs. Llewellan-Jones said.

"Good. And have a tub and hot water brought to my wife's room right away, and another to my room, as well," he said, taking Esme's hand to lead her from the kitchen.

As they walked toward the stairs, Quinn noted

the dark circles under Esme's eyes and how pale she was beneath the soot. He considered picking her up and carrying her up the stairs, but refrained—until she stumbled. He immediately swept her into his arms.

"Don't tell me to put you down," he warned as he started up the stairs.

She didn't even try. Instead, with a weary sigh that made him curse his absence anew, she laid her head against his shoulder.

"Are you sure you're not injured?" he demanded with quiet concern. "Sometimes you don't realize you are until after the crisis."

"No, I'm not hurt, just tired."

He carried her down the hall and into her bedroom, kicking the door shut before he put her down. She didn't complain about that, either, thank God, because what he had to say was for her ears alone.

"Esme, I'm so sorry I wasn't here," he said, his gaze faltering as guilt overwhelmed him again. "If anything had happened to you…"

She laid her hand on his shoulder, offering him the sort of comfort her brother probably took for granted. At once a pang of longing swept over him, to have that sort of love and devotion from a woman like Esme...

"It's quite all right," she replied softly. "No serious harm was done. It was a very small fire and only a little damage was done to the house. Fortunately, Mrs. Llewellan-Jones was already up and about and saw the smoke. It was a simple matter to organize the servants to put it out."

Her cheeks reddened with a blush. "I forgot I was supposed to be merely decorative."

She felt guilty? He should have been here to protect her instead of wasting his time in another club. "Considering I wasn't here, I'm glad you did."

Or perhaps she was upset by his kiss in the kitchen.

He decided not to speak of it, and to try not to think of it, either. "McSweeney told me the fire started after a lantern was dropped near some straw and crates left after a wine delivery. Do you think it was an accident, or deliberate?"

Her delicate arched eyebrows knit with thought. "I did consider the possibility that it had been deliberately set by someone who had come from the mews through the back gate, but not until the fire was out. By then, the gate was open. However, it could have been opened from the inside. Nevertheless, I made certain all the servants were accounted for at once, and none of them were missing. Of course, it could be that the fire was started, then the perpetrator came into the house and up to the servants' quarters before Mrs. Llewellan-Jones raised the alarm."

She thought of everything, just as he was sure she was capable of anything, including fighting a fire single-handedly, or summoning and guiding any available assistance.

"Someone could have climbed the wall, of course," she went on, "and it's possible they lit the lantern inside the garden, so nobody saw them in the mews. But why would someone try to set fire to your brother's house? What enemies does he have here? Or do you think somebody knows we aren't who we claim to be and that they mean to frighten us into leaving Edinburgh?"

"Whether it was an accident or not, I'm not willing to take any chances with your safety, Esme," Quinn said firmly. "I'm hiring a coach to take you back to London tomorrow."

Esme stared at him with dismay, her fatigue

from the early excitement of the fire vanishing in an instant. "It could just as easily have been an accident, not set by some villain out to harm us. After all, I should think somebody who genuinely wanted to hurt us would have gone about it in a better way, don't you? There was only enough wood and straw for a very small blaze, hardly enough to destroy the house or even cause much damage."

She straightened her shoulders and faced him squarely. "Besides, I'm not a coward who flees at the first sign of trouble. I came here because Jamie asked me to, and I won't leave until I can give him a satisfactory answer about Catriona's father."

An equally stubborn glint appeared in Quinn's blue eyes. "We've found nothing to indicate the earl is being swindled, so there's no need for you to stay. Before I returned this morning, I was going to suggest we both go back to London, but now I shall remain in case the fire was set on purpose, to find out who did it and why."

"If this fire was set by someone who knows who we really are and to discourage us, that is proof that there's something amiss here after all, and I don't intend to leave until we know what," she replied just as sternly.

"Whatever is happening here, I doubt your legal expertise will be required," he countered.

"You don't know that," she retorted. "And how would you explain your wife's sudden departure?"

"I can simply say you went to London to visit friends or buy some new clothes."

"But—!"

"Enough, Esme," he declared. "You're leaving. Tomorrow."

"I will not!"

"I won't put your life at risk!"

"You aren't," she decisively pointed out. "*I* am—or Jamie did when he first suggested this plan, so you may absolve yourself of any responsibility for me."

"Whether you agree or not, I am responsible for you and I'm not going to put you at risk," he said, his patience clearly running out.

She didn't care if it was, or what he said. She wasn't going to run away. Did he think she was a child he could order about? Or an underling? Or a coward, that she would be too afraid to stay after this mere hint of danger? After all, the fire might have been an accident, caused by a servant too afraid of dismissal to confess, rather than a threat or warning.

She was no servant, no child, no coward. She had agreed to help her brother find out the truth about what was happening here, and by God, she would.

But what could she say that would make Quinn understand that?

If he was like most men, there were some things he couldn't abide. If she had to resort to such tactics, she would, because he was forcing her to. "I am a grown woman, not a child. Nor am I your wife or your sister, so you have no authority to order me to go. And if you try, I'll make a fuss the likes of which you have never seen."

His brow furrowed and she guessed he was trying to imagine what that sort of fuss might be. "What, you'll cry?"

"Believe me, I'll do much more than that," she replied. "I'll kick and scream and have to be carried out bodily. How would you explain that to the servants? And even if you manage to do that, I'll simply go to Catriona."

There was a soft knock on the bedroom door,

followed by a maid's breathless voice. "My lady, we've brought your bath."

There was nothing to be done except open the door and since Quinn was standing there like some kind of irate warrior, Esme marched to the door to admit a panting maid carrying a hip bath. Behind her came three more maids bearing tall, metal pitchers of hot water and Mrs. Llewellan-Jones with an armload of fresh linen.

"I'll leave you to it, then," Quinn muttered as he went to the dressing room door. "We'll discuss your shopping trip later."

No, they would not, Esme silently replied. As far as she was concerned, the matter was settled and the only way he could make her leave was to bind and gag her.

A short time later, after washing and changing his clothes, and accompanied by a policeman and a high constable, Quinn stood in the back garden surveying the damage from the fire.

The back wall of the house was black from smoke above the smoldering ruins of several crates. Soaking wet ashes covered the ground and nearby flowerbed, and the closest tree's branches had been singed. Near the wall were the remains of a broken lantern and the area around it still reeked of whale oil. A closer inspection had revealed that several panes of glass in the lower windows had cracked from the heat and would have to be replaced.

Still, it could have been worse. Much worse.

As for Esme, he was still determined that she return to London; unfortunately, she was obviously equally determined to stay. Even more unfortunately, she was right in that he had no authority over her to force her to return. There was only one man in the world who held that sway over her, and Jamie…

The answer came to him like a spark from the smoldering ruins of the crates.

He would write to Jamie and tell him that he should summon Esme home. When her brother learned of the fire, surely he would agree that Esme had to leave.

As relieved by that decision as he'd been to discover that Esme hadn't been hurt, Quinn turned his attention to his companions—the sandy-haired policeman in an ill-fitting uniform who prodded the sodden debris with the toe of his boot while

scratching his head under his hat, and the constable, who was a butcher when not engaged in
his official duties.

The constable, Mr. Russell, was dressed in
clothes befitting a prosperous merchant, which he
was. In face and figure and manner, however, he
reminded Quinn of nothing so much as a rooster.
His jowls even wiggled like a wattle.

"Nobody's confessed to dropping the lantern,
eh?" Mr. Russell said when he realized Quinn
was looking at him.

"Not yet," Quinn said. "I'll speak with them
now."

Quinn escorted them to the library, telling one
of the footmen to summon the butler along the
way.

When they reached the mahogany-panelled
room lined with books that Augustus had probably never read, Saunders, the policeman, took his
place near the door and shifted as if ill at ease. Mr.
Russell, however, settled into the chair Quinn offered as if he planned to linger until dinner was
served.

Quinn was not filled with hope that either of
these men would be able to find out who was re-

sponsible for the fire, or indeed, anything much about it at all. Still, proper protocol had to be observed.

"Any reason anyone would want to set your house on fire, my lord?" the constable asked.

"None that I'm aware of," Quinn replied.

"I'd like to conduct the interviews, if you don't mind," he continued, not only because he didn't have any faith in the detecting abilities of the public officials, but also because he would be able to avoid any possible problems regarding his own activities. "Of course, you'll be free to ask any questions yourself, as well."

"As you like, my lord," the constable amiably agreed.

Saunders was apparently too overwhelmed by the magnificence around him to do anything except nod.

A weary-looking, but neatly attired and freshly shaven McSweeney arrived. He paid no heed at all to the constable or policeman and spoke only to Quinn. "You wished to see me, my lord?"

"Yes. Naturally we have some questions about what happened last night—or rather, early this morning," Quinn said as he stood behind a large walnut desk with his hands clasped behind him, as his father had so often stood when questioning or berating his youngest son. "Do you have any idea who might have been in the garden with a lantern?"

"No one should have been there at that hour, my lord, with a lantern or without it," the butler flatly replied.

"You saw nothing unusual before you retired?"

"No, sir. I went to my room at my regular time and left the hall boy in the foyer awaiting your return. The next thing I heard was Mrs. Llewellan-Jones calling for help."

"What time was this?"

"I don't know exactly, my lord. I didn't stop to look at my pocket watch. It was near dawn, although it was still dark."

"Do you know why Mrs. Llewellan-Jones was up at that hour?"

"It's her custom to rise early, my lord. She doesn't trust the maids to be up and about their chores unless she's awake to ensure it. She's a very conscientious woman."

"I'm sure she is," Quinn replied.

Nevertheless, no one in the house except Esme was above suspicion, not even McSweeney.

Even so, he found it difficult to believe McSweeney could be a criminal. The butler had always been kind to him and taken the time to talk to him when he found him alone with a book, or simply looking out the window wondering what the rest of the world was like.

Yet McSweeney hadn't recognized him, so who could say what else had changed with the passage of time? He had, so perhaps McSweeney had, as well, although he hated to think so.

"All the servants have excellent references, my lord. Mr. McHeath and I went through them personally," McSweeney continued.

McHeath.

With the solicitor in charge of hiring their servants, it would have been easy for him to get an associate or accomplice into their household, to spy or cause trouble.

"Thank you, McSweeney. I think that will be all, unless the constable or policeman have any questions?"

"You seem to have thought of everything, my

lord," the constable replied, while Saunders simply nodded.

"I think you deserve a nap, McSweeney," Quinn said, "but first send in Mrs. Llewellan-Jones."

The butler bowed and left the room just as Esme entered it.

She was obviously fresh from the bath. Tendrils of still-damp hair clustered at her neck and around her pretty face. Her gown was like something a water nymph would wear, of flowing green and blue silk, cut square about the neck, with short puffed sleeves exposing her arms. Draped around her was a cashmere shawl that looked as soft as her skin.

The constable leapt to his feet and stuck out both chin and chest. Quinn half expected him to start crowing.

Esme blushed like an innocent maid caught *en déshabillé*. "Oh, am I interrupting, Ducky?"

When did that soubriquet start to sound attractive?

"Mr. Russell, allow me to present my wife," he said, tamping down the wish that she could be. "My lady, this is Mr. Russell, one of the high constables of Edinburgh, and that young man is a policeman."

His mouth agape, the young man bobbed his head. "S-Saunders, my lady."

Quinn couldn't blame the fellow for being stunned into incoherence by Esme's presence. He was finding it difficult to concentrate with her in the room, too.

"How do you do, Mr. Russell, Mr. Saunders," Esme replied with a smile. "I do hope we can find out what happened. I was never so frightened in my life!"

Of course she'd been afraid when she'd seen the fire. And where had he been? Off on some wild-goose chase and trying to avoid her. Once again remorse and regret, his familiar companions, gnawed at him.

"We'll catch the culprits, my lady, never you fear!" Mr. Russell manfully vowed.

His mouth still gaping, Saunders nodded eagerly.

"I'm sure you will," Esme replied as she ran a swift gaze over Quinn. Of approval? Of desire? Of simple acknowledgment of his existence? He wished he knew.

"I'm sorry, but I didn't see or hear anything until Mrs. Llewellan-Jones shouted 'fire'," Esme said, sitting on one of the chairs beside the desk.

"And you, my lord?" Mr. Russell said. "You didn't see or hear anything unusual, either?"

"I was not at home."

Saunders looked dismayed, as well he might, while the butcher blushed as if he'd stepped in something he shouldn't.

"I was at my club, as several other members will attest."

Mr. Russell flushed and looked about to choke. "I never meant to suggest—"

"I take no offence," Quinn said as Mrs. Llewellan-Jones, as neatly and plainly dressed as always, appeared on the threshold. In spite of her neat appearance, there was no disguising the puffiness around her eyes and the strain evident at the corners of her thin lips.

Like McSweeney, she ignored the other two men and addressed Quinn. "You wish to speak to me, my lord?"

"Yes, please sit down."

Chapter Fourteen

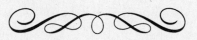

As the housekeeper did as Quinn asked, Esme forced herself to concentrate on the purpose of this interview. She mustn't be distracted by the incredibly handsome Quinn, with his still-damp hair and freshly shaven face, even if he had been so obviously upset by the fire and so relieved that she was unharmed.

And who had kissed her in front of the servants with such fervent passion, although she couldn't be sure if that was because of his feelings for her, or because he felt it necessary for the roles they were still playing.

She must concentrate on what the housekeeper had to say—and she should have been present at the questioning of Mr. McSweeney, too, despite having to act the dim-witted wife.

"This is Mr. Russell, a high constable, and Mr. Saunders of the Edinburgh police," Quinn began.

Mrs. Llewellan-Jones nodded an acknowledgment of the other men.

"I'm going to ask you some questions about the events of last night," Quinn said. "Then I'm going to give you the same order I gave Mr. McSweeney—take a nap."

The housekeeper responded with a hint of a smile. "Thank you, my lord."

"I understand it was you who raised the alarm."

"I did, my lord."

"Before dawn."

The housekeeper's cheeks turned slightly pink as she answered. "Yes, my lord, shortly before. It's my custom to rise early, to ensure that the maids are about their chores in good time."

"So I understand. How did you discover the fire?"

"I smelled smoke, my lord. I was coming into the kitchen and immediately smelled the smoke. I ran outside, saw the flames and called for help."

"I see. Thank you, Mrs. Llewellan-Jones."

The housekeeper nodded, rose and started for the door.

Was that all he was going to ask? And weren't the constable or policeman going to question her? Esme could think of at least one more pertinent fact to ascertain. "You were already dressed when you saw the fire?"

Mrs. Llewellan-Jones slowly turned back. "I was."

Esme smiled, in part to maintain her role and in part to avert any suspicions she might be raising in Mrs. Llewellan-Jones, who struck Esme as the type of woman who could thwart any efforts to get honest answers, if she so chose. "You must be a very early riser indeed! I had no idea."

"I've always been an early riser, my lady," Mrs. Llewellan-Jones replied evenly. She looked from Esme to the others. "Is there anything else?"

"Well, I was just wondering," Esme said, determined to ask her questions while doing her best to maintain her role, "where you were when the men were actually putting out the fire. I don't remember seeing you."

"Since you had everything under control, my lady," Mrs. Llewellan-Jones calmly replied, "I saw no need to stay in the garden. I went inside to make sure the cook was preparing breakfast."

Esme could tell that however serenely Mrs. Llewellan-Jones answered, she hadn't liked that question.

That was interesting.

"And was Mr. McSweeney assisting you in the kitchen?" she asked with apparent wide-eyed inno-cence.

"Mr. McSweeney had gone to fetch the police, my lady, as I'm sure Mr. Saunders can attest. I thought he would have told you that."

"I didn't speak to him myself this morning," Esme replied. She looked at the young policeman.

"Y-yes, that's right, my lady," he stammered. "The butler f-fetched me."

Mrs. Llewellan-Jones regarded Esme with a frown. "Surely you don't suspect Mr. McSweeney?"

"Certainly not!" Quinn declared. "I don't suspect anyone in this household. We merely want to know what happened this morning. Since the house could have burned to the ground if you hadn't been awake to call out an alarm, you have my deepest gratitude, Mrs. Llewellan-Jones. You can be sure my gratitude will find another expression in your wages this month."

The housekeeper's eyes flared with surprise before she gave another little half smile and nodded. "Thank you, my lord. If there's nothing else?"

She glanced at Esme, who decided she'd asked enough.

"I'm satisfied," Quinn said. He turned to the constable and policeman. "Unless you gentlemen…?"

"No, I think everything important has been asked and answered," Mr. Russell said.

Saunders nodded.

After Mrs. Llewellan-Jones had departed, Saunders started sidling toward the door. "I—I think…if you'll excuse me, my lord, m-my lady, Mr. Russell…"

"I'm glad to see you're eager to get to work!" Quinn cried. "I have every faith that the perpetrators of this crime will be speedily captured and I assure you that you, too, will receive a suitable expression of my gratitude on that happy day."

Mr. Russell rose and posed in an attitude unfortunately reminiscent of Napoleon Bonaparte. "Have no fear, my lord. The Edinburgh constabulary is up to the mark! Come along, Saunders."

With that, the butcher strutted out of the room,

followed by the humble policeman who did, after all, have the capacity for speech.

After they had gone, Quinn stood behind the desk like an admiral on the quarterdeck, and Esme mentally girded her loins for another confrontation. He could make any argument he liked; she wasn't going to leave Edinburgh unless he physically forced her.

But instead of launching into another demand that she follow his orders and depart, he sighed, sat heavily and said, "I can't say I'm filled with confidence that those two will be able to find out what happened."

Was he going to pretend that other conversation hadn't happened? Did he simply assume she was going to go because he thought it best? "That's *another* reason I should stay."

Instead of looking annoyed, he shrugged his shoulders and spoke with a tone of unexpected acquiescence. "Since I agree that it's pointless for me to attempt to force you to leave, I'm not going to say anything more about it."

He wasn't? He'd finally realized she wasn't going to give in just because he was a man and *he* thought it best? "Good," she said, not disguising her relief.

"You say all the servants were accounted for?"

This was more like it—a discussion in a moderate, business-like tone, not one fraught with underlying currents of emotion. That was what she preferred, or so she told herself as she sat on the nearest chair and answered. "Yes, at least once the fire was out. Until then, it was unfortunately chaotic. Do you think it was one of our servants?"

"Perhaps, but I'm sure it wasn't McSweeney. I've known him since I was a boy and I can't see any reason he'd want to harm us, or Augustus, either. If he felt any animosity toward us, he would have refused to return."

"What about the housekeeper?" Esme suggested, recalling Mrs. Llewellyn-Jones's demeanor when she'd answered her questions. "I have a strong feeling she isn't being completely forthcoming."

"You think she's hiding something?"

"I do."

Quinn frowned as if considering her statement, then he said, "My experience tells me she's being truthful."

"Mine says otherwise. Men are always too ready and willing to believe women are too stupid or ignorant or virtuous or loving to be capable of wrongdoing. I would that it were so, but women, especially desperate ones, are unfortunately every bit as willing and capable as men of doing whatever they think will help them, or that will remove a difficulty, whether real or perceived. Women can also be as greedy or malicious as men. So I say again, I think Mrs. Llewellan-Jones was *not* being completely forthcoming."

Quinn rose and started to pace, his hands behind his back. "Let's assume you're correct," he began.

"I am," she insisted, certain she was. She had seen too many woman pass through her brother's offices, had known too many girls at school, to doubt her instincts now.

"Why would Mrs. Llewellan-Jones hide any information? And of what sort? If she set the fire, why would she do it? What possible motive could she have?"

Esme could think of one, for truly, hell had no fury like that of a woman scorned or abandoned.

"Since this is a woman of whom we speak, what do you know of your brother's past indiscretions?"

Quinn slowly wheeled toward her.

"Perhaps Mrs. Llewellan-Jones was a victim of his lust."

"If that were so, wouldn't she realize I'm not Augustus?"

"Would she?" Esme countered. "McSweeney didn't recognize you. Or she may not have been the victim. It could be that she was related to a woman your brother wronged, or perhaps someone he harmed in another way—a cheated tradesman, or one who thinks he was. Perhaps your brother held a mortgage and foreclosed. Do you know anything of your brother's business dealings?"

Quinn shook his head. "No. McHeath would know, but he wouldn't be privy to information about Augustus's past love affairs. As I said, my brother has a horror of scandal, so if he kept anything secret, it would be that sort of thing."

"Past business dealings will give us a place to start, at least," she replied. "Unfortunately Mr. McHeath would surely find it odd if you asked him about your own business. I, on the other hand, could reasonably plead ignorance of your financial affairs. Mr. McHeath also hired all the servants, so it would be natural for your wife to ask him about them."

Quinn toyed with the edge of the desk blotter. "I see your point," he conceded, and she couldn't help feeling a surge of triumph at the admission. It was as if he was finally acknowledging her contribution to this endeavor.

"Nor do I believe we should assume the fire was an act of violence against us," she continued. "As I said before, we should also entertain the possibility that it was an accident. Still, I'm well aware it could be otherwise, so I suggest ordering the footmen to keep watch, one at the front of the house, one at the back."

Quinn nodded his agreement. "I'll hire a few more, too. I don't think anyone will question that after what's happened."

"I'll visit Mr. McHeath this afternoon and see what I can learn about the servants."

"Since he was responsible for hiring them," Quinn said grimly, "it could be that he—"

"Deliberately hired a criminal associate or he may be in league with one?" Esme interrupted as her mind leapt to the obvious conclusion. "That perhaps he even hired the perpetrator for that purpose, or to spy on us? Yes, it could be," she reluctantly admitted.

"That would mean McHeath is a dangerous man. Perhaps I should accompany you."

At least it wasn't a demand. Nevertheless…"I think not," she replied. "He won't be as forthcoming if you're with me, and I can hardly imply I have doubts about your financial competence if you're in the room."

He sighed and a look of resignation, almost…defeat…appeared on his features. "Very well, Esme. But be careful and if he seems the least bit suspicious—"

"I'll leave," she assured him.

She rose, ready to go to Mr. McHeath's without delay, but MacLachlann's next words made her hesitate. "Your brother will have to be informed of this."

Did he? What good would it do to worry Jamie over something that might be immaterial to their reason for being in Edinburgh?

Or did MacLachlann have another motive? What if, in spite of his apparent change of heart,

MacLachlann still wanted her to go back to London? He would surely describe the fire in the worst possible terms, making it sound as if their lives had been in grave danger. Since Jamie would then be worried about her, he would no doubt summon her back to London.

Unless, of course, MacLachlann's letter never arrived.

"If you must, but note that the fire could have been accidental," she said pertly, as if she hadn't realized what he might be up to. "I don't want you to worry him unnecessarily."

"And if he wants you to go home to London?"

She sighed heavily as she proceeded to the door, taking some small satisfaction from seeing through his scheme. "I shall, of course, abide by his wishes, although I sincerely hope he doesn't."

"Good afternoon, Lady Dubhagen. This is a most pleasant surprise. Please, sit down," Mr. McHeath said as Esme was shown into his office by his clerk, a neatly dressed young man with red hair and freckles.

She did as the solicitor asked, noting the quality of his desk—carved oak with mahogany inlays, as well as the fine oak panelling and shelves of law books. He had a few papers on his desk and the silver ink set was polished as bright as a mirror. The windows of his chamber were large, although no sunlight could penetrate the fog outside, so clean-burning lamps that were as shiny as the ink set had been lit to provide more illumination.

"What can I do for you, my lady?" Mr. McHeath asked as he took a seat behind his desk, concern in every feature.

Was it really possible he was a scoundrel? That despite his apparent solicitude, his kind demeanor, that he sought to steal from his clients and even do bodily harm? Every instinct, every bit of experience and intuition Esme possessed, told her that it couldn't be so. Nevertheless, she must be wary and careful, and give him no cause to suspect she was anything except what she claimed, in case MacLachlann was right and she was wrong.

"I've come to ask you about our servants, Mr. McHeath, particularly Mrs. Llewellan-Jones," she said, chewing her lip to denote anxiety. "You see, there was a fire in our garden shortly before dawn—a small one," she hastened to add when she saw the shock on his face.

"What happened? Was anyone injured?"

If he was feigning his reactions, he should be on the stage of the Theatre Royal in Drury Lane.

"Everyone was quite all right, thank heavens, and we aren't sure what happened," she said, twisting her reticule in her hands. "It was started by a dropped lantern, although who had it and what they were doing there at that time of night, I have no idea! I thought it must have been a servant, but none of them have confessed, so I thought I ought to check their references."

Mr. McHeath immediately rose and went to a wooden cabinet with brass handles, from which he produced a sheaf of papers. "Here are the letters of reference for all your servants, if you'd care to examine them, although I assure you I made the usual inquiries about them."

She eagerly accepted the references. "Thank you."

She immediately began to the read the first one, which pertained to Mrs. Llewellan-Jones. If this reference was credible, she was indeed a paragon among housekeepers.

The next one referred to Mr. McSweeney and the next to the head footman. It soon became apparent that every servant came with an excellent character and recommendations from past employers, right down to the scullery maid.

As she read, Esme realized that Mr. McHeath had come closer. A bit too close, perhaps—at least close enough to make her uncomfortable and begin to wonder if Quinn was right about Mr. McHeath's attraction to her. As for her feelings for the solicitor...

To be sure, he was a good-looking man about the same age as Quinn, respectable, intelligent, a fellow Scot and a solicitor to boot, yet he didn't stir her heart in any way. Nor, she had been sure until this moment and despite whatever Quinn suspected, did she stir his.

She got quickly to her feet. "I shouldn't take up so much of your time."

"There's something else the matter, isn't there?" the solicitor gently prodded as he took the papers from her and put them on his desk.

"I don't know what you mean," she said, wishing he wasn't standing between her and the door, wondering if that position was a deliberate attempt to block her exit.

"There is another explanation for the lantern and the fire," Mr. McHeath said. "Might I ask where your husband was when the fire broke out?"

She wasn't sure what to say. She could lie and say he'd been home, but there was the chance that Mr. McHeath had heard about MacLachlann's nocturnal activities from other clients or members of the clubs. "He was…out," she said.

The solicitor looked at her with sympathy. "I'm afraid that confirms other things I've heard, my lady, and leads me to wonder if it was your husband who dropped the lantern."

Quinn would have told her if he'd dropped the lantern while returning from one of his investigative escapades in a men's club, wouldn't he? Why would he pretend otherwise to her?

Unless he hadn't been alone. Perhaps *he* had been with a servant.

Or maybe he thought the potential threat of physical harm would be a good way to make her leave.

As she sank back onto the chair, Mr. McHeath spoke with gentle compassion. "I'm sorry to distress you so, but I'm afraid we must consider that possibility and if so…"

If so, what?

"My lady, I've seen the way he treats you. I'm very concerned for your safety as well as your happiness. Please, let me help."

The last person she wanted to talk to right now was Mr. McHeath. She wanted to get away from him, to be alone to think. "Thank you for your concern," she said, getting quickly to her feet, "but now if you'll excuse me, I ought to go home."

Instead of going to the door and opening it for her, as she expected, McHeath took hold of her hands and gazed anxiously into her face. "If he's mistreating you in any way, I can help you get away from him. If you fear retribution or that you will be left penniless because he has control of the estate, there are means to get an income for you, or even a divorce."

"Let me help you, my lady," the solicitor pleaded. "No woman deserves to be miserably married."

"Please, Mr. McHeath, let me go!"

He did, but he nevertheless stood between her and the door. "Then before you go, please answer me this," he said, regarding her intently. "Why are you trying to deceive me and everyone else in Edinburgh?"

Chapter Fifteen

Desperately trying to keep her wits about her, Esme did the only thing she could—she continued pretending to be Quinn's vapid wife, regarding Mr. McHeath with apparently mystified confusion. "Whatever do you mean, Mr. McHeath?"

The solicitor took a step closer, his expression not angry or upset, but compassionate and sincere. "Why are you pretending to be stupid? Is it to pacify your husband? Do you fear him? Does he fly into a rage if you express an opinion that contradicts his own?"

It hadn't occurred to her that her portrayal of a dim-witted, slightly intimidated wife would arouse any man's sense of chivalry. What should she say? How could she explain her relationship with Quinn without giving away too much of the truth?

"I'm very touched you're concerned about my welfare," she answered honestly, "but you needn't be. I fear I've given you the wrong idea, Mr. McHeath. I wouldn't want to stop being the Countess of Dubhagen. I only wanted to find out about Mrs. Llewellan-Jones. A man will have his recreation, after all. I just wouldn't like it to be with a servant in our own house."

She saw the solicitor's respect for her dwindle and was sorry for it, but what else could she do?

"Now you really must excuse me, Mr. McHeath," she continued as she hurried to the door.

Once more he stepped in front of her to block her exit. "My lady, if your husband is the callous brute I fear he is—"

"No, he's not," she insisted just as the door to the office burst open.

"What the devil are you doing with my wife?" Quinn demanded, glaring at Mr. McHeath as if he'd gladly kill him.

Esme stared at him with stunned dismay. He had known she was coming here and why, and he had agreed, so why had he followed her? Did he think she was incapable of conducting an independent investigation? Or was he really that convinced Mr. McHeath had seductive designs on her—and that she might succumb?

"I'm telling her that if she wishes to be free of an unhappy marriage, I'll help her," the solicitor admitted without fear and with reproach.

"Get away from her," Quinn warned.

"Don't be upset, Ducky," Esme said before she turned to the solicitor, who was glaring at MacLachlann as if he wanted to have him arrested. "It's all right, really, Mr. McHeath."

"What's he been accusing me of?" Quinn demanded.

"Nothing, Ducky, really."

"I have been hearing some very disturbing accounts of certain visits you've made to various unsavoury establishments in Edinburgh since your return," McHeath said, regardless of Esme's interjection. "Establishments that may not only cause financial and social embarrassment for your wife, but possibly harm her health."

Esme slowly turned to face Quinn. "What does he mean?" she asked softly, although she was worldly enough to understand the implication of Mr. McHeath's words.

"We'll discuss this in private," Quinn said

through clenched teeth, reaching out to take her hand.

McHeath moved between them.

"Get away from my wife," Quinn growled, "and mind your own business."

"If your wife requests my aid, she'll get it," McHeath returned just as sternly.

Jamie had often said that Quinn was a fierce and skilled fighter with more lives than a cat, so Esme hurried to intercede, moving to stand in front of Quinn and splaying her hands on his chest to hold him there. "Calm yourself, Ducky." She looked back over her shoulder at the indignantly angry McHeath. "I'll be quite all right, although naturally I'm touched by your concern. Come along, my dear," she said as she took Quinn's arm.

For a moment, she feared he wasn't going to move, but he did, mercifully letting her lead him from the office.

The moment they were seated in the carriage, and regardless of Quinn's defensive sulking in the corner, Esme demanded to know what on earth he thought he was doing, coming to the solicitor's office. "Or do you think me incompetent to ask questions?"

"Of course I think you're competent," Quinn growled in reply. "I wanted to see what he'd do if I arrived unexpectedly. Surprise generally results in an unguarded reaction and so a better understanding of the person I suspect."

"And what of me? What of my unguarded reaction?"

That earned her the sort of smirking grin she hadn't seen on Quinn's face for several days, and hadn't missed. "I assumed you would continue to play your role, which you did, and very well."

She warmed beneath his steadfast gaze, but wasn't prepared to relinquish her indignation just yet. "What do you make of Mr. McHeath's reaction then? I hope his chivalrous behavior has caused him to rise in your estimation, as he has in mine."

MacLachlann regarded her as if she had completely missed the point. "Chivalrous? Is that what you think?"

She had just said so, hadn't she? "What else, when he was so keen to help a woman he believed trapped in a terrible marriage?"

"The man doesn't see you as some sort of damsel in distress," Quinn replied as if she were a simpleton. "He wants you in his bed."

She didn't believe that for an instant. "Just because he tried to help me—or rather, the woman he believes is your brother's wife—you assume he has selfish motives. And can't you see that if there is a woman he wants, it's Catriona, not me?"

"If you had any real experience of the world, you'd know that I'm right."

"I do have real experience of the world, as you call it," she retorted. "How could I not, hearing what Jamie has to deal with every day? Unfaithful, lazy husbands who abandon their wives, leaving them to the mercy of their creditors. Poor widows and orphans left destitute. Servant girls who are turned out, often with a child to support because their employers raped them. Women shopkeepers who must sue to get what they're owed because men think they can cheat women without consequences. I assure you, MacLachlann, I've seen a great deal of the world and much I wish I had not, including what can happen to the health of a wife whose husband frequents brothels."

Quinn had the decency to blush.

"Yes, whatever you may think, I'm worldly enough to have understood what Mr. McHeath meant. You've been going to brothels."

"Just one," Quinn defiantly replied. "And only to ask questions."

This time, it was Esme who smirked. "No doubt."

His gaze hardened. "That's the truth, Esme. The only reason I went to that place was for information. And how did Mr. McHeath come by the knowledge of my activities, do you suppose?"

"I suspect he has his sources, the same as you," she replied.

"And one of my sources is Mollie MacDonald, who happens to be a whore." Quinn crossed his arms and regarded her without shame or remorse. "Maybe in some things you aren't as naive as I thought, but I still don't trust McHeath. He either wants you, or he wants something from you. I'm sure of it."

"Perhaps all he seeks is the satisfaction of being kind and helpful."

MacLachlann made a disdainful sniff.

"Why do you persist in seeing vulgar or untrustworthy motives everywhere?"

He straightened and slid forward on the seat. "Because, my little plum cake, you're a beautiful woman and it's my experience that no man wants to be merely a *friend* to a beautiful woman."

She wasn't beautiful. She was plain Esme McCallan, so he had to be lying, or exaggerating in an attempt to excuse his own ridiculous behavior in Mr. McHeath's office.

He frowned and his brows lowered as if with confusion. "What's the matter, Esme? Hasn't anybody ever told you that you're beautiful before?"

"Of course not," she retorted, "because it isn't true."

"Yes, it is," he said, his voice low but resolute, as if the words must be spoken whether he wanted to say them or not. "You're beautiful, Esme, and you always have been in spite of those hideous gowns you usually wear and your ink-stained fingers and poker-straight hair."

"That's a lie," she insisted. It had to be. No man had looked at her twice, except to complain that, like a child, a woman should be seen and not heard. No man had ever complimented her on her beauty, and certainly no man had ever tried to be intimate with her, except for Quinn, of course.

"No, it isn't, but you've been too immersed in the law and devoted to your brother to realize it."

"Then why hasn't anyone else ever said so? Why hasn't any man ever pursued me?"

"Likely they would have if they hadn't feared your sharp tongue."

"You don't."

"I like your sharp tongue. I admire your clever mind, although other men might not, and your independence, and your devotion to your brother." He looked at her directly then, his eyes full of a yearning so strong, it seemed to pull her toward him like a rope. "And I've wanted you from the first time I saw you."

That couldn't possibly be true. Surely she would have realized...seen...guessed... And he wouldn't have been so scornful, so mocking.

Yet as she looked into his eyes, she believed what he was telling her. The evidence of his sincerity was there, plain as if it were written on parchment.

As if it were decreed by law, she moved to sit beside him and reached out to touch his cheek. How long had she wanted him, too? When he arrived in his fine new clothes the day they left for Edinburgh?

Since last month, when he and Jamie had been laughing together over a story Quinn was telling?

Or from that first meeting when Quinn had been so devilishly dashing in spite of his state and his less-than-fashionable attire?

Whenever it had happened, all that truly mattered was that it had, and now she wanted to kiss him. So she did, and as she kissed him, every muscle, every sinew, every nerve within her seemed to come alive as it never had before.

Every part of her told her she wanted this man, needed him, as she had never needed or wanted another. He alone could kindle this incredible excitement. He alone could rouse her passion and make her wanton in her desire. He alone provided the fire she had thought never to experience, or even to need as other women did.

How wrong she'd been about that, and him! How blind and ignorant!

Her heartbeat began to race as he returned her embrace with equal fervor. Her body thrummed with warmth, with desire, with the excitement of mutual passion, as he gathered her into his arms and kissed her deeply.

His fingers worked the buttons of her pelisse until it was undone and he could slip his hand inside to cup her breast through her gown. Kneading gently, he encircled her with his other arm and pulled her closer, while she pushed his hat from his hand to run her fingers through his mane of dark waving hair.

Mouths locked, hands caressed and stroked. His fingertips grazed over her gown, until he finally insinuated one hand inside her bodice to cup her. She moaned with yearning encouragement and tugged his shirt from the waistband of his trousers so she could reach beneath it and feel the hard muscles of his chest beneath the fine fabric.

He gathered the skirt of her gown in one hand, sliding the other underneath and between her legs with slow deliberation.

She arched against him as his lips left hers and grazed her jaw, then her neck. She attacked the buttons of his shirt, wanting to feel more of his skin. When she succeeded and laid her hand against his naked chest, he groaned, the sound coming from deep within his chest, primal and raw, like her own tumultuous desire.

She forgot she was supposed to be well-mannered and morally upright. That they were not married, or engaged. That no promises of any kind had been given. No marriage agreement spoken or signed.

They were simply a man and a woman caught up in their shared yearning and lust and want. Unrestrained. Unguarded.

His fingers worked at the drawstring of her pantelettes until he had them undone. She should be modest. Embarrassed. Ashamed. But she was not. She even wiggled her hips to help him lower them.

She knew what was about to happen. What she wanted to happen. What she'd been trying not to imagine since the first time she had ever seen Quintus MacLachlann. What she'd been telling herself could not happen, no matter her wayward thoughts, because he was a rogue. A seductive scoundrel. A disgrace.

Now she knew better. He was a man who had thrown away his advantages—and lived to regret it. Who felt remorse and had suffered for his mistakes. Who was as alone and lonely in his way as she was in hers.

Yet he wanted and needed her. He roused her primitive, natural longing as no man ever had, or likely ever would.

He licked the little indent at the base of her throat as he cupped her below and pressed the heel of his hand against her. She writhed and gasped when he slid a finger inside the slick opening. He pressed again and another finger joined the first. And then—and then, it was as if her body had been slumbering all her life and suddenly awakened. Gritting her teeth to keep from crying out, she half rose as the tension snapped and threw her out of herself, into some other realm without thought, without logic, without laws or rules or modes of conduct. Only feeling. And raw, primal sensation.

This was loving. This was being intimate. This was pleasure—and she would give the same to him.

Yet as her hand went to his trousers, he suddenly drew back and tugged down her skirts as if she'd pulled a knife.

"No," he said, his voice raw and hoarse, stern and unyielding. As if he were ashamed.

Or she should be.

As swiftly as she'd experienced that astonishing release, shame flooded through her. In spite of all her resolve, of the inner fortitude she thought she possessed, she had been as weak and willing as any woman to give in to the demands of her flesh—and in a carriage, too.

She should have remembered she was a good and decent woman who wanted his respect, and giving in to her lust was not the way to earn it.

Although the very notion would have struck her as utterly ludicrous only a few days ago, what she really should want—what she did want—was to be married to Quinn, to be his wife and the mother of their children.

Except that would mean giving up the law, for surely she wouldn't be able to continue to help her brother if she was married, even to Quinn.

As she fixed her underclothes and smoothed down her skirt, she avoided looking at Quinn. Trying to ignore the longings of her heart, she forced herself to consider the practicalities of marriage to him. He would be passionate in bed, but otherwise? What sort of security could he offer her? What sort of profession could a disgraced heir with a dubious past find? What sort of life?

What if their feelings for each other were only lust? She had seen too many marriages crumble and decay because there had been no love, no trust, no security.

She must avoid a similar fate. She should stay away from Quinn and prevent any more such intimate encounters unless and until she was certain there was more to their feelings than lustful desire. Otherwise, she would truly be no better and no smarter than so many of the women who'd sought Jamie's help after losing everything because they thought they were in love.

The carriage stopped moving.

"Thank God," Quinn muttered, his voice husky as he finished buttoning his shirt.

When the footman opened the door, Quinn didn't wait for her. He didn't even look at her before he disembarked and strode into the house, leaving the footman to help her down from the carriage.

Nevertheless, Esme held her head high as she went into the house, although inwardly she felt as desolate and ashamed as if she'd been abandoned at the altar.

Esme McCallan had been humbled at last—and not by a man.

By her own lustful desire.

Quinn strode into his brother's library and went straight to the brandy, pouring himself a drink that he tossed back in a single gulp.

What the devil had he done? How could he have gone so far? In another passion-fuelled moment, he would have taken Esme's virginity. How could he have been so selfish? How could he have forgotten what he owed to Jamie and come so close to deflowering his sister?

Although he supposed he could take some pride in the fact that he'd left her before things had gone too far, he had still let himself get swept along by his longing and desire and need.

The only way Esme should lose her virginity was when she married, and she could never marry a man like him.

What did he have to offer her, after all? Nothing, except a handsome man in her bed, and he knew precisely what that was worth. It had been proven to him often enough in his youth by women who'd flattered and teased, only to discard him once they tired of him, until he learned to leave them first.

If he'd been wise, he would have realized how hollow and unfulfilling those relationships were, and sought something—someone—better.

Someone like Esme, who stirred both his passion and his heart. Who made him feel so good... and yet so bad.

He poured a second drink that swiftly followed the first.

He'd made an ass of himself at McHeath's office, too. He hadn't gone there because he didn't trust Esme's ability to defend herself or ward off unwanted attention; he had gone because he didn't trust McHeath. Although Esme didn't believe McHeath had any lascivious interest in her, she wasn't a man, with a man's knowledge of his own sex.

He poured a third drink, then hesitated with the glass partway to his lips as he remembered that he'd told Esme he never drank to excess anymore.

His glass stayed on the tabletop, and he threw himself into a thickly cushioned wing chair of an ugly shade of green. He'd acted like a jealous husband in some sort of cheap melodrama.

Except that he hadn't been acting. Seeing Esme with McHeath, hearing the man's accusations, he'd been overcome by primitive and possessive rage—something Esme obviously found distasteful and uncivilized.

Because it was.

Quinn got to his feet and strode over to the window that overlooked the garden and the mews. The mess from the fire had been cleaned up and he could hear the glaziers as they went about inserting new glass in the kitchen window.

He couldn't wait for Jamie to order his sister back to London. He would have to make her go, for her sake as well as his.

Chapter Sixteen

"Is something the matter, my lord?" McSweeney asked as Quinn paced the foyer of the town house that evening. He hadn't seen or spoken to Esme since they'd returned from the solicitor's office, nor had she made any attempt to speak to him.

Why should she? After his lack of self-restraint the last time they were together, he wouldn't be surprised if she never wanted to see him again. "I fear my wife might be too unwell to attend the party this evening."

The butler's brows rose ever so slightly. "Indeed, my lord? She summoned her maid to help her dress an hour ago."

"Ah. Delightful," Quinn murmured, trying not to betray the full extent of his relief.

"I don't wish to speak out of turn, my lord, but I must tell you that the servants are all quite taken with her. Her behavior during the fire was most exemplary."

Quinn turned to face the older man. "How so?"

"She kept an amazingly cool head, my lord."

"I wish I'd been here," Quinn replied, the words slipping out as if he were a boy again, confiding in the only ally he had in his father's house.

"If I may venture an opinion…" McSweeney began, only to fall silent when Esme, attired in gown and cloak, appeared at the top of the stairs.

Her hair was more simply dressed than it had been recently, pulled back the way she wore it in London, although there were dainty curls on her forehead and brushing her cheeks. She likewise wore simple pearl earrings and the single strand of pearls, and the gown peeping out from beneath her evening cloak had only two rows of ruffles at the hem.

Even so, she was as lovely as any young woman dressed in the height of fashion. No, lovelier, because no amount of fine attire could match the bright intelligence of her eyes, and the fullness of her ruby lips that could kiss with such passion.

He had to stop thinking like that. He had to

forget how it felt to hold Esme in his arms and kiss her.

Or so he commanded himself all the way to Lady Elvira's, one of the more overdecorated domiciles he'd ever had the misfortune to enter.

His discomfort regarding the surroundings grew when an unfortunately familiar voice called his name as soon as they entered the drawing room.

Ramsley. Of all the vain, young asses... And so far, he'd managed to keep Ramsley far away from Esme. Unfortunately, Ramsley wasn't alone; a group of equally overdressed popinjays were with him.

A broad smile on his round, freckled face, Ramsley came to a halt in front to them and gestured at his companions, who were obviously more than half-inebriated.

"May I present Dougal McSudderland, Lord Ramsley of Tarn," Quinn reluctantly said to Esme as the young idiot bowed. "Ramsley, my wife."

"Charmed, absolutely charmed!" the younger man enthused as he took Esme's hand and kissed the back of it. "By God, Dubhagen, what a prize!"

The corners of Quinn's lips tightened, while

Esme put on another vacuous smile and said, "It's a pleasure to meet you, Lord Ramsley."

"More so for me to meet you, my lady. You're even more lovely than I'd heard."

Esme giggled, while Quinn took hold of her elbow. If he couldn't risk being alone with her, the least he could do was get her away from Ramsley.

"If you'll excuse us, Ramsley, I have something I wish to discuss with the Earl of Duncombe," he said, steering her toward the older nobleman, who was seated a short distance away with his daughter beside him.

Esme didn't protest as Quinn led her away from the young noblemen who'd all been leering at her as if she was a Cyprian on display.

Yet as the weight of his hand on her arm warmed her and made her remember the excitement of his embrace and kiss, she realized it was even more of a mistake to come here with him. She should have pleaded an aching head and stayed in her room.

Perhaps she should capitulate and go back to London, as distressing as that would be. If she couldn't control her desire when she was near him, she might have to get away from him, even if that meant disappointing Jamie.

When they reached the earl, Quinn leaned down so that he could be heard over the music. "I wonder if I could have a word with you about mortgages. It's occurred to me I could be doing more of that sort of thing. You make such financial bargains, do you not?"

"A few. This is hardly the place to talk about money," the earl replied, fidgeting and sliding a sidelong glance at his daughter.

Catriona looked lovely in a gown of pale green silk with dark green satin ribbons around the hem and bodice, and tight-fitting sleeves that emphasized her slender, graceful arms. Many of the women were equally well-attired and most of the men looked good in their evening dress, although none so fine as Quinn.

"I believe we'll find brandy, as well as privacy, in the library," Quinn replied.

The earl's brows lifted. "Never thought of that! A *much* better place to talk, man to man," he said, rising with Quinn and Catriona's assistance.

As Esme watched them go, marvelling again at the way Quinn moved with such lithe, athletic grace, Catriona sidled back toward the corner. The young woman's manner was furtive, as if she didn't want to be seen.

"Is something the matter?" Esme asked, following her.

"No, not really," Catriona replied, toying with the tassel of her fan, her nervous action reminding Esme of the other changes within the young woman, who seemed to have truly suffered.

But then, so had Jamie.

"I didn't mean to alarm you," Catriona said softly. "I find it preferable to keep out of the way of people, that's all. They can make gossip out of the most meaningless word or gesture and after Jamie…" She colored, then went doggedly on. "I've been gossiped about enough to last a lifetime."

Esme had always resented Catriona for making it necessary for her and Jamie to leave Edinburgh. Now, however, it occurred to her that it might have been more difficult to stay and endure the gossip and whispers, as Catriona had.

"Your brother is the finest man I've ever met, or ever shall," Catriona went on, gazing at Esme with sorrowful eyes.

It sounded as if Catriona still loved him.

Was it possible that she'd completely misjudged the young woman?

If Catriona had loved Jamie enough to love him still, despite the passage of time, why had she jilted him? Did her father truly have that much control over her?

Would she give up the man she loved rather than upset or risk offending a beloved parent? Was she that devoted? If she was, she might be capable of continuing to love a man she believed she couldn't have...

Esme suddenly felt a little dizzy. Was this to be *her* fate, too?

"What are two of the prettiest women in Edinburgh doing whispering in a corner?" Lord Ramsley asked, coming to stand before them.

Four of his cronies were with him, each with red eyes and redder noses, as if they'd been into the wine for hours.

"If you'll excuse us, Lord Ramsley," Esme began, starting to move forward until he blocked her path.

"You must allow me to introduce my friends, who are on tenterhooks to be introduced to you,"

Ramsley continued without letting either Esme or Catriona respond. "This is Lord Luchbracken, Lord Esterton and the Honorable George Teannet."

The three other men made attempts at bowing and Lord Esterton, who was at least three stone too heavy for his height, slurred, "'Lighted, ladies, qui' de-lighted."

"If you'll pardon us," Esme said, prepared to push her way past them if necessary.

Ramsley moved forward, making her back up to prevent a collision. "We just want to talk to you."

"*We* don't wish to talk to *you*," Esme retorted, taking Catriona's hand.

"What in the name of God do you young asses think you're doing?"

Esme had never been so glad to see or hear Quinn in her life.

Right behind him came a furiously indignant Mr. McHeath, who appeared like an avenging angel materializing from on high.

The other gentlemen moved away as fast as their state would permit, but Ramsley stood his ground. "I was merely talking to them."

"And now you can stop talking to them and go away," Quinn commanded.

"You have no right to order me to do anything!"

"Perhaps not, but if you're wise, you'll do as I say."

"Why? Because you're rich and your family's an old one?" Ramsley scoffed. "Old and degenerate, if half of what I've heard is true. And you are as bad as any of them."

"I suggest that you cease and desist, Lord Ramsley," Mr. McHeath said with quiet but stern resolve. "Move away from the ladies."

Instead of following that sage advice, Ramsley scowled. "So you would order me, too? I'm even less likely to listen to you, McHeath, despite the money your family's made.

"Why don't you go back to Jamaica?" he continued with a smirk as he again addressed Quinn. "You can leave the wife, though. I daresay I can make her forget you soon enough."

Quinn stiffened as if he'd been struck by a bolt of lightning. Then his brows lowered ominously and his hands balled into fists at his sides. Esme took Catriona by the elbow to get her away, while Mr. McHeath quickly moved to get between the two men.

"You shouldn't do anything rash, my lord," Mr.

McHeath said to Quinn. "There are, however, grounds for—"

"Get out of the way, McHeath," Quinn growled, his voice low and stern.

"Yes, get out of the way," Ramsley taunted. "As if his lordship could hurt me."

"Oh, I can," Quinn replied, so coldly and calmly that Esme could well believe he intended to murder the fool.

"Ducky, please, let's go home," Esme urged, leaving Catriona and taking hold of Quinn's arm.

"An excellent idea," Mr. McHeath seconded, clearly just as concerned about what might happen. Meanwhile Catriona inched closer to the solicitor.

"Yes, run away, my lord," Ramsley taunted. "Isn't that what you always do? Isn't that why you went to Jamaica?"

Instead of replying to Ramsley, Quinn gave Esme a strained smile. "Come, my love. I quite agree that this gnat isn't worth the effort it would take to swat him."

Esme stifled a sigh of relief. Then, while Quinn's attention was still on her, Ramsley threw a punch at Quinn's head. Esme cried a warning at the cowardly attack, but Quinn had already ducked and turned in one fluid motion. Despite his defensive action, the blow landed on his nose and blood trickled down his chin onto his once-pristine cravat.

With a roar like an enraged lion, Quinn retaliated, landing a series of swift blows that sent Ramsley stumbling backward. More people came to see what was going on, while those nearby moved just as swiftly out of the way.

"Stop!"

At the sound of Esme's distraught voice, Quinn glanced over his shoulder. Ramsley saw his chance and charged forward to hit him again.

But Quinn was ready and spun around to avoid the blow, lunging forward. Using his shoulder, he shoved Ramsley to the polished floor now splattered with blood from his nose, then he grabbed the man's arm and in one swift move, broke it.

Ramsley screamed as the bone snapped, then turned pale as bleached table linen and fainted dead away.

Panting and satisfied, Quinn straightened, to see Esme staring at him as if she couldn't believe the evidence of her own eyes.

He'd reacted instinctively to protect himself, but to her, he must have looked like a savage—or her previous poor opinion of him brought to life.

So he feared, until she ran up to him, exclaiming, "What a cowardly, dastardly attack! Ramsley should be arrested!"

Suddenly, his nose didn't hurt quite so much, although as Lord Luchbracken shouted for a doctor, he just as suddenly remembered he was supposed to be Augustus.

He hadn't fought like a gentleman. He'd learned to defend himself in the streets and pubs and gambling hells of London, not in some boxing club for the idle rich.

Augustus had been away from Edinburgh for years, Quinn reasoned as he tried not to notice that Esme had thrown her arms around him. Who could say what he'd learned in that time?

"Is your nose broken?" Esme demanded as she stopped hugging him. She pulled his handkerchief from his jacket and began dabbing at his bleeding nose.

Despite his sincere wish to keep his distance, Quinn had the most intense desire to reassure her with a kiss.

Instead he reached up to feel his nose and cheek, wincing when he encountered swelling. "No, although it hurts like h— It hurts," he said as he took his handkerchief from her and wiped the blood from his chin. "I trust the insolent dog has learned a lesson."

"I should think so," McHeath said as he joined them, followed by a worried Catriona. "Since he struck the first blow, you could charge him with assault."

"And sue him for the value of your ruined clothes," Esme added.

She sounded exactly like Jamie discussing a case. Quinn cleared his throat, hoping she would realize she might be revealing too much legal knowledge, although what she had said was much less worse in terms of risking their ruse than his actions.

"At least, I—I think so," she stammered. "Dear Papa was in a similar situation after a coach splashed mud and dung all over his best greatcoat and ruined it completely."

"I think justice has been adequately served," he replied.

Lady Elvira thrust her way through a knot of

women nearby. "Is he dead?" she cried, staring in horror at the sight of Lord Ramsley. His friends had rolled him over so he was faceup, but he was still lying on the floor.

"He's alive and likely to stay that way, as am I," Quinn calmly answered. "If my blood has stained your floor, I'll happily pay for the repairs."

"Stained my…?" Lady Elvira murmured as she scrutinized the floor. "Is that *blood?*"

"Somebody catch her," Quinn ordered when Lady Elvira began to sway.

As several of the women hurried to help their swooning hostess, Esme leaned close to Quinn and whispered, "I think we'd better be going."

"I couldn't agree more," he replied.

The open flap covering the window of the carriage taking Esme and Quinn back to the Earl of Dubhagen's town house allowed light from the side lanterns to illuminate the interior. Quinn, however, was mostly in shadow, save for the occasional glimpse of his face when the carriage turned, as if the lantern and the road were conspiring to tease Esme with brief glimpses of her handsome companion's injured face.

It was clear Quinn was in pain but, like many men, he was trying not to show it. A man like Quinn would probably make light of a broken rib, so she doubted asking him how he felt, or mentioning the circumstances leading up to his injury, would illicit a welcome response.

She also wanted to tell him how relieved she'd been to see him when she and Catriona had been cornered by those oafs. She wanted to thank him for his intervention, even if she'd also been afraid he was either going to kill Ramsley or be hurt himself. But she was too aware of what had happened the last time they were alone in a carriage to risk either a compliment or what he might take as a criticism, and soon enough, the carriage jolted to a halt.

When the footman opened the door, he stared at Quinn as if he'd grown another nose.

"Just a little spot of bother at the party," Quinn said lightly as he got down from the carriage and held out his hand to help Esme and escort her inside.

When they reached the front door, they encountered McSweeney, who was just as shocked by Quinn's appearance. "Do you need anything, my

lord?" he asked in a whisper. "Bandages, oint-
ment, or…anything?"

"I'm quite all right. Go to bed, McSweeney."

There was no point trying to gloss over how
Quinn had gotten hurt, Esme reasoned. The servants would hear all about what had happened
soon enough. "He looks a fright, I know, but it's
only a bloody nose," she said with a giggle. "That
will teach him to get into a brawl at a party, I
hope!"

"Yes, my lady," the butler muttered, obviously
still taken aback as they started up the stairs.

Whatever Quinn might think about his wound,
she wasn't going to leave him alone tonight. She
had heard of cases where injuries to the head appeared to be minor, only to lead to death, so she
would stay with Quinn to make sure he didn't
begin to manifest more serious symptoms.

Quinn didn't speak until he saw his valet and
her maid waiting for them outside their bedrooms.
"You can go," he said to his valet. "I'll take care
of myself tonight."

The man seemed relieved and didn't hesitate
to head for the servants' stairs before Quinn dis-

appeared into his room without even a glance in Esme's direction.

"You may go, too," Esme said to her maid, who dutifully and quickly obeyed.

Then she opened Quinn's door.

Chapter Seventeen

Quinn's bedroom was as ornately and elaborately decorated as an oriental potentate's palace, full of dark oak furniture intricately carved, with gold and scarlet brocade curtains on the bed, heavy gold velvet draperies drawn across the windows, a thick Aubusson carpet on the floor, and bronze candleholders full of tall white candles making pools of light. A fire had been kindled in the hearth, and the flames flickered and made the shadows dance as Quinn whirled around to face her. "Esme? What are you—?"

"I think we should send for a doctor or an apothecary," she replied as she closed the door, her tone brisk and matter-of-fact. A man like Quinn wouldn't want her pity, or coddling. "Head injuries can seem minor, but prove disastrous."

"This is nothing," he said dismissively, proving to her that she was right to think he wouldn't take kindly to maternal ministrations. "I've been more badly hurt."

"Perhaps you have, but I was not in the vicinity and you were not in my care."

"I'm not dying and I'm not in your care!" he protested as he vigorously stirred the fire so that the flames leapt even higher. "If you want to play nurse, find another patient."

"I don't want to play nurse, as you call it, but since I'm pretending to be your wife, the responsibility for your health resides with me. Are you injured anywhere else?"

"No! Damn it, Esme—!"

"Foul language won't encourage me to leave, either. And I refuse to believe that after what I witnessed, you aren't injured anywhere else."

He threw himself into one of the upholstered armchairs. "I suppose there may be a few bruises," he grudgingly conceded.

A trickle of blood appeared at the bottom of his swollen nose. When Esme saw it, she felt the same fear she'd experienced when Ramsley had attacked him—but she didn't dare show it. "Your nose is bleeding. Put your head back," she ordered as she hurried over to his washstand.

Mercifully he did as he was told without objection, and she began to wipe the blood away with a cool, damp cloth. "Is your nose very painful?"

"It's not broken," he replied. "I'm sure I look a treat," he added sarcastically.

"I hope your pugilistic skills don't suggest to anyone that you're not your brother."

"I acted on instinct—as you did, I assume, when you suggested I sue."

She couldn't disagree. "I only noted your style of fighting because we should have some sort of plausible explanation for your unusual methods, should that become necessary."

"We can say I learned fisticuffs as a hobby. Many gentlemen do."

"That may be enough to satisfy," she agreed, as deliberately dispassionate as a lawyer questioning a witness. "Why did your brother go to Jamaica?"

"He left Edinburgh after I was disowned, so I don't really know. But it could well be that he fled to avoid a scandal, or any hint of one. I told you he has an aversion to scandal."

"The bleeding's stopped for now, so if you'll

stand up, I'll help you take off your jacket," she said, moving to do so.

He jumped up, tore off his jacket and threw it on the bed. "I don't need your help to get undressed. Go to your own room, Esme, and leave me alone."

His sharp angry words were worse than a blow, but she wasn't going to obey until she was satisfied he was going to be all right. "No."

Quinn glared at her like an impassioned emperor. "Esme, stop arguing with me. Your presence is no longer required, either in this room, or in Edinburgh. You're going back to London as soon as I can have your bags packed and the carriage prepared."

Her stomach twisted with a combination of dismay and disbelief even though she glared at him. She didn't want to leave before they'd finished their task and she didn't feel that she was in danger, not so long as Quinn was with her. But more importantly, deep in her heart, she didn't want to go back to London for a reason that had nothing to do with her safety or their investigation. London would seem lonely and empty now, lacking excitement except for those few times she might see Quinn. See, but never touch. To speak to, but never kiss.

"I won't. I won't leave until *I'm* satisfied we've pursued every avenue of our investigation. I came here to help my brother, and unless I'm convinced I'm in immediate physical danger, that's what I intend to do. You can't force me to go."

"That fire and those louts at the party tell me you *are* in imminent danger, so you're going to go, even if I have to tie you up like a bale of wool and put you in the carriage myself."

"You wouldn't dare!"

"I assure you, I would, and I will."

She could see that he meant it, so she had to find another reason to stay.

And she did, one that was new as of this evening, but valid nonetheless. "I've come to believe Catriona still cares for Jamie. If he still loves her, as you seem to think and our presence here apparently attests, I owe it to him to try to mend the breach between them. An incident at a party, a slight fire—what is that compared to my brother's future happiness? So I tell you again, I will not leave. And I won't leave this room until I'm sure you aren't seriously injured."

Swallowing hard but determined to show him she meant what she said, she began to undo his bloodstained cravat, willing her fingers not to tremble.

"I said I don't want your help," he repeated sternly.

"I'm merely removing your cravat."

He put his warm, calloused hand over hers. *"Stop."*

She ignored that order, too. If he really wanted her to stop, he was going to have to push her away.

He didn't. His hands fell to his sides.

Perhaps he wanted to see how determined she was, or expected her maidenly modesty would make her cease if his orders wouldn't.

If so, he was about to discover that he was wrong.

"This is ruined," she noted as she tossed his cravat into the basin.

Pressing her lips together, she began to undo the buttons of his equally bloodstained shirt. "So is this."

His breathing grew more erratic, his chest rising and falling as rapidly as hers, but he still made no attempt to stop her.

Once his shirt was open, she pushed it back from his shoulders, exposing his leanly muscular torso. There were a few bruises, and many small scars that proved he had not led a charmed or easy life.

He suddenly stepped back as if she'd slapped him.

"Esme, for the love of God, have mercy on me, and go!" he ordered hoarsely, anguish in his eyes as he dropped to his knees. "I'm a wastrel, a fool who squandered his privileged heritage. I'm everything wicked you've ever thought of me and I'll prove it if you stay."

"No!" she cried, horrified that he would kneel to her. She swiftly reached down to bring him to his feet. "You're a good man—a kind and generous man, intelligent and brave, and if you've made mistakes in your past, you've more than atoned for them since."

Shaking his head, he backed away.

She must and would tell the truth. "Whatever you've done in the past, you have my affection, as well as my admiration and respect."

His eyes seemed to bore into her very soul. "If I

could hope, Esme, I'd want more than your affection, admiration and respect. I'd want your love."

"Do you truly mean that?" she whispered, afraid to believe it could be true.

"Pretending to be my brother isn't the first time I've acted a part. I've been acting ever since I met you, Esme," he quietly replied. "I mocked and teased you because I didn't want you to know how I really felt."

He spoke with such heartfelt yearning, it was as if a rope had been thrown around her and was pulling her slowly toward him. "How *do* you really feel, Quinn? Please, tell me."

"I love you," he whispered, and with absolute sincerity. "I think I've been in love with you from the first time I met you, in spite of that ghastly brown gown you were wearing, but I didn't want to admit it, not even to myself, because that would mean acknowledging everything I've done to make me unworthy of you. If only I'd behaved differently, made better choices, been a better, stronger man, I could have hoped that you could love me in return. As it is…"

He reached out and took her hands in his. When he spoke, she saw raw honesty and vulnerability in the depths of his eyes, a soul stripped bare of all its masks and defences. "No other woman has ever touched my heart the way you do, Esme. They've had my body, but never my love. Only you."

It was no lofty declaration made in a rose-filled garden, no vow on bended knee, no promise in a sunlit church. It was a simple statement of fact, clear and concise.

As her heart leapt with joy, she resolved to be as honest about her feelings as he had been about his. "I've always felt something for you, too," she confessed. "No other man ever attracted me as much as you, although I wouldn't show it. At first, it was only desire, but it was so strong, I was afraid of what would happen if I let you see how you affected me. And I feared I was being as foolish as any love-struck girl. So I told myself over and over that you were a rogue, a scoundrel, a bad man."

"But I *am* a rogue and a wastrel and not nearly good enough for you, Esme."

"Let me finish!" she commanded desperately, grabbing his shoulders. "I've been in love with you for months, but I was sure you'd never care for a woman like me, so I tried to convince myself that what I felt for you was wrong and a terrible mistake.

"For a long time, I managed to fool myself. Ever since I stole that coin and vowed I would never do anything like that again, I've prided myself on my honesty and moral integrity, only to live a colossal lie when it came to my feelings for you.

"But no longer. I want to admit what I feel. I'm *glad* I feel it and I wouldn't change it for the world."

He looked at her with hopeful, anxious eyes. "I love you, Esme," he said softly. "I've loved you for months, but only realized it here, where I have never been happy before."

As he had opened his heart to her, she would to him. "I love you, too, Quinn, with all my heart."

She splayed her hands on his rapidly rising and falling chest, feeling the warmth of his flesh beneath her fingers, sensing the beating of his heart and the throbbing of his blood. "I want to be with you as if we really were husband and wife."

He took hold of her wrists and shook his head even as desire flared in his dark eyes. "I should make you leave. Carry you to your room."

"If you try, I shall only come back," she vowed as she took his hand and led him toward the bed, despite the risks.

For risks there were, especially for her. They weren't married and she could get with child. She was courting scandal and shame and worst of all, she would have to leave Jamie, to whom she'd been both companion and clerk. She'd have to give up the law.

Be with Quinn. Love him completely and risk losing the life she knew, or leave him and never discover what it was like to be in the arms of the man she loved and desired, who made her feel as no one else ever had or, she suspected, ever would.

The choice was easy. "I know exactly what I'm doing," she assured him. "What I'm offering. What I want. *Who* I want. I love you, Quintus MacLachlann."

"Thank God!" he whispered as he took her in his arms and kissed her with all the fervent longing she could ever hope for.

It was wonderful, and exciting and thrilling as her body warmed and waited, her heart throbbing with desire, the need growing as his fingers toyed with the knot of the lacing at the back of her gown.

She broke the kiss and turned around, presenting her back to him in silent invitation.

He understood at once and began to undo the lacing of her gown, his lips brushing across the nape of her neck and sending shivers down her spine. "You don't know how often I've dreamed of this."

"Or you how often I've dreamed of being in your arms."

He laughed softly as the laces parted. "You're right. I had no idea, or I assure you, I would have risked the lashing of your scathing tongue and tried to kiss you much sooner."

Holding her bodice to her breasts, she turned to face him. "I am as I am, Quinn. You must take me as I am, or not at all."

His smile instantly reassured her even before he said, "That wasn't a criticism, Esme. I want you just as you are, stubborn and resolute and intelligent and proud and neat as an elderly spinster. I want you because you are as you are, not in spite of it."

He stepped back and spread his arms. "But you

must take me as I am, too, Esme, past sins and scars and all."

"We are none of us perfect," she said. "I do want you, Quinn, just as you are."

His eyes blazed with admiration and longing as his lips curved up in the joyous smile of a man who begins to believe his impossible dream might be achievable after all.

Esme stepped out of her gown and, clad only in her chemise and pantelettes, into his open arms.

"You're so beautiful," he said as he brushed his lips across her cheeks, her nose, her jaw, before coming to her mouth, his kiss deep and loving and passionate.

She relaxed against him and gave herself up to the pleasure and exhilaration his kisses and caresses aroused. His tongue slid between her lips while his hands slipped her chemise from her shoulders, his action briefly shocking her back into the full awareness of who she was, where she was and what she was doing.

But she was still confident this was the right choice. The place she wanted to be. The man she wanted to be with.

Never had a man seen her without her clothes

on. Never had she wanted one to—until tonight. Until Quinn.

She backed away and slowly lowered her chemise. His breathing quickened and his face flushed as he watched, but he made no move to come closer. Not then, or when she undid the drawstring of her pantelettes and they, too, puddled at her feet.

As his heated gaze traveled over her naked body, she instinctively put one arm across her breasts, and her other hand below her naval.

"Don't," he said softly. "Let me see you. Let me admire you in the candlelight. God, Esme, I had no idea… Those terrible gowns… No, I should be glad you wore them or too many other, finer, richer men would be vying for your love."

"They could have vied all they liked," she said as she lowered her arms, feeling safe and cherished, admired and respected. "It seems I prefer rogues—and since you have seen me thus, I think it only fair that you disrobe completely, too."

"I've never been so inclined to strip naked before," he huskily replied.

Chapter Eighteen

Esme discovered she wasn't quite as bold as she thought, or perhaps it was the last gasp of her maidenly modesty, but as Quinn started to remove his white satin knee breeches, she hurried to the bed and scrambled beneath the satin coverlet.

"I may have a few scars, but I'm not as frightening as all that, surely."

"It's not fear," she retorted from the warm confines of the bedclothes, her voice muffled. "I've just…I've never seen a completely naked man before."

"Ah," he sighed. "Well, for a neat woman, you've left your gown in peril of serious wrinkles."

What was he doing? Picking it up?

She opened her eyes a bit, to see that was indeed the case. He had picked up her gown and was in the process of laying it over the back of a chair. And he was completely naked.

She opened her eyes wider to get a better look at his taut buttocks and long, muscular legs, his skin glowing bronze in the candlelight. He had not an ounce of fat on his lean body. Like his chest, his back bore a few scars, some obviously old, others more recent.

He turned and she quickly closed her eyes. In another moment she felt the bed dip as he joined her.

"No need to look away, my little plum cake," he said as he reached for her. "It's only fair that you see me as God made me, since I've seen you that way."

She opened her eyes to find him regarding her with passion glinting in his eyes. "You've been hurt so many times," she murmured, running her fingertips over a scar below his collarbone on the left side of his body.

And in other ways, as well, she thought.

"Never get into a knife fight with a Gypsy." He skimmed his hand up her arm. "You, I notice, have no scars at all."

"I've led a very uneventful life." *Until now.*

"Good." He sidled closer, bringing his body into full contact with hers, once more capturing her mouth with his.

Gloriously happy and still firm in her resolve, she shivered with desire and anticipation. He leaned down to drag his tongue across her nipple. Never had she felt anything like the sensations that aroused—yet there was more to come, as he put his mouth over the pebbled tip and sucked it inside.

She moaned and arched upward, too surprised and excited to do more, until he broke that contact.

"I—I didn't…know…." she stammered in a whisper.

"There's a lot more I want to show you."

She felt liberated, unbound by convention, able to do exactly as she desired. "Oh, yes, please!"

He did, letting his fingertips glide with agonizing slowness up her arm, then down her cleavage and below her navel, then back up again until she was squirming.

He lifted her arm and pressed a kiss upon the pulse of her wrist before he let his lips go where his fingertips had been—with one important difference. When he was on the return to her neck, he paused to lick and suck her breasts until she could scarcely stand the growing tension.

Hoping to ease that, wondering if she could, she began to do the same to him, letting her hands move up his arms and down his chest, brushing her palms across his equally taut nipples, watching his reaction to see if she was succeeding.

Judging by the strained tendons in his neck, the length and firmness of his shaft, she was. Even more excited, she put her hands on his chest to force him upward a little. She raised her head and began to pleasure his hardened nipples as he had pleasured hers.

His skin tasted ever so slightly of salt, smelled of soap and bay rum, and the little hairs that crossed his chest tickled her nose, but as he moaned, a heady thrill of delight rushed through her.

Here, in this chamber, in this bed, as they stroked and caressed, they were equal as they could never be outside. They were partners, both wanting to give and receive, and doing so.

He rolled her onto her back and positioned himself between her legs. "I can't wait any longer, Esme," he said as he reached below her waist, to where she was hot and wet and needy.

"Nor I," she replied, ready for what came next. Anxious for it.

To prove that, and that she was still certain of her choice, she encircled him with her hand and shifted to get into better position for him.

His gaze upon her face, he pushed forward. She let go and took hold of his upper arms as he thrust farther inside.

She felt the slight tear of flesh—a brief pain—and winced.

"I'm sorry," he whispered, his brow wrinkling with concern.

"No need," she assured him, sliding her hands to his buttocks to show that she had no regrets. "I want this, Quinn. I want you and I want you to love me."

He gave her what she desired, filling her completely, as with another low groan, he began to thrust. At the same time, he leaned his weight on his left elbow and with his right hand, caressed her breasts. His touch, the feel of him inside her, all combined to fuel her growing excitement.

This was beyond anything she'd ever imagined. This was making love. This was being loved.

Such was her last coherent thought as the excitement and anticipation and tension grew and grew again, almost beyond bearing. Quinn's breath was hot upon her face, his body as tense as her own as he drove himself with increasing speed and need and passion. She wrapped her legs around his waist, holding him closer and tighter, her own breathing hoarse and swiftly shallow.

The need and desire increased. Her whole body tightened, her mind a blank, aware only of the pleasure of his mouth and tongue on her skin, his hands on her body. She wiggled and squirmed and held him close—until the tautness snapped, like a line holding a ship at anchor in a rough sea, so that the vessel rocked and bucked and rode the waves without control or pilot.

He, too, groaned, loud and rough, as he stiffened, then jerked like a puppet on twisted strings. Afterward, drawing in great, deep breaths, he lowered himself to rest his head upon her breasts.

They lay thus for a long time as their breathing slowed.

Esme opened her eyes and looked at him, and the bed and the room around them. How could these all be the same, she wondered, when she felt so different? Perhaps she looked the same, too, although she could never be quite the same Esme.

She had always believed that she wanted something more than the usual fate reserved for her sex, marriage and children and endless domesticity. She'd believed she had found a better life, working with her brother.

Now she knew that no matter how much she loved the law and helping people who needed a good solicitor, she loved Quinn even more. Perhaps they should have waited until they were truly married, behaved with more propriety, told Jamie about their feelings. Instead, she'd acted impetuously, selfishly, wildly...

Like Quinn in his youth.

Now she could truly understand how emotions could rule the mind. And she was older than he had been, so presumably should have had more self-control.

But if he loved her as she believed he did, they would always be together, and life as his wife was the one thing that could promise her even more happiness.

Since coming of age she'd trod her own path, made her own way, in a world that expected little of women except compliance and duty, but never had she done anything as unconventional as what she was about to do now.

Nevertheless, she would do it.

She took Quinn's face gently between her hands and, looking steadily into his eyes, asked, "Will you marry me?"

At Esme's softly spoken request, the full weight of what they'd done came crashing down on Quinn like a huge and heavy tree. He'd made love to the woman he adored and respected above all others without benefit of marriage. He'd taken the virginity of his best friend's sister without a word or pledge of promise. No matter what she had said before, her judgment had been clouded by desire and she would surely come to regret what they'd done tonight, even if they married.

Perhaps especially if they married, for whatever hopes he harbored for the future, the past could not be changed.

He got to his feet and tugged on his breeches without looking at her, knowing there was only one thing to do, one way to protect and preserve her happy life in London. "No, Esme, I won't marry you. I'm nobody. I'm *nothing*. I have no title, no estate, no home, no wealth, nothing to offer you at all."

Her loose hair her only covering, Esme also rose from the bed. "Are those your only objections?"

"Aren't they enough?" he demanded, grabbing his shirt. "They should be."

"I'm well aware of your past, Quinn, and know you've done things any man of sense and honor should be ashamed of—as you are, which only proves to me that you *are* a man of sense and honor. If you weren't, your past wouldn't disturb you as it does. Whatever you've done in the past, you're a fine, worthy man and I'm not going to let you go."

She didn't really understand. She couldn't, or she wouldn't want to marry him.

He would have to try a different tack. "Generally, it's the man who makes the proposal, Esme, and I note that I did not. I have no wish to marry. Why should I, when I can enjoy the benefits without any legal entanglement? Surely you can appreciate how much easier it makes things when I tire of my lover."

"There was a time I would have taken those

words at face value and believed you must not really love me," she said, as calm and cool as if they were discussing an entailment. "I would have thought that you had, after all, only lusted after me and having seduced me, were finished with me. But I know you too well to believe that now. You love me as much as any man ever loved a woman, and the proof of that is your refusal to bind us by law or contract because you've got the foolish notion that you're not good enough for me.

"Even if you truly don't wish to marry me, I have no regrets for what we've done. After we finish our task here, I'll go back to Jamie's house and you can go back to yours. We can meet there, if that's what you'd prefer. With no legal entanglements."

Convinced at last that what she felt went far deeper than mere desire and that she did, indeed, realize what she was doing, a hope unlike anything he'd ever experienced blossomed in Quinn's lonely heart. Esme McCallan loved him, and she would accept him as he was, in spite of his past. She would take him for her husband and give him the chance to be part of a family again. Only this time, it would be a loving one.

And yet… "What about your brother? How can I go back to London and tell Jamie, the man who helped me when I was at my lowest—and low it was!—who has seen me at my worst—and it was terrible—that I want to marry his sister?"

"We'll tell him together," she replied, regarding him with resolute serenity. "Or I shall tell him myself, if you'd prefer."

As if he were a coward. "I'm not afraid of Jamie."

"Aren't you?" she asked softly. "Aren't you afraid you'll lose his friendship? Aren't you afraid that he'll hate you?"

She came to him and took him in her arms, her voice steady and sure, her breath warm on his cheek. "He won't, because he loves me and he knows I'm no flighty, silly girl to be swept off my feet by something I only *think* is love."

"Oh, Esme," he whispered as he embraced her. "Yes, yes, I'll marry you, and I'll gladly spend the rest of my life trying to be worthy of you."

"You already are," she assured him as she held him close, until she felt something damp on her shoulder. "Quinn, your nose! It's bleeding again!"

He muttered a curse as he hurried to the washstand and dunked a towel into the pitcher of cold water.

Esme grabbed a sheet to wrap around herself and dragged a chair closer. "Sit down and put your head back."

He did as she commanded and she wiped the blood from his upper lip with the cold towel.

"There. The bleeding's stopped for now. I really think a doctor should examine you."

He shook his head. "It's nothing. I've had worse injuries. And as you may have noticed, I'm quite a healthy, virile specimen."

His gaze flicked to the towel in his lap, which wasn't quite in the same position it had been before, having been raised by an obviously aroused portion of his anatomy.

Despite their recent intimacy, Esme blushed. "I thought men were always rather…exhausted… after such exertions," she said as she rinsed out the cloth.

"Some men are," he replied from where he still sat, "and sometimes I am. But not tonight. Not with you."

"But your nose—"

"Is fine," he said, his voice low and seductive

as he reached out to take hold of her arm and bring her to him. "Let's go back to bed, Esme, my wife-to-be."

She smiled the most devilish smile he'd ever seen on a woman's face. "I don't see why we have to go back to the bed when you look so comfortable here, my husband-to-be," she said as she straddled him, her thighs resting on his hips.

"Good God," he murmured, delightfully surprised as he put his arms loosely about her. "If I had realized what an adventurous, brazen woman existed beneath those dowdy clothes you wore, I would have set about wooing you the day we met and not stopped until you were mine in body, name and law."

Her arms around his neck, she inched forward. "We have achieved one of those objectives, and one more. You have my heart and my body, too. All that remains is for the law to be satisfied," she said before she kissed him.

Instantly, passionate desire flamed into life between them. Their tongues entwined, their kiss deep and exciting as Esme's naked breasts brushed against Quinn's chest.

"I want to make love with you again," he whispered, his mouth against her cheek, "but I don't want to hurt you."

"If it hurts, we'll stop," she promised, raising herself to take him inside again.

"Esme?"

"It's all right," she assured him as the pleasure overtook a little twinge of pain. "I don't want to stop."

"Rock forward," he prompted as he brushed his lips across hers.

She did as he suggested, the sensation making her breath catch.

"Keep rocking," he whispered, holding her with his left hand while stroking her pebbled nipple with the pad of his right thumb.

Then his mouth was on her breasts, sucking, licking, pleasuring her with his lips and tongue. She began to rock faster, with fervent need and longing, as that wondrous tension built to a new crescendo.

A low growl began in Quinn's throat, rising almost to a roar, and she clenched her teeth to keep herself from screaming with ecstasy when they both reached an explosive climax. Her eyes closed tight as wave after wave of release swept through her and over and around her, taking her to blissful satisfaction.

He held her close, his chin resting on her sweat-slicked shoulder, until she moved back and examined his face.

"I'm not bleeding again, am I?" he asked.

"No," she said, relieved.

"And you? How are you?"

"I feel wonderful," she said, until he moved a little, and she again felt a painful twinge.

"Not quite," he said with a frown. "Can you move?"

"Yes," she said, easing herself away from him. "I'll be all right in a little while."

"Soon, I hope. In the meantime, you should rest. With me," he said, nodding toward the bed.

Weary, sore, but joyously happy, Esme didn't protest. After all, they were supposed to be husband and wife, weren't they? And one day soon, they would be.

She nestled against him, blissful and secure. "I love you, Quinn," she whispered.

"I love you, Esme," he said, kissing her tenderly and holding her as they fell asleep.

* * *

They were still entwined in each other's arms and slumbering peacefully when they were startled awake by the sound of footsteps thundering up the stairs.

Jamie McCallan burst into the bedroom. Clad in his indigo greatcoat and hat, face pale and hair dishevelled, he stared at the tableau before him as if Esme and Quinn were standing over a body in blood up to their elbows.

"Jamie! What are you doing here?" Esme cried, clutching the sheet to her breasts while Quinn scrambled from the bed and grabbed the coverlet to wrap around his waist.

Jamie turned away from Esme to address Quinn, as if he couldn't even bear to look at her. "I trusted you," he charged. "I trusted you to take care of her, not—"

"This is my fault, not his," Esme interrupted, getting out of bed and draping the sheet around her like a toga.

Jamie regarded her in a way that cut her to the quick, as if she were no more than any other foolish, pitiful woman easily seduced by a cad. "I thought you, of all women—"

McSweeney arrived, panting, on the threshold. "I'm sorry, my lord! The gentleman wouldn't wait."

"So I see. Who do you think you are, McCallan, to burst into our bedchamber in this barbarous fashion? Have you completely lost your mind?" Quinn demanded, his manner suddenly haughty and disdainful—as befit an outraged earl. He had his mask firmly back in place, as she and Jamie should, too. This plan had been Jamie's idea, after all. If he now had any cause to regret—

"I have important news for his lordship," Jamie announced. "Very important news."

She suddenly noticed how pale her brother was and that he had dark circles under his eyes, as if he hadn't slept for days. Or had come from London as fast as humanly possible.

Her maid appeared at the door, with Esme's robe over her arm and a very surprised look on her face.

Quinn took it from her, dismissed her with a brisk order to go, then said to McSweeney, "This man is my solicitor in London. See that we're not disturbed."

"Very good, my lord," McSweeney murmured as he went out and closed the door behind him.

Chapter Nineteen

Quinn had regretted many things in his life, but nothing more than what he'd done with Esme as he faced her righteously indignant brother. No matter how much he loved Esme, he should have had more self-control and waited to make love with her until they were legally married.

Then he realized that Jamie apparently wasn't angry anymore. Now he looked…sorry. And perhaps even sad.

"What is it?" he demanded. "What's happened?"

Jamie met Quinn's gaze squarely and answered without further preamble, although with obvious sympathy. "Your brother and his wife died of ague in Jamaica a month ago. You are now officially the Earl of Dubhagen."

For a moment, Quinn felt…nothing. Not sorrow, not regret, not joy. Nothing, as if Jamie's announcement applied to somebody else, and that person was a stranger.

Until Esme's hand, warm and soft and vital, slipped into his.

"I received a letter from an associate of mine in the office of the earl's solicitor in Jamaica," Jamie explained. "He was also writing to the family solicitor here in Edinburgh, so I thought I should make haste to tell you of the change in your circumstances and to decide how best to proceed."

"But I can't be the earl," Quinn protested. "My father disinherited me."

"So he may have threatened or even planned to do, but he never did. There's not a single legal reason you would be barred from the title. And since Augustus has left no heirs, everything goes to you—title, estate and income. You're a rich man, Quinn—or should I say, my lord."

He hadn't been disinherited? He could scarcely believe it, but if Jamie said it was so…

"Your father must have loved you, after all," Esme said softly.

"Perhaps he did," Quinn agreed after clearing the lump that had come to his throat. "I wish I'd known it when he was alive. It would have…it would have made a difference. I wouldn't have felt so alone."

"You aren't alone anymore," Esme said as she squeezed his hand, her presence and love a comfort.

Jamie cleared his throat, the sound loud in the silence. "I'm sorry to have to be practical at such a time, but your family's solicitor here in Edinburgh will be learning of your brother's fate any day. Perhaps it would be best if you both returned to London."

"Mr. McHeath and the rest of Edinburgh society are in for a shock whether we stay or go," Quinn replied. "Since I've really been the earl for a few months now, I haven't been breaking the law. If people assumed I was Augustus and Esme was Hortense, well…"

"The only lie we've really told is that we're already married," Esme said. "I never actually said I was from Jamaica. I just said it was hot—which it is."

"As for the married part, we intend to rectify that as soon as possible," Quinn said. "Thank God the laws of Scotland are more accommodating in that respect."

Jamie felt for a chair and sat heavily. "Married?"

"While I should like your blessing, Jamie, I'm of legal age, so I don't require your permission to marry," Esme quietly noted, as if speaking to a person taken ill. Her expression and voice softened, almost to a plea. "You like Quinn, don't you? I love him and he loves me, and we're going to be married."

"You truly want to marry him," Jamie said, looking as taken aback as Quinn would have, too, if somebody had made that suggestion even a fortnight ago.

"Yes, I do. I also want to make it clear that Quinn didn't seduce me. It was my decision to spend the night with him without benefit of clergy, despite his efforts to dissuade me, so if you must be angry with anyone about that, it is I."

"I know I'm not nearly good enough for her," Quinn said, "and despite the love I feel for her, I should have waited until we were married to share a bed. But since we didn't, I hope you'll forgive me. I do love her, Jamie, with all my heart, and I give you my word that she'll always be first in my life. I'll do everything I can to make her happy."

Before Jamie could reply, there was a sharp, insistent rap on the door.

"My lord!" McSweeney called from the other side. "I'm sorry to disturb you, but a footman has come with an urgent message from Lady Catriona. It's the earl. He's had a fit of apoplexy. He's dying, the footman says."

Esme and Quinn dressed as quickly as they could, then joined an equally anxious Jamie in the carriage. On their way to the earl's, Esme and Quinn told Jamie what they'd discovered about the earl's finances, and what they had not.

Esme doubted he heard half of it.

They were admitted to the earl's house immediately and shown into the drawing room, while the butler dispatched a maid to summon Catriona. The house was hushed, as if no one dared to speak, or were afraid of what might happen if they did. Esme sat beside Quinn on one of the sofas and held his hand while Jamie began to pace in front of the hearth.

"Apoplexy isn't always fatal," she said, desperate to break the unnerving silence. "He may yet rally."

"Perhaps," Quinn agreed.

"Remember Mrs. Beesdale?" Esme said to her brother. "She was on death's door from that very cause at least three times that we're aware of and always recovered. She made a new will every time," she added for Quinn's benefit.

Jamie didn't seem to hear that, either, but at the sound of light, rapid footsteps, all eyes, including his, darted to the hanging stairs beyond the door.

Catriona came hurrying down the steps. Her hair was in a long braid, and she wore the most simple of frocks for the day, a printed green muslin with only a single row of darker trim—proof that she'd dressed quickly and that the earl's attack had probably happened in the night. She was pale, and it looked as if she'd been weeping.

Esme glanced at Jamie, who stood unmoving, as if the sight of Catriona had rooted him to the floor.

"Thank you both for coming," Catriona said, rushing toward Esme with outstretched hands.

Until she saw Jamie. The remaining color drained from her face and she began to sway.

As Esme cried a warning, Jamie raced forward and caught Catriona before she fell, then carried her to the sofa. Esme followed, desperate to help in some way and regretting they hadn't given the poor girl some warning of Jamie's presence. Quinn, meanwhile, ran to the door and called for assistance.

Esme watched helplessly as Jamie sat half on the edge of the cabriole sofa, looking at Catriona as if she might evaporate or expire on the spot. He gently brushed her hair from her face, his expression and action proving to Esme, more than any declaration, that her brother still loved Catriona, and probably always would.

Now aware of what love between a man and woman could be, she couldn't fault him for his devotion, in spite of what had happened in the past and the years since. She could only admire and respect her brother more.

The butler appeared and lost some of his stony calm.

"She swooned," Esme explained. "Is the doctor still here?"

"No, no!" Catriona cried weakly as she opened her eyes and looked at Jamie as if uncertain he was real. "Let Dr. Seamus stay with my father. I was just… Is it you, Jamie? Is it really you?"

"Yes, it's really me," Jamie assured her.

"Bring some tea and brandy," Quinn told the butler.

The man immediately departed, while Catriona grabbed Jamie's hand. "Papa's fallen ill. Suddenly. Just this morning and I sent for the doctor, who says there's no hope, so I wanted…I thought… Oh, Jamie, how I've missed you!" she cried, throwing her arms around Esme's brother and sobbing against his shoulder.

Esme had no idea what to do, or say. She glanced at Quinn, but he looked equally lost at sea.

"Perhaps Esme and I should leave," he ventured.

"No!" Catriona cried. "Please, stay. I want Esme to hear everything, even though she hates me, and justly so, because of what happened between her brother and me."

"I don't hate you, Catriona," Esme quickly said. "I was angry and resented you before, but not anymore."

The young woman's lips quivered as she spoke. "Oh, I'm glad! But I still want…need…to explain, to tell you all—but especially you, Jamie. I lied to you when I said I wouldn't marry a man who worked for his living. I lied for your sake, because my father threatened to ruin you if I didn't give you up—and he could do it, too!"

Her expression grew more determined and impassioned. "I wanted to marry you, Jamie, oh, so much! I told him what a fine man you were and how much I loved you, but Papa still wouldn't agree. I even threatened to run away with you, but then he said he would destroy you.

"He's a powerful man with influential friends," Catriona went on, her voice shaking with emotion. "He could have ruined the career you worked so hard for, Jamie, even if we went to America or Australia. I couldn't risk that. I wouldn't, even though I broke your heart, and my own, too."

Esme suddenly wished she was somewhere—anywhere—else. This was the sort of conversation no one but the principals should be privy to. She began sidling toward the door, while Quinn stared out the window as if he'd been turned to stone.

"But that's not the worst of it. He's been lying about his finances, too," Catriona said, arresting Esme's attempt to leave. "After the doctor had told him…told him this attack might be fatal, Papa confessed to me that he hasn't been losing money at all. That was a lie, every time, to keep me near him. To make me think he was in danger so I wouldn't leave him."

His expression unreadable, Quinn slowly swivelled on his heel to look at the couple.

"It's not because he loves me," Catriona bitterly continued. "Who would be his hostess if I married and left him? Who would fuss over him and tend to his needs, his whims? Who else except a dutiful daughter? He only told me now because he wants to die in a state of grace, or at least with God's forgiveness."

The earl sounded monstrously selfish and many would likely have a difficult time believing that Catriona could be telling the truth, but Esme could, and so could Jamie, or Quinn, or anyone familiar with the sort of cases that crossed a solicitor's desk: the disputed wills, the bitter settlements, the quarrels among family members, the marriage contracts drawn up with no thought of love or happiness or even contentment. Everyone in that room had seen enough to believe that a selfish, arrogant old man could and would do just as Catriona described, and for no other motive than self-interest.

Catriona wiped her eyes with the back of her hand. "I'm not crying over him—not anymore," she said with trembling defiance. "I'm crying because of what he did to us, Jamie. And because I'm so happy to see you again."

She lowered her eyes and twisted her hands in her lap. "I didn't think to ask…" She raised her eyes, hopeful and yet frightened, too. "Are you married?"

Esme's brother smiled as she hadn't seen him smile since the night Catriona had jilted him. This was the Jamie she had known in her childhood, the Jamie who'd been absent for so long. "How could I marry when my wife-to-be is here? You will marry me, won't you, Catriona?"

"Oh, yes!" she cried, throwing her arms around Jamie's neck and kissing him passionately.

The butler appeared at the entrance of the drawing room. His eyes widened, but duty demanded he keep his voice expressionless, and he did. "If you please, my lady, the doctor says you should come at once."

Catriona's breath caught before she nodded and got to her feet, holding on to the arm of the sofa for support, until Jamie put his arm around her. "Would you rather see him alone?" he asked softly.

She leaned against Jamie and looked up at him as if he were her champion come at last to save her. "I need you, Jamie, now and always," she said before she turned to Esme and Quinn. "I would be grateful for your company, too. I would like to have friends nearby if this is to be goodbye."

The earl's large bedchamber was like a tomb, full of dark, heavy furniture. Thick velvet draperies surrounded the bed and more were drawn across the tall, closed windows. The only light came from a small candle on the table beside the curtained bed, and the air was stale and smelled of the sick room. The earl himself seemed dwarfed by the pillows and covers, as if he'd shrunk, or was already dead, his face gaunt and cadaverous.

Yet his bony chest still rose and fell, albeit with shallow, gasping breaths.

The doctor, waiting by the bed like a high priest about to administer the last rites, turned toward them when they entered the room. If he was surprised to see four people, he hid it well. Esme supposed that he, like a lawyer, had seen too many things in his life to be surprised by much.

"Papa, I'm here," Catriona whispered as she sat on the edge of the bed beside him. She took his hand and held it gently, like the dutiful daughter she was.

Like the loving wife she would be.

"I fear his lordship has lost the capacity to speak," the doctor said quietly, and his grave expression told them he didn't expect the earl to last much longer.

Nevertheless, the earl's eyelids fluttered—or rather, his right one did. His left, like that side of his face, stayed immobile, and the left side of his mouth sloped down.

"Papa?" Catriona said again. "Can you hear me?"

His eyelid moved again, this time opening a little. His gaze meandered for a moment before focusing on her face.

"Papa, I forgive you," she said softly, and sincerely.

Esme had believed she would never, ever admire or respect Catriona McNare, but she did then, and forever after.

She also felt both proud and humbled when Jamie stepped forward, put his hand on Catriona's shoulder and, with compassion on his face and in his voice, said, "So do I, my lord."

There was a fleeting flicker of recognition in the old earl's face, a moment when Esme was sure he knew who had spoken and what he had said, before the old man closed his eye and let out a long sigh.

The doctor checked his pulse, then shook his head.

"Oh, Jamie!" Catriona cried, turning toward him.

Jamie held her close as she sobbed, while Quinn gently tapped on Esme's arm. "I think we should wait below," he whispered.

She nodded her agreement and together they left the room, and the couple reunited at last.

The earl's butler, who had obviously been waiting by the door, stepped forward when they walked out. "Has the earl gone to his reward?" he gravely inquired.

"Yes," Quinn replied, taking hold of Esme's hand. "I believe he has and I only hope he gets what he deserves."

The butler frowned for a moment, then assumed an appropriately funereal demeanor. "I shall, of course, be pleased to stay on if the countess wishes."

"I'll mention it to her if she asks," Quinn replied. "I daresay she has other things on her mind at present."

The butler nodded. "The earl's solicitor is waiting in the drawing room, my lord. Lady Duncombe summoned him, as well. Shall I tell him to return tomorrow?"

"No, we'll speak to him and apprise him of the earl's demise," Quinn replied.

Chapter Twenty

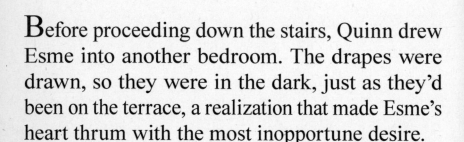

Before proceeding down the stairs, Quinn drew Esme into another bedroom. The drapes were drawn, so they were in the dark, just as they'd been on the terrace, a realization that made Esme's heart thrum with the most inopportune desire.

"I suppose it's necessary, but I have no wish to discuss anything with Mr. McHeath," Quinn muttered. "I'd rather stay here with you."

"I'd rather be alone with you, too, but this is hardly a suitable location."

"You've come up with the perfect argument again," Quinn noted with amusement in his deep voice. "This is what happens, I suppose, when you fall in love with a lawyer—or a woman who should have been."

Esme felt overwhelmed with gratitude and pride. There probably wasn't another man in a million who would accept her other passion without quibble or protest. "At least now we can be sure Mr. McHeath wasn't involved in any wrongdoing," she said, "although I never really believed he was."

"You are far too trusting of those in the legal profession, my dear."

"Not at all," she replied, running her hands up his chest. "I've heard too many tales of legal wrongdoing. However, I've learned to trust my own instincts, and I felt in my bones that he was an honest man."

"Then I shall learn to trust your instincts and your bones, too," Quinn said as he drew her close enough to kiss, "although there are certain other parts of your body I believe I shall enjoy more."

"Quinn, you wouldn't! Not here!"

"I didn't mean here and now, and I must say, if that's what you were thinking, you are far more adventurous than I ever imagined."

"It's not what I was thinking!" she hastened to assure him. "Not until you pulled me into this room and when we have such news to impart."

"Indeed," Quinn agreed, letting go of her with obvious reluctance. "A day of shocks and surprises."

"Yes," Esme said quietly, remembering the stunned, vacant expression on Quinn's face when he'd heard about his brother and sister-in-law's death. "I'm sorry about Augustus and his wife."

"I am, too, and that I'll never have the chance to reconcile with him, or my father," Quinn said sadly. He sighed, then managed a little smile. "I was also sorry when I thought my letter had brought Jamie to Edinburgh in such haste. I was sure he'd send for you and make you go back. I should have realized that there hadn't been enough time for my letter to arrive and him to get to Edinburgh."

"Quinn?" Esme said in a small voice.

Puzzled by her tone, he pulled back to try to get a better look at her face in the darkness.

"I have a confession to make. I intercepted your letter to Jamie."

"Intercepted?" he repeated warily.

"It never left the house," she confessed. "I took it from the hall table before it was posted. I feared Jamie would want me to go back to London, but I wanted to stay here, with you. And since your fears proved unfounded—"

"I wouldn't say that just yet," Quinn interjected.

"We still don't know who dropped that lantern. Despite what the good Mr. McHeath suggested, I assure you that I wasn't in the garden with a lantern, or another woman."

"I know that, Quinn. And speaking of Mr. McHeath, I think we've kept him waiting long enough."

"Aye," Quinn quietly agreed.

When they entered the drawing room, they found Gordon McHeath, his hands behind his back, marching back and forth on the carpet in front of the marble hearth like a soldier awaiting his marching orders.

When he saw them, he came to an abrupt halt and his brows rose. "Where's Lady Catriona?"

"Upstairs," Esme said, moving toward him. "Her father has passed away."

As Esme sat in a delicate gilded chair, the solicitor's expression flickered with dismay before he assumed what she recognized as a lawyer's dispassionate mask. Quinn stayed where he was, halfway between the door and the hearth, as if, even now, he didn't care to get too close to Mr. McHeath.

"She wrote in her note that he had taken ill," the solicitor said, "and her handwriting suggested…" He cleared his throat, then spoke in a more normal tone, albeit with sympathy. "How is she taking it?"

Quinn answered before Esme could. "Better that we might have expected, but I suppose we could put that down to the arrival of her fiancé."

The poor man rocked back on his heels as if he'd been hit, confirming Esme's suspicions that his feelings for Catriona weren't strictly professional. "She is *engaged?*"

"Yes, to the young man she wanted to marry years ago," Esme said. "Please, sit down, Mr. McHeath. We have other news to impart, as well."

"Other news?" he asked as one in a daze as he sank onto the sofa.

"Yes—good news. It seems the earl was lying about his financial difficulties. He confessed as much to Catriona this morning."

"This morning?"

"After he was taken ill," Quinn said.

"And she told you?"

Esme looked at the young man with compassion. "Yes. You see, Mr. McHeath, that was one reason we came to Edinburgh. Catriona has been afraid her father was being swindled and she wanted help to discover the truth."

McHeath shot to his feet. "She asked you, not me? Good God, she didn't trust...?" He looked even more upset as he exclaimed, "Surely she didn't think *I*—?"

"I'm afraid she couldn't be sure about anyone in Edinburgh, so that's why she wrote to my brother," Esme explained.

"Your brother?" Mr. McHeath repeated. "Who the devil is he that she would write to him?"

"Perhaps, my dear, further explanation can wait until another time, when emotions are less fraught," Quinn suggested.

Thinking he was right, Esme nodded her agreement just as Jamie and Catriona appeared on the threshold. Catriona's eyes were red and puffy, but she nevertheless looked happy.

McHeath stiffened as his gaze swept over Jamie before coming to rest on Catriona. "I'm sorry for your loss, my lady," he said stiffly, "and that you felt you couldn't trust me. If you still doubt my honesty—"

"I don't! I never really did," she said as she left

Jamie and went to him, looking up at the solicitor with her soft, gentle eyes. "But I couldn't be *completely* certain. I know that you have…certain feelings…for me, and I'm sorry if anything I've done has hurt you."

Mr. McHeath stepped back as if he feared contagion. "I understand that your affections have been otherwise engaged," he said as he bowed. "I…" He took a deep breath and when he spoke, it was with a little less bitterness and more sincerity. "I wish you every happiness, my lady."

"Thank you, Gordon. Your kindness and concern have always meant a good deal to me."

"I had better consult with the doctor about the death certificate," the solicitor brusquely replied.

Esme's heart ached for the young lawyer, even though there could have been no other outcome given Catriona's love for Jamie, and his for her.

McHeath started to leave, then hesitated. "If you need me for any other help, my lady," he said, "please ask."

"I shall," she replied.

With a nod, McHeath hurriedly left the room.

"Well," Quinn said, the word an exhalation of relief. "Now that the legalities are in hand and you two are finally reconciled, I suppose Esme and I are free to go? There's an important matter that we ought to take care of right away."

"What's that?" Esme asked, baffled by his tone as well as the look in his eyes.

"Why, our marriage, little plum cake. Thankfully we're in Scotland, so we can attend to it right away. Or would you rather wait?"

"No!" she cried without hesitation.

"You'll need a witness," Jamie offered.

"They'll need two," Catriona said, showing a spark of sudden resolve. "And perhaps you two will stand witness for Jamie and me—unless you'd rather wait?" she asked Jamie.

"I've waited five years," he replied, "but your father—"

"Is dead. And it's because of him we've lost five years of happiness, so I won't worry about propriety now."

"Gad, Esme, I think you're catching!" Quinn exclaimed.

He spoke not with wariness or distain, but with an undisguised pride that thrilled her as much as his most intimate touch. He really was a remarkable man.

Jamie smiled at the woman he loved. "Thank God!"

"So to the church it is," Quinn declared, making a sweeping bow to his bride-to-be as he gave Esme a devilish grin that made her whole body warm. "And propriety be damned!"

A few hours later, the Earl of Dubhagen and his wife, suitably grave after attending the deathbed of the Earl of Duncombe, dismissed their butler and went, with a little less decorum, into the drawing room.

Once there, Esme wasted no time pulling Quinn into her arms and kissing him.

"My sainted aunt, I've unleashed a tigress," Quinn murmured through his laughter as he kissed the tip of his newly wedded wife's nose.

"Surely you're not regretting that?" Esme teased, gloriously happy as she tilted her head to look into his merry blue eyes.

"Not a bit," he replied, holding her close. "I only regret it took me so long to realize that you were the only woman who could make me truly happy."

"We were both blind, stubborn fools," Esme said

with a sigh. "I was a ninny to try to keep you at arm's length."

"Arm's length?" Quinn cried before kissing her again. "I was under the impression you wanted me in another country."

"Well, there was a time I truly thought I did— but because I was finding you irresistible."

"I find you irresistible, too, little plum cake," he said, giving her yet another physical indication of that truth.

"Quinn, please! It's the middle of the afternoon," she protested, although only halfheartedly.

"Of our wedding day," he reminded her.

She sighed and relaxed against him. "I hope the poor reverend eventually recovers from the surprise of two couples arriving and asking to be married immediately."

"The sum I gave him should more than compensate for any distress he may have felt," Quinn assured her.

"As well as the look in your eye told him quite clearly you wouldn't accept a refusal."

"I don't doubt it," he agreed, stroking her cheek. "However, I must point out, my little plum cake, that your own expression was hardly less determined."

Laughing, Esme took his face between her hands and brought him close for a brief kiss. "Now what shall we do, husband? Stay here and face society, or return to London?"

Quinn grew serious. "What do you think?"

"Stay," she said firmly. "Although we now know the earl's finances were never in trouble, there's still the matter of the fire in the garden. I don't want to leave until we know who's responsible and see them arrested and charged."

"I'd expect no less from you," Quinn said with a nod. "And I agree." His hands began to wander. "If it wasn't likely to upset the servants, I'd carry you upstairs and keep you there a week."

"You can't hold me prisoner," she chided as she began to caress his magnificent, muscular body, something she now had every right to do.

"The Habeas Corpus act. I remember," he replied, as he sat on the sofa and drew her down on his lap. "I'd just have to make sure you *wanted* to stay."

Esme wound her arms around his neck. "I'm sure you could. We would get hungry, though."

"McSweeney could bring us provisions from time to time. Speaking of which..." He drew back. "I should speak to McSweeney and tell him the truth about who we are. He was always kind to me as a lad and I'd like him to know who I really am before the news of Augustus's death becomes public."

Esme saw no reason to disagree. "If you think that would be best."

Quinn smiled with relief. "I thought I might have to convince you."

She shook her head. "If you think it's the right thing to do, that's all I need to know."

"I don't have to tell him how long we've been married, though," he added with a wicked grin. "Or where the ceremony was performed."

"Or that I'm a solicitor's sister?"

"Nobody in Edinburgh has asked me about my wife's family," Quinn noted.

"There is something else that worries me," she confessed as she toyed with the ends of his cravat. "I don't know how to be a lady. I could manage for a few weeks, but I've spent all my time studying the rules of law, not the rules of etiquette. I don't know what should be served for dinners, or how to organize a ball."

"Surely it can't be any more difficult than learning the proper way to write a will so that it can't be disputed," Quinn replied. "It's been so long since I was in society, I'll probably make a thousand mistakes for every one you do," he added as he kissed her lightly.

"I beg your pardon, my lord, my lady," McSweeney intoned from the doorway.

Blushing, although she was only a little embarrassed, Esme quickly got to her feet.

"Yes?" Quinn replied, addressing the butler and looking not a whit ashamed as he grabbed Esme's hand and gently pulled her back down.

"The high constable wishes to speak with you, my lord."

"Perhaps they've finally discovered who set the fire," Esme said hopefully.

Quinn looked equally hopeful as he told McSweeney to show the constable in. Esme went to another chair and Quinn stood by the hearth in an attitude that suggested he'd been in a position of power and command the whole of his adult life.

With a jolt of humility, she suddenly realized

that their marriage hadn't conveyed legitimacy and worthiness on a disowned rakehell. By taking her for his wife, Quinn had raised her social status far beyond anything a woman of her class could normally aspire to. He had made her, the sister of a solicitor without wealth or title, a countess.

What had she to offer such a man, except her love and devotion? Yet it seemed, of all things in the world, that he wanted nothing so much as that, just as she had always craved a love coupled with respect and equality.

Quinn would give her that, and with him for a husband, she was surely one of the most fortunate young women in England.

"Well, Mr. Russell," Quinn said as the constable strutted into the room. "What news?"

"Unfortunately, my lord," he began in a sepulchral tone after he had taken the chair Quinn had silently offered him, "despite our best efforts— our very best efforts—we haven't been able to discover who's responsible for the fire."

Leading with his chin, Mr. Russell leaned forward on the chair. "Frankly, my lord, I think it's rebels who want to overthrow the monarchy. They no doubt got the idea from the French."

"What makes you think so?" Quinn asked, obviously just as baffled as she was by the suggestion.

"Because there are so many anarchists and discontented rascals in Edinburgh, my lord," Mr. Russell replied, leaning back with obvious satisfaction, as if he'd offered the only possible explanation. "The rebellion in France has given such rabble too many ideas. But rest assured, my lord, we *will* find the culprits and they *will* feel the full force of the law!"

"Interesting notion," Quinn said evenly, clasping his hands behind his back and rocking on his heels. "You've found no evidence of any other possible perpetrators?"

"No, my lord, not a whit."

"You don't think it could have been an accident?" Esme asked.

The constable's expression as he looked at her was so patronizing, she had to clench her teeth to maintain a semblance of serenity. "Bless your heart, my lady, if it was, why wouldn't that person admit it?" He smiled at Quinn. "That's women for you, my lord, isn't it? Always ready to excuse any villainy."

"If it was an accident, the person responsible

might not speak up because he or she fears punishment and having to pay for the repairs," Esme said.

At her firmly spoken response, the constable's expression turned a little doubtful. "That could be," he allowed.

"Thank you for keeping us informed, Mr. Russell," Quinn said briskly. "Good day."

The man looked so shocked and disappointed at Quinn's dismissal, Esme almost felt sorry for him.

As Mr. Russell got to his feet, Quinn strode to the door and called for the butler. "Please show Mr. Russell to the door," he said when McSweeney appeared. "Then return here. I have something to say to you, McSweeney."

Quinn watched Esme sitting expectantly on that too-ornate chair while they waited for McSweeney to return. She was far more worthy than many another woman to be a countess. How many other women could bring such intelligence and life experience to that role?

How many other countesses would be so passionate? And how many other women would accept him as he was and make him so happy?

McSweeney appeared at the drawing room door. "You wished to see me, my lord?"

Quinn took a deep breath. This wasn't going to be an easy confession, even though he was sure it was the right thing to do. "I have something to tell you, McSweeney. Something rather shocking."

The butler raised a brow. "Indeed, my lord?"

"Yes. I want to make something clear, something I should have told you from the start." He took a deep breath. "I'm not Augustus. I'm Quintus."

The man didn't look the least bit surprised.

"Don't you have anything to say?" Quinn asked incredulously. "Aren't you surprised by my news?"

"Perhaps I should have made it clear, my lord, that I knew who you were the moment you arrived," the butler calmly replied. "Your brothers never carried themselves the way you did, especially Augustus. A more clumsy man than he never existed and you, my lord, are far from clumsy."

McSweeney had known the truth from the start? "Why the devil didn't you say anything?"

"It's not my place to question you, my lord."

Quinn wondered if he'd ever be surprised by anything again. "Then do you know about

Augustus and his wife in Jamaica? That they're recently deceased?"

"I had assumed that your brother was deceased, or you wouldn't be the earl," the butler matter-of-factly replied. "As for official notification, I assumed you had your reasons for not announcing their deaths in the customary manner. Speaking for myself, my lord, I'm glad you've inherited the title and estate. You always were the best of the bunch—if you don't mind me saying so."

As Esme relaxed in her chair, Quinn couldn't help wishing McSweeney had spoken sooner. Pretending to be Hortense had gone against her morals and her nature, and he doubted she would have done it for anyone except her brother.

Well, perhaps for him, now.

The butler cleared his throat and shuffled his feet. "My lord, since honesty is to be the order of the day..." He hesitated and, in a shocking breach of butlery decorum, stuck his finger between his throat and his cravat as if the fabric had grown too tight. "I have a request to make, my lord. Mrs. Llewellan-Jones and I wish to be married and we hope you'll allow us to keep our positions if we do."

With a cry of triumph that made both the men start as if she'd fired a canon at their heads, Esme leapt to her feet. "*You* were in the garden that night!" she cried, pointing at McSweeney. "You and Mrs. Llewellan-Jones! Of course! That explains why Mrs. Llewellan-Jones was already awake and dressed! I should have thought of that before."

"Good God!" Quinn gasped.

He would never in a hundred years suspect McSweeney of such a thing, but the man had such a miserably contrite expression on his face, Esme had to be right.

"It was I who dropped the lantern," the butler sorrowfully admitted. "I kicked it with my foot while we were… I kicked it over by mistake."

"Why didn't you say so at the time instead of making us think there was some sort of evil villain out to murder us or destroy the house?" Quinn demanded, relieved yet frustrated, too. If it hadn't been for the fire, he wouldn't have believed he had to send Esme away.

On the other hand, if he hadn't faced losing her, perhaps they never would have spoken of their feelings, or acted on them, either, and the rest of his life would have been as lonely as the beginning.

"Delia…Mrs. Llewellan-Jones was afraid we'd lose our place and if the reason was, ahem, what it would be, she'd never get another," McSweeney contritely explained. "She's very proud of her reputation and didn't want it smirched. Although I felt sure you wouldn't dismiss us, she was so upset about the possible consequences, I decided to say nothing, something I truly regret, my lord."

His cause for remorse seemed so minor to Quinn, he almost laughed, except that he knew how painful genuine remorse could be.

"Love has a way of making us all do things we wouldn't normally do, for good or ill," Esme said gently.

McSweeney looked at her as if she'd started spouting poetry. She did sound different—but Quinn had heard that tone from her before, in bed, so was not quite so surprised.

"Since I have no desire to lose two excellent servants," Quinn assured him, "of course you may marry and remain in our employ as long as we're in Edinburgh, unless there comes a day there may be little McSweeneys running about."

The butler grinned with relief. "Thank you, my lord."

"Be off with you now, McSweeney," Quinn ordered. "Go tell Mrs. Llewellan-Jones you can be married and keep your position—but no more nocturnal rendezvous in the garden, if you please."

"Y-yes, my lord. Thank you, my lord," a chastised yet nevertheless joyful McSweeney stammered and, apparently totally forgetting the rules of proper conduct, he ran to the door. However, he managed to return to proper form and closed the door quietly.

"Well, that's a relief," Quinn said with a sigh as he sat on the sofa. "We'll have to let Mr. Russell know it was an accident after all, although I fear the poor fellow will be disappointed that it wasn't part of a massive, rebellious conspiracy."

"Maybe then Mr. Russell will also realize that women's suspicions should not be dismissed out of hand," Esme pertly observed.

"Perhaps, but I must point out, plum cake, that he doesn't know how clever you are—just as we didn't know about McSweeney and Mrs. Llewellan-Jones. I must say it's difficult to imagine McSweeney in the role of a lover."

"Why? Because he isn't as young and dashing and handsome as some other men I could name?" Esme said, her expression softening as she stood just out of Quinn's reach. "Love isn't dependent on age. I've seen several gentlemen of more mature years so overpowered by it, they were willing to make the most outrageous concessions in marriage settlements."

"Which you—or your brother—talked them out of, I suppose?"

"It's a solicitor's duty to look after his client's interests."

"I have an interest, Esme, and it's one I think my wife should address."

"Oh?" she replied with mock innocence. "What is that?"

"Come sit beside me and I'll tell you."

If she acquiesced, she suspected there would be little talking and much kissing and caressing, perhaps even leading to lovemaking right there on the sofa.

She immediately sat beside him and assumed a serious demeanor quite at odds with her rapidly beating heart and the growing heat of her desire. "Yes, my lord?"

To her surprise, he kept his hands clasped and turned to her with a truly serious expression. "There's a lot of legal business when you have an estate and a town house in Edinburgh and another in London. I want you to be our solicitor."

"Oh, Quinn!" she cried with both delight and regret. She was overjoyed by his words, but aware of reality. "I can't. I'm a woman."

"You most definitely are," he agreed. "A beautiful, amazing woman, so I realize you can't officially be my counsel, although I'm sure you're every bit as good at drawing up a contract as any male solicitor could be, if not better than most. Still, you could be my de facto solicitor, and we can let McHeath and Jamie be the ostensible ones."

"Mr. McHeath might not appreciate my interference," she felt compelled to note.

"Then I'll hire another solicitor."

"I hope that won't be necessary," she replied. "I feel sorry for the poor man. He clearly cared a good deal for Catriona."

"And too much for you, considering you were supposed to be my wife."

"He only wanted to help a woman he thought

was unhappily married," she replied. "I didn't enjoy having to trick him."

"I know it's been difficult for you," he said, brushing a lock of hair from her forehead before he kissed her there. "It was much harder for you to play the ninny than it was for me to play the overbearing nobleman."

"You *were* rather good at that," she said with a gleam of mischief in her eye. "I suspect you could become quite the tyrant if I let you."

"Which means the point is moot, because you never will. One condemning look from those eyes of yours, and I shall capitulate—so I suppose I'm doomed to do whatever you wish."

"*Whatever* I wish?" she said, her voice low and sultry as she edged closer.

"There are some orders I would more gladly obey than others, my queen."

"Then there's only one more thing for me to hope for, since I have the most wonderful husband in the world," she said, caressing his chest.

"You have my heart and I'll gladly give you anything else your heart desires."

"I'm sure you'll do your best to provide it," she said, kissing him with tender passion.

"How can I, if you don't tell me what it is?" he asked, smiling even as he returned her kiss.

"Children," she whispered with her lips against his cheek. "I want to have our children."

Quinn laughed softly as he held her close. "I promise to do my zealous best, my little plum cake."

And he did.

* * * * *